Crow Like Thunder

Jean Ann Hudson

Jean Ann Hudson

Published by Jean Ann Hudson

This book is a work of fiction. Names, characters, places and incidents either are products of the author's imagination or are used fictitiously. Any resemblance to actual events or locales or persons, past or present, living or dead, is entirely coincidental.

Copyright © 2014 by Jean Ann Hudson

All rights reserved. Without limiting the rights under the copyright requested above, no part of this publication may be reproduced, stored in or introduced into a retrieval system or transmitted in any form or by any means (electric, mechanical, photocopying, recording or otherwise) without prior written permission of both the copyright owner and the above publisher of this book.

visit www.jeanannhudson.com

Manufactured in the United States of America
1 3 5 7 9 8 6 4 2

ISBN-13: 978-1499690903
ISBN-10: 1499690908

for all those who love and care for animals

1

An Unexpected Guest for Dinner

A cold autumn air was settling over the spruce and pine-covered mountainside, but inside the massive stone walls of Wilker castle, Ambrose leaned comfortably against the blazing fireplace mantle and silently watched. Through a bustling and noisy dining room full of lively guests, servants brought food on large trays and set them on a side table in preparation for the guests of honor. Ambrose did not chat or mingle with any of them while waiting for the meal to begin, although he did watch the food go by with a certain envy, raising his nose with a faint hope of catching a whiff of the roast boar going past. Finally something of real interest to Ambrose was about to arrive and he looked toward the door. Just then his son appeared, but no one else took much notice. So like him to enter unobtrusively and prefer it that way. Tall and dark-haired and just like Ambrose at that age, Harz came into the dining hall and glanced around. A servant immediately presented him with a tankard of ale and he took one sip but continued glancing around the room. He was arriving a minute before his cousin, Count Gustav, just in case there was anything untoward, but there wasn't. At least nothing he could see.

Harz came over to the fireplace next to his father, as Ambrose had known he would, and placed his tankard on the mantle, then leaned against it and gazed into the flames. Something was distracting him, some memory, his father could tell. He didn't usually brood like this, but rather kept his eyes and ears open. Ambrose studied his son admiringly; Harz was a well-regarded and indispensable member of the court, taking the place Ambrose had thought *he* would occupy, what with all his accumulated knowledge of Wilker, its people and its politics; what with being the former Count's brother and the current Count's uncle. But no one came to Ambrose now. No one even noticed him, not even his son who, instead of leaning toward his father for confidence or advice or just to smile, merely turned around as all the revelers were turning to watch Count Gustav and his companion Sparrow come through the door. The meal could now begin, and although everyone appeared in a celebratory mood as they took their seats, no one acknowledged the day or person whose anniversary it was. For it was one year ago today that Ambrose had died.

Ambrose didn't bother to sit at the dining table. He no longer knew yearning hunger nor sated stomach, but he reminisced for the old satisfaction of food, for the taste of wine. He listened from the hearth and watched his son, whom he had not wanted to leave alone to this job of helping the Count. Although Harz of course was not the only help Gustav had. But Harz was going to be very important to the Count, Ambrose had warned him of that, and had made him promise, just as Ambrose's life was draining away, to stay close to Gustav, as it felt as if his royal line was in peril. In fact, it did not appear to Ambrose that it was going to continue at all; Gustav was going to die without heirs.

Now, being dead, Ambrose had no way of telling his son that, no way of warning Gustav. Even so, Ambrose stayed nearby, trying to determine if his death-bed premonitions were real or not. In this in-between world he sensed he needed to do something, but couldn't tell exactly what. How was it that a whole year had passed before Ambrose had woken up from dying? Strange how timeless it was now. Time didn't matter. When there was something important about, then there was time, so right now he was here. That's when Ambrose noticed that the little woman next to Gustav kept looking across the room at him.

She wasn't his wife, not by law; Ambrose had known Gustav's wife, the Countess Gertrudis. He never had liked her, and was happy that she had been sent back to her home country for trying to harm Gustav's friends, of whom she was jealous. Gertrudis couldn't stand to be anything but the center of attention and had even been jealous of

3

their own infant son, Dane. No, this little woman next to Gustav was not married to him, not formally. But she was close to him and loyal to him and was raising their son in the castle nursery along with several other babies recently born. If only Harz had a woman like that. What would it matter if they couldn't be legally married? People put too much stock in that; faith belonged to those who felt it, not those who swore it. This young lady, seated next to Gustav and trying not to notice Ambrose, had come from the forest where she had lived all her life with her parents, learning all the wisdom of nature and communicating with the animals easily. Ambrose now wondered if this girl might just as easily communicate with him. Ambrose moved his image slowly to stand right behind Harz and face directly across the table at Sparrow. If he frightened her, she might get up and run away. But she just gazed at him over Harz's head.

Ambrose had been noticed by others in the castle, mostly other ghosts. The castle certainly had plenty. Most of them hung about enjoying festivities or listening in on conversations; they drifted off after a while. One ghost had been in Wilker a long time; Ambrose believed she was his great great great great aunt, probably. She had died young while running through the castle to her husband's bedroom and had tumbled down a flight of stairs. She had died so suddenly that instead of realizing what had happened, her spirit merely got up and kept running. She was of the belief that her husband was being unfaithful, and ran from room to room bursting through doors expecting to find him guilty of the fact. Ambrose tried to talk to her, tell her this man had in fact been true to her and mourned her early death all his life and never remarried, but she just kept running up and down hallways.

Then there were people, living people, who might seem to notice Ambrose. They would pause while walking by him as he lounged in a chair or waited by a doorway with nothing better to do. They would rub their goose bumps, wrap their arms over their chests and move on. Most took no notice at all; they would walk right by or through him. But still, Ambrose stayed because he felt that Harz was lost or confused, not seeing some truth in front of him.

Earlier that year, it had seemed as if Harz would find that woman who should have been his wife. They had walked into the village together as if equals, even though she was just Genivee, a dairy maid. They had visited the old woman who told fortunes with cards – the old woman who in fact made the cards – the woman named Mona. She had tried to convince them they belonged together. In fact, as Harz had later watched this fine girl with braided blonde hair tap on lily pads by the river's edge, he had wanted to kiss her, had wanted to very much. But Harz was not one to forget his place. To kiss a woman of equal rank would be flirtation. To kiss a dairy maid far below his station, someone who could not object without fearing consequences, that would be to take advantage. So he had left Genivee unkissed on the banks of the river, and now she was attached to someone else. And Harz was alone while his father stood right behind him, willing Sparrow to notice. She could be so helpful to Harz.

Instead, Harz began to be unnerved by the sight of Sparrow gazing over him as if to something beyond. He looked into her eyes, plain and brown, and although they were not wide and filled with wonder, they did perceive things of importance that others missed; things his cousin would do well to notice. Gustav was lucky this girl had decided to follow him back to the castle and raise their son together with the other children instead of remaining where she was comfortable. She saw things Gustav didn't.

Sparrow did not know what to make of Ambrose, and after a time she wished he would fade away. She noticed Harz looking at her, perhaps annoyed at her rudeness to keep gazing beyond him. Gustav's elbow touched hers and she looked at him and smiled. She busied herself with the food in front of her and sipped the wine. It burned her throat and she glanced around the table at all the others who were drinking heartily, not sipping lightly. She imagined what heat would be building up in their bodies and wondered if they would know what to do with it. When she glanced around the room, the mysterious man with the beard was drifting toward the door that led to the kitchen. Not for the first time, she wondered if her unusual (to everyone else) abilities were changing inside the castle walls. Ambrose drifted into the hallway to the kitchen, leaning against the wall and watching closely as the desserts and hot drinks went by. *Sparrow doesn't know me*, Ambrose thought to himself. *But she does see me and can't ignore me.*

Harz continued with his meal and continued to watch Sparrow appear to see something that no one else was noticing. He glanced once to see what it was, but of course no one was standing by the fireplace or the hallway door, certainly not with all this food on the table and a place for anyone who wanted any. Harz knew she was unaccustomed to having servants bring things, scurry to and fro. But Sparrow was not observing any servant. She was, as usual, in a world of her own. Harz looked down at his own food without much interest.

So also was Genivee in a world of her own now, he thought. And in a world apart from him. He was remembering what had been said at the hunting lodge in the forest from where they had recently returned after the annual summer hunting trip: *Genivee is interested in another.* Of course, the mere page who had made this statement might know nothing at all, might be merely gossiping for sport. But he had no reason to lie or make things up, and so Harz had believed it. He had combined it with all the other tiny observations that by themselves, meant nothing at all, but taken all together, meant a great deal and meant, above all else that Genivee *was* attached, and not to him.

After dinner, Gustav and Sparrow took the usual amble up to the castle's towering keep to gaze across the courtyard and castle walls, into the mountains beyond as the sun set beneath some purple clouds. A thin band of cloudless sky stood out bright and yellow just above the horizon and below the storm bank. Gustav wrapped his arms around Sparrow as she gazed into the distance, the chilly evening air shivering down the hills, shooing off the warmth of the day. Sparrow said, "Our little son Kasch is very clever; when Luna started crying this morning he rolled over and patted her head." Gustav was getting used to having these small reports of nursery tidings. How anyone could spend an entire day with three babies mystified him, although at times he thought it could be preferable to some of the company he was obliged to keep when conducting a royal audience. Wishing to sound interested, he asked,

"And is Beth a useful caretaker for Dane?" Sparrow replied,

"Shy and slight Beth looks after your firstborn with gigantic devotion." Gustav had been considering sending Beth on her way to avert any conflicts between women. Better to head it off than have to deal with it full blown. He suggested,

"I was thinking I might dismiss her. With both you and Liesse there to look after the little ones she's hardly needed." Sparrow was appalled, although not surprised to hear a man's grand solution to a non-existent problem. She protested,

"That thought is extravagant; both your sons have caretakers perfect for each of them. They will not suffer for it. Liesse has plenty to do with her own little Luna to look after."

"Very well, your request is granted." This was a statement his subjects loved hearing. Sparrow regarded neither the weight of its truth nor the hint of its mocking. Her mind was on other things. She said,

"I have heard tell of ghosts in the castle. Is this so?"

"The tales are mostly made up; the ghosts are surely real." Sparrow wondered then if she should be as fearful of ghosts as everyone else was. Gustav answered her unspoken question saying, "Pay no attention to ghosts, my love. They only try to cause trouble, frightening subjects into making a fuss over nothing." Sparrow had never encountered ghosts in the forest. She decided she had better follow Gustav's advice on this for he would know about his own castle.

Relieved for now, Sparrow gazed at the brilliant band of gold between the purple clouds and the dark gray mountaintop. She noticed specks of black fluttering in the dying light, a flock of black birds too far away to count but clear against the yellow horizon. Sparrow cocked her head and wondered what they could be, but instead of asking the birds themselves wondered out loud, "Why are they gathering like that?" Gustav had put his lips on her neck, which needed to be warmed by his kiss.

"Hmmm," was his only answer, but when he realized she might not be referring to birds, he looked up, said, "It's just ravens," then returned to her neck.

"Why are they gathering like that, at this hour over the headwaters?" Sparrow wondered out loud. Gustav responded,

"Maybe a dead animal, a carefree mountain goat perhaps, lost his balance, slipped and fell and met his end." Then he remembered an old saying and decided it would apply, for he didn't want Sparrow to busy herself now communicating with animals unless that animal was him. "*A flock of birds, a purple sky, Is not a time to idle by.*" And with that he swung Sparrow around to face him.

In the courtyard below, Harz made his way to the magazine where Vatra, Squire Constable, was presiding over an inventory of weapons, mostly old swords that had not been used in anything like a real battle in ages. Harz began by asking him, "Where is your brother?" This was a question people asked whenever they wanted to be completely sure they weren't in fact addressing that other brother, his identical twin. In this case, Harz knew whom he was addressing and he really did want to know Trevka's whereabouts. Vatra said,

"I believe Trevka is on the lookout for more spies around the nursery." Harz had been expecting something like that, some excuse to hang around the nursery in the hopes of suddenly being useful to Beth or of learning more about her. But really, what more was there to discover? She was now simply a nursemaid in the castle. She didn't warrant his attention. Harz said, mostly to himself, "I shall have to give him a new assignment." Vatra didn't pause in his sorting, but said quietly,

"He'll be sorry about that." Harz disregarded the impertinence of expressing such an opinion, which he was aware of anyway. He replied,

"Perhaps, but he should be more productively occupied." The two men looked at each other. It was a debate whether anything Trevka spent his time on was productive, although of late he had done some extraordinary things: He had discovered and thwarted an attempted kidnapping of the Viscount Dane, even capturing the perpetrators, Beth and her cousins. Whether it had been serendipitous luck or actual sleuthing that led to the apprehension, no one could be sure. But lingering about the nursery cultivating an attachment to Beth was something that should probably be discouraged. "Beth is busy enough with her responsibilities and need not suffer distractions." Vatra knew his brother liked Beth and responded,

"Considering her past antics, keeping an eye on her might not be such a bad thing. She's been overlooked by most since coming here." Just then a flock of ravens flew overhead, calling out stridently and making a raucous noise that was just as suddenly gone. Ravens were usually solitary, not in a crowd unless mobbing an owl. Vatra looked up at them and recited a line he remembered,

"A flock of birds, a purple sky, Is not a time to idle by," and returned to his task with renewed vigor, not wishing to offend any omens from the sky. He spoke to a page nearby when he noticed they had mixed up some of the broadswords they were sorting and said, "Set those aside, they need polishing." Harz left them to their task and stepped out into the courtyard proper to look around, but nothing seemed amiss. No one other than a few evening amblers were about. He crossed the courtyard and headed to his own lodgings in the castle, finishing the rhyme from childhood in his head, *Notice what is lying under, When the ravens crow like thunder.*

It rained all night over the mountains but it was an isolated squall and there was only damp ground, no mud, as Magnus headed out to spend the day with a party of tax collectors. It was not a job officials usually enjoyed but Magnus had succeeded, as a foreigner advancing a new scheme, in convincing Gustav to implement a different revenue structure. It was the practice in Wilker for the Treasurer to impose a heavy tax burden on his knights and lords. To meet this demand, they in turn imposed heavy taxes on their heralds and squires, who in turn taxed their villeins and peasants. Magnus had been trying for years to convince Gustav that this actually resulted in *less* revenue overall. Ironic but true was the fact that the more one demanded of others, the less they seemed to have. Merchants especially were adept at holding back business if they felt too much of it would be going to a greedy crown that would misspend it anyway. (For no matter how royals spent their revenue, it was viewed as poorly done by the ignobles who worked hard to earn it.) Even farmers tended to harvest less when taxes were high. However, when people had extra coins in their fists, they busied themselves happily counting and spending instead of complaining and revolting. Therefore, the percentage levied would now be the same for all and less than usual, and the knights and lords were instructed to impose the same structure on those below them. It had taken quite a while for Gustav to accept this logic, but there was no one in the court with the experience and intelligence of his foreign-born adviser, and he came from the richest country known.

Magnus was along to make sure that the tax collectors were not pocketing anything on the side. On horseback, riding in front of two young men, he couldn't help hear what they were saying, even though they spoke in low voices. One said to the other, "What about that girl then, she had any announcements for you?" The other one answered,

"No news, I'm glad to say. It would appear I'm in the clear."

"You are lucky that way."

"I like being lucky; it's better than being good."

"It is easier." Then they spoke of other things which Magnus also did not wish to hear of and so he rode ahead and caught up to the officer in front. He asked the man,

"Are those two riding at the end trustworthy? There will be a full accounting." The officer glanced back and replied,

"Those two are only along for their horses; if any of ours go lame, they end up sharing or walking back. Be assured, my lord, I wouldn't trust them with anything other than moving an animal." Magnus considered the two and didn't like the similarities between himself and them. Did Genivee have an announcement for him? He didn't feel lucky or good, although in truth he was both. One night together was enough to make him a future father, but it apparently hadn't happened.

Genivee was entering the nursery that morning when it was unusually empty and sat down on one of the sofas. Only Liesse and Luna were there. "Where is everybody?" Genivee asked. Liesse replied,

"Beth took Dane to the apothecary, she thought he had a cough. Sparrow took Kasch to the forest, something about meeting the maple trees." The two looked at each other and wondered what they were missing. "And today Luna is four!" she said and jiggled the baby. "Luna *and* Kasch." The two babies were born on the same day four months ago, Kasch in the forest and Luna in the castle. Genivee thought for a minute and said,

"Sparrow didn't go alone to the forest, did she?"

"She would have, but no, Vatra is with her."

"Good." Genivee was quiet for a while and waited for her friend to get any gossip out of the way before she commenced her own. But Liesse could see she had something on her mind and ventured to guess what it was.

"Seen anything of Harz lately?" Genivee shook her head. Then she said,

"No, and I don't expect to. He's far too close to the Count to consider the likes of me."

"So is Boris close to the Count and he married me."

"Yes, but Boris is not the Count's cousin." Genivee watched Luna examine a sock and then put it in her mouth. "No, I'm not thinking of Harz now." She looked up at Liesse to make sure she was listening. "I spent the night with Magnus right before the hunting trip last month." They looked at each other. Liesse thought it was all happening over again, for it was a year ago on last's years hunting trip that she and Boris had spent a night together, and now the proof was drooling on a sock. Liesse said in a breathless voice,

"You're not-" Genivee shook her head.

"No," she confirmed with less pleasure than confidence. "But it doesn't really matter, does it? Now he's obligated, as a gentleman. And he is a gentleman." Liesse wondered, if she wasn't pregnant, how far that obligation extended. She reminded Genivee, as Liesse was good at reminding others of the obvious,

"Yes but you weren't a virgin, and you must have been quite agreeable if it happened at all."

"We both were agreeable."

"He must know you aren't trying to corner him into marrying you."

"He's been kind enough not to act as if I'm trying to corner him by not wiggling urgently to get away. Like other men I've known." Liesse smiled. There must be some entertainment in watching a few men squirm. Women did enough squirming thanks to them.

"Then what are you worried about?" Genivee got up from the sofa and went to a window. Looking into the courtyard, there were only errand boys and scullery maids about, most of them resting for a few minutes in the shade of a tree. She wondered what she was worried about. She mused,

"Once you connect with someone that way, even if it is just for fun and nothing comes of it, isn't there something terribly sad in that although you might have created a child, now both can walk away and never think of the other again? How is it something so fleeting can have such eternal consequences as a new life?" Liesse wondered. She had always known she was lucky to be married *and* have Luna. Although having a baby alone was not so terribly bad. There were young girls who had babies at home with their parents helping. It wasn't scandalous. But it was a lonely, difficult road. And if the parents were old or ill and unable to help much, then having a child by one's self could be arduous indeed, but some did it. Genivee turned around to tell her friend a story from the hunting trip.

"Did you know that that surgeon who was on the trip last month, that Dr. Quillin, he actually asked Magnus how his first wife had died? And at the supper table no less! I thought we would all die of embarrassment. My god, most people don't even know he is a widower. And I think probably only the Count knew why."

"What did he say?" Liesse was always wanting to know every last juicy, bitter detail.

"He coolly answered that she, and her baby, had died in childbirth." Liesse shook her head at the sadness of it. To lose so much when so much is at hand. They were silent for a while. Dying in childbirth happened too often, even in a country as forward as Magnus's. Losing a baby was even less uncommon. Then Liesse blurted out,

"Then that's it! He's terrified of having it happen again. Lonely but terrified." But Genivee shook her head slowly, the explanation too simple.

"Does he look and act like a man terrified?" Liesse had to shake her head too. He was the most calmly detached, intelligent man around. He had nothing to prove to anyone; his heritage and reputation preceded him to everyone who knew him and to those who did not, he was just as happy to be anonymous. Genivee couldn't say she regretted her night with Magnus, but it did seem to be having consequences she couldn't simplify. "I just wish there had been a way to say I was interested in him without seeming to promote myself to his level, as if he must consider me a possible wife or not at all. The idea of his courting me is ridiculous, haughty." Then after remembering that romantic summer evening she added, "And I really *did* want to be with him."

Liesse reached over to her friend and looked into her eyes, saying, "You are plenty to ask for, from anyone. I think he would be lucky to have you. He's probably thinking you are so easy-going that you hardly even miss him." Needing more detail, though, she added, "Did you have any more nights together since then?"

"We could have, at the lodge. But I didn't want to risk really obligating him. And the lodge is small, quiet, you know." Liesse nodded her head. Even her and Boris's tryst had been outside the lodge in the smoke shed. "I just wish I knew how he really felt." Liesse added,

"And he probably wished he knew how you felt. How do you feel?"

Genivee turned back to the window; the loiterers were all gone, back to their work.

"I miss him," she said. Just then Luna lost sudden interest in her sock. She threw it down and glanced around, then started to whine and whimper. Liesse picked her up and cuddled her, saying,

"When will Sparrow come back from visiting trees? Luna always gets this way when Kasch is not here to play with." Liesse bounced Luna on her knee and saw Genivee gaze at the baby with fondness. Having a child and a husband was preferable to being a lonely dairy maid whose youth was fading away. She said with confidence, "I think he will ask you to marry him, being a gentleman." Genivee nodded and said,

"And I'll say yes because I like him, not because I caught him." She threw up her hands and quipped, "If you sleep with them they pretend to lose interest; if you don't sleep with them they think you are insincere. Either way, they think you are trying to trap them."

"They trap themselves," Liesse countered. "If they didn't want sex so much, they wouldn't be so in its thrall. Listen, Genivee, being married is not a trap for men, although they will always protest that it is. The truth is, we are the ones getting caught and they are the ones getting what they wanted all along. And we keep sleeping with them even though they never again show the kind of yearning that melted our hearts in the first place. If you think he cares for you now, hold onto that. He won't keep reminding you of it forever." Genivee wondered how hardened Liesse's heart was becoming, not getting occasionally melted, as she claimed. She hoped a man like Magnus would be wise enough to dole out some affection, but then she knew people changed after marriage, once the struggle was over.

2

A Winter Wedding

Magnus pored over numerous papers spread out on the large table in the royal antechamber that showed the accounting and accomplishments of the latest tax collection. At the window with the best light, Harz stood next to the small desk where the secrctary sat ready with paper, quill and inkwell. While they waited for Gustav to arrive, Harz gazed out the window, scanning the people milling about in the courtyard at mid-morning. The dairymaids would all be done with their morning work and Genivee would certainly be elsewhere by now, but still he checked each person in view just to see if she was among them. He now had a reason to seek her out and speak to her. Word had come to him that Mona, their somewhat mutual friend, was saddened by the recent death of her favorite tabby cat. Knowing how old ladies must cherish feline companions, and knowing that the dairy was usually full of kittens, he was going to suggest to Genivee that she take one of them as a gift for the old woman. Perhaps one that resembled her late topaz tabby, for Genivee had seen the cat when they both visited about a year ago.

Gustav arrived and Harz turned away from the window. Boris continued chewing on a turkey leg, silently mistrusting Magnus to create any sort of interest for him in regard to a tax accounting. Magnus was studying the page with the summary of all the names and numbers the tax collection had gathered. Gustav stood next to him and perused the numbers as well, but didn't say anything until Magnus pointed to a number at the bottom and said, "That is the total collected for this year." Gustav was quiet a moment and then responded with,

"It is more than was collected last year, although not by much; it would seem a lot of trouble for little difference in revenue." But Magnus countered,

"This is the number of knights and lords we collected from this year; much more than in past years. When they were offered the choice of paying a month of service or paying a small tax, many of them decided to remain at their homes."

"Let's hope we don't need them to fight any battles," Gustav warned.

"Just so," Magnus replied. The results of battles were only rarely profitable and Gustav knew this. There had been no battles since Magnus had arrived years ago. He continued, "We made it clear they must in turn collect a lesser amount but diligently from all their own chattels; whenever peasants find out that others have managed to escape paying anything, the fever of not paying catches everyone. They aren't used to the new structure, but in years hence the benefit will accumulate. It is worth the effort to visit every knight and lord, and much better than spending more time with the richest few, listening to their tales of penury. Then the choice is either to believe them or confiscate some of their property, which only leaves them worse off. Either way, one of us gets robbed." Boris pushed up from the corner of the table and went casually over to look at the figures. Magnus concluded, "By not demanding so much of them, the knights will have more means to help those below them, and they prefer distributing alms to those below them than to handing over levies to the Count above. Then *they* can look generous instead of you looking generous." Gustav could well believe that knights enjoyed playing the part of beneficent master but being the Count he had to ask,

"And how does that profit the Court?"

"A kingdom is not rich when the ruler holds all the wealth. A rich kingdom is one in which everyone is busy doing what they are good at. But everyone must have some wealth to get started, and that means not having it locked in a coffer. You should not hope to gather the most money, but take pride in moving the greatest amount of it along."

Gustav doubted it; he had been told that a ruler should have all the money, for only he knew what to do with it. What would poor people do with sudden wealth? Perhaps, foolishly, they would merely hold onto it and stash it under their pillows at night, but Magnus knew this was not true. He said, "Believe me, they will spend their new-found money as quickly as they acquire it, and then it will be out in the realm again, circulating. A realm with money flying about is rich; one in which the money grows cold in their lockboxes is dead." Gustav raised his eyebrows but didn't ask any more questions. He had always hoped Magnus would bring more wealth into Wilker, but his richness was in ideas, not silver or gold. Gustav decided not to debate the matter further, for he had no experience with such a system. So he simply said,

"I shall look forward to next year's accounting." He promised himself he'd be rid of Magnus if things were not better by then, but had to admit he had thought that before and could never justify doing so. Then as if the next year had already arrived and there were extra revenue to spend, Magnus added his own suggestion for using it. This made both Harz and Boris look over at him in wonderment.

"New revenue might be put to good use building a bridge closer to the village and the castle. Saving several days on a trip to get to the merchants on the other side would benefit both this county and the next. As it is, many don't trade with Wilker because it is just too far to travel to do so."

"Hmmm," Gustav said. He wondered if qualified bridge builders could be found in Wilker but he didn't want to admit this to Magnus. If he had to pay the cost of foreign bridge builders, it would become impossible. "An interesting suggestion," he merely commented. He looked up from the figures and asked Boris if he had heard any comments about the recent tax collection or anything else of interest around the village but when there wasn't any, he turned to Magnus to query him on his own news. "And when is this wedding of yours and Genivee's to take place?"

"Three months hence. She wants a winter wedding when all is quiet." Boris, a picked bone in his hand, snorted that,

"Dead of winter is the best time to have a warm bride." Knowing such coarseness might offend his friend, Gustav quickly added,

"Any time is good, but women of course like to have things their own way. Or so my Sparrow tells me." They made further banter but Harz had closed his eyes and wasn't listening.

A week later, against his initial reluctance, Harz found himself riding into the village with a curious kitten tucked inside his jacket. Although he had been uncomfortable around Mona when he initially met her, he had decided that an old woman bereft of her favorite cat was an unfortunate and easily helped situation. Besides, the kitten had trotted out to him one morning while he was in the courtyard.

One unauthorized kitten removed from the castle would be part of his duty in serving the Count.

He arrived at Mona's abode at the edge of the village and as he had hoped, she was on her front porch with a shawl wrapped tightly around her. She paused in her rocking chair, leaned forward a bit to peruse her visitor and then welcomed him over with an indifferent wave. He walked through her small front yard now full of gone-by flowers falling over. He stepped onto her porch and took off his hat and swept it in front of him which made her smile. She pointed to a chair next to her and he sat down. She said,

"You're a kind man to visit an old woman who criticized him." Harz looked up at the sky and pondered.

"I don't recall that," he said. "I remember a woman who made excellent tea and cake."

"That's true, although I've no cake today, and anyway, it would seem I was mistaken about my ideas for you. I hear Genivee is to be married to some widower from across the river." Amazing what an old woman alone managed to know. Harz doubted that Mona had been wrong about anything, and thought it likely she was just being kind to say so. He hadn't pursued Genivee as perhaps she might have liked him to. He remembered why he was there and retrieved the sleepy-eyed kitten from his jacket and laid it down on Mona's lap. The kitten blinked, gazed around, then met Mona's eyes as she reached out to stroke the kitten's ears. The two looked at each other, the kitten stretched and took three turns around Mona's lap, then plopped down again, satisfied. Mona said, "Thank you for the gift, good sir. I do miss my Topaz, but little Gem here will bat away some of the sadness." Mona stroked Gem's ears and the kitten purred and rubbed its face against Mona's adoring fingers. The fingers stopped for a moment as Mona raised her eyes to look past Harz onto the far side of her porch, but only for a moment. She didn't want to try explaining to Harz how his father, long dead, happened to be standing there with them. Instead she was quiet for a spell and then asked Harz, "And how is that squire, the one with the cards, what is his name?"

"Trevka," Harz answered.

"Yes, Trevka."

"He is well. He is more favored by the Count as time goes on."

"I thought as much," Mona said. "He was thoughtful to give those cards back to me."

"Now you can tell fortunes again," Harz said.

"Oh, I have many cards, but I'm not so busy with them now." She stroked Gem's ears again. "I'm going to leave the fortune telling to you for now. I think you are up to it." Harz wondered at such an assessment, surely just an old woman feeling tired. Then she asked him, "Has Trevka found that wife he's looking for yet? I saw her close by." Harz wondered how she imagined such things. He knew Trevka seemed fond of Beth, or perhaps he was just protective and confusing the two. Harz wasn't certain that either was right for the other, either quite good enough for the other. Which one had more status in his mind was hard for him to separate.

"Perhaps," was all Harz could think of to say. Mona looked up from her new feline companion and gazed into Harz's eyes saying,

"Trevka does want for a wife, and many girls about the town and castle think highly of him for being the Viscount's rescuer. They gossip and giggle and ask me to read their palms to see if they might marry a noble man." Harz looked askance at Mona. Of course girls could be silly creatures, but was Mona making this up? Mona looked at him seriously and asked, "If you had a daughter, would you want her to marry Trevka? Do you think he is worthy of that?" Harz gazed at Mona while wondering how she came upon her theories. She did have a way of unsettling him, but along with the truth in her eyes there was also kindness. He replied finally, as he had thought much about it already and his answer was not difficult,

"Trevka has surprised me. He seems able to handle the unexpected with determination and imagination. I would like to be sure that he has not however, just encountered several occasions of good luck. He is still young and it takes more than bravado to carry one through." Mona thought about this and concluded,

"I think the same can be said about this girl he fancies, is it not so?" Harz thought about it, and Beth had acted not only with courage but faith.

"Yes, that's so," Harz said. After more consideration, Mona added,

"So they are alike that way. But what of their parents, their ancestors? Trevka is a squire and important at court. This girl came from far away. Perhaps that means they are too unequal." When Harz didn't comment, Mona concluded, "Yes, too unequal. I wonder what will happen to this girl then, if she does not find someone to protect her. She has no family, is that not so? A husband would be most advantageous to have, for when her tasks for the Count are finished, she will likely be sent on her way. And who knows where that will be." Harz finally had to interrupt her musings and told her,

"The Count is not so unfeeling as that. She has earned a place at court."

"By kidnapping his son? He can't forget that. No, she will need something else to keep her secure, otherwise she and all her children, should she ever have any, will be lost. Of course she would likely not have children, being on her own in the world. Such a sad, solitary life. A marriage of more than convenience would make her secure. One of love and status would do her well." Mona leaned over and squeezed Harz's hand. "Make sure she has that, she does deserve it." The bearded man at the end of the porch smiled at Mona and she knew she had said what he wanted her to. She leaned back and admired her new kitten. After a minute, Harz stood up to leave and smiled at her. He walked through the fading garden of her front yard and got back on his horse and turned to doff his hat. She raised her arm to wave good-bye, Gem batting at the tassels of her shawl. Ambrose was still on the porch with Mona and when Harz was out of sight he turned to her and said *Thank you*. Mona said to him,

"Well I'm glad you won't be needing to haunt me about it, but how long are you going to keep after him? Is it so important this mouse of a girl marries so well?"

"It is to Harz, more than he realizes. He'll be very glad one day he didn't let this opportunity go by. As you said, there are many other ladies with their unmarried eyes on Trevka and although he's fond of Beth today, he has been known to change his mind about these things in the past. And you never know how scheming young girls might be." Ambrose more thought his words than spoke them, but Mona understood him nevertheless. Looking back over her own life she mused,

"I may indeed know how scheming young girls can be, being one once myself. I used to go out and watch the royal processions and I remember you well." Mona cocked her head to one side and asked, "What made you die, anyway?" Ambrose thought about it, as he had before, but unfortunately he didn't know any more than anyone else. Maybe he would when he got beyond this in-between state where he seemed to be at the moment. He tried to answer Mona.

"I don't know. All I do know is that when I was about to die, I began to know things beyond my own self and time. I knew that the present Count was going to end up having to give his throne away to someone he was not expecting to give it to, maybe even to someone he wasn't even acquainted with. I also knew Harz was the only person close enough to him to prevent this happening, although I'm still not sure if even he can save the crown for someone with the same blood." Mona, not being royal herself and having an outsider's somewhat haughty opinion of the even haughtier said,

"Maybe that wouldn't be such a bad idea. I heard that his treasurer has some new ideas and some people seemed to be quite happy about it."

"Who is to know," Ambrose pondered. "I'm stuck here myself and hardly know what to do any better than when I was alive. One must move forward as best they can and try to help others. Perhaps there will be rest for me later at some point. For now..." He glanced at the road where Harz had ambled down and without thinking, got up and began to follow him. Mona watched him go and didn't know for whom she felt more sympathy; the ghost or the one he haunted. She petted Gem and felt glad to be neither.

Just before Christmas, Trevka's interest in Beth having not yet faded, he was in the courtyard on a quiet afternoon, gazing up toward the nursery. He knew when Sparrow would take Kasch out for a stroll and Beth would stay inside, unable to stand the cold air that Sparrow barely noticed. He didn't know where Liesse would be but he'd take his chances, for although he had made eyes at her once, she was now married. He had a page with him who played the lute and decided the time was right to tap his shoulder to begin playing. He placed one hand on his heart and held the other out and began singing,

"Lo, how a Rose e'er blooming from tender stem hath sprung!
It came a floweret bright, amid the cold of winter,
When half spent was the night.
The Flower, whose fragrance tender with sweetness fills the air,
Dispels with glorious splendor the darkness everywhere."

Inside the nursery, Liesse and Beth were listening. As Trevka repeated the chorus Liesse commented,

"He's forgetting some of the lyrics!" But Beth blushed a little, even though it was really just a Christmas carol. Liesse then looked at Beth and said, "He's not singing to me. If you go to the window it's a sign you accept his gift, probably the only one a poor Squire has." The lutist's fingers were getting cold and numb and the last notes were twanging in the still air. Snowflakes began to scatter and the two troubadours stood silently below the window. The lutist rubbed his hands together and blew on his fingers while Trevka scanned the window.

"Again," Trevka said as he indicated for the page to play. He sang again. Inside, Liesse, wondering how long they would be out there and noticing what must be very cold air to sing in, leaned over and said to Beth,

"You'd better show your appreciation before they both freeze to death." So Beth put Dane down and went to the window. She looked down on the two and smiled, then waved her hand. As they finished the second verse, she tapped her hands together in silent applause. Trevka looked up at her and smiled, forgetting to bow deeply as he had planned.

In January, Beth was on her way to the wedding of Magnus and Genivee, walking by herself to the old stone chapel and wondering how she had come to be invited. Although she knew something of Genivee, it was only because Liesse liked to talk about her friend, as in fact she liked to talk about everyone. Beth knew only very few people in the castle, spending most of her time in the nursery and sleeping next door to it. Beth had met the Count and his cousin Harz, but only briefly. As she approached, she admired the quaint chapel with steeply peaked roof and small round windows of stained glass framed by large stones in a radial pattern that contrasted with the squarely placed blocks of the building. There was an enormous yew tree at one corner that hung over the whole chapel and small cemetery. It was certainly a fairy tale place to have a wedding but as Beth thought this, she realized the chapel resembled another fairy tale house made of gingerbread and a candy roof.

Beth entered the building and took a seat at the far side in the shadows. Her inclination had been to stay in the nursery with all the babies but she didn't want to snub the only invitation she had received since being here. Musicians were playing a flute and a violin. She heard men whispering behind her and expected that very soon one of them would request she leave but instead one came around and said, "Can my fortune be so great as to find you here in need of an escort? Or has your escort stepped away?" Trevka awaited an answer. Beth said,

"He has just arrived," and she indicated the empty seat next to her. Trevka sat down and straightened the sleeves of his jacket. Beth asked him, "How well do you know the bride?" He was about to answer with his usual swagger something like, 'Quite well, she's an old flame,' but decided that would be both untrue and ungentlemanly.

"I have known her several years and she is a very fine lady."

"And the groom?" Trevka could go on for quite a while about Magnus's wide knowledge, equanimity, of his being a foreigner who was better regarded than some natives. Instead he said,

"A man whose status I could not do justice describing." Beth wondered how it was that Genivee, whom Liesse described as a milkmaid, was coming to marry this man who advised the Count, but Trevka was not as inclined to gossip as she had been led to believe. Perhaps Liesse made much of that up, or else he was changing his ways. She also wondered if Trevka was actually here because he liked her, as Liesse also gossiped, or whether he was still here under instructions not to let her out of his sight. She imagined the Count was suspicious of her, even though he was letting her stay and giving her charge of his son. Beth glanced around at the chapel, decorated with pine sprigs and holly berries. It was a beautiful place for a wedding and several stoves warmed the chapel suitably.

The music changed to a processional and everyone turned to watch Liesse, the brown-haired matron of honor enter the chapel, and then the bride in an ivory silk dress and carrying a bundle of holly and ivy. Gazes followed their progress down the aisle and then watched as words were spoken and exchanged. The officiant's aged voice did not carry well and so the ceremony was muffled and vague at their distance. Beth therefore studied their faces, what she could discern from her vantage. The man was somewhat older, very refined. The bride was lovely and graceful. The marriage was declared sanctified and they kissed. Beth thought perhaps they would be happy in spite of the vast difference in their rank. They were certainly handsome together.

The ceremony was over and the bride and groom left the chapel with their friends closely following. Beth waited in her seat, not wishing to dash toward the door nor follow quickly behind these people who did not know her and likely didn't want to. Trevka waited patiently until Beth indicated she wanted to leave. She had thought everyone of importance had left but then noticed Harz walking by and studying her again. She had only seen him once before, and that was when she had been brought before the Count after her kidnapping attempt. She had been certain she would be interrogated and punished for the scheme. Instead they had just studied her and for some reason Harz had decided she wasn't a threat and from then on her job was to watch over Dane, which was all that she wanted. Now Harz looked at them both intently and she deduced that Harz had been instructing Trevka to keep his eyes on her. *And I had hoped it was because Trevka favored me*, she thought.

When they were outside the chapel and most everyone had driven away in carriages or on horseback, Beth commenced her walk back to the castle, not very far away, but Trevka insisted she not walk alone. "The forest can be full of vagabonds," he warned. Beth replied,

"Yes, I used to be one of them," and they smiled at each other. As they walked, Trevka regaled her with an accounting of the lore of the forest they were passing through and the fortune of a sunny and not-too-cold winter day. Perhaps he was hoping she would relax her guard and give away some scheme working in her mind, but she didn't say much. As they reached the edge of the forest and the castle came into view, Beth asked him suddenly, "Trevka is this your job? Do you keep an eye on me because that is what you are told to do?" Trevka stopped talking, surprised to hear anger in her voice. He said,

"No, in fact Harz hasn't given me any assignment of late." Then thinking that didn't sound very complimentary to himself added, "But I think he may be sizing me up for something important."

"Oh," Beth said. She had thought being spied on was an insult, but now it seemed *not* being spied on was even more of one. They were now safely within the castle walls and Beth said, "Thank-you for walking with me, then. How fortunate that you didn't have to risk your life protecting mine from vagabonds. I know you would have." She turned to walk across the courtyard and head up to the nursery. Trevka watched until she was safely inside, then turned toward the reception hall certainly filled with food, a welcome thought against the chill creeping into his bones. He had taken a mere step or two when Harz caught up to him and said,

"Trevka! There is a new assignment for you and it begins right away."

Trevka glanced in the direction of the banquet hall and pointed in its direction. Harz continued, "The Count requests a party to travel to Uluvost and ascertain that the Countess Gertrudis is fairly accommodated. You are to take charge of the traveling party." Trevka was not responding with his usual exuberance for a new escapade. Instead, he was hoping Harz would notice the blustery wind battering at them both. "Can you undertake the task or shall it fall to someone else?" Harz asked him, impatient with his lack of attention.

"Uluvost?" Trevka remarked. It was less an adventure and more of a punishment.

"Yes, you must be ready in two days." *Two days?*, Trevka thought: he would spend the whole time eating at the reception they were now missing.

"And how long shall I be gone?" Trevka asked.

"As long as is necessary. The Count wants a complete assurance that every effort is made to talk to the Countess and register any complaints or needs she may have. Uluvost has not been known as the most luxurious of places and she merits at least as much as she was promised when she married out of it." Trevka could hardly object unless he wanted to lose all hopes of moving up in the court. If he didn't take on every task asked of him, he would never become a knight one day. But Uluvost would be an unwelcoming, hostile place from both the inhabitants and the land. The roads would be poorly kept and likely deep in mud. The forest would be rampant with wild animals as well as the poachers sure to be shadowing them. Trevka said offhandedly,

"There should be at least six in the party, thieves abound."

"Yes," Harz answered, "six is suitable." Trevka nodded his head in acknowledgment of the assignment and was stiffly waiting for Harz to leave so that he could begin shaking his head in disbelief and muttering in disgust. But Harz wasn't finished and added, "And when you return, if you return, we shall see if Beth has cared enough to warrant your courting her formally, as you should if you have an interest in her. For otherwise, you must end your attention to her all together and right away. Anything less is dishonorable." Trevka looked surprised at Harz but he wasn't jesting; he was actually saying that Trevka would have the Count's permission to court and marry Beth. Harz suddenly turned and walked away. Trevka wondered for a moment if Harz himself had an interest in Beth. He almost acted jealous, or maybe he was just protective. Or maybe the Count did not want this girl to be without a husband to keep her in check.

Days later, having seen nothing of Trevka, Beth asked Liesse, her earpiece to the goings-on in the rest of the castle, if she had happened to see him about. She teased that she might do something dastardly just to make sure he was watching as usual. But Liesse wasn't in the mood for jesting. She said with a somber tone, "Trevka is busy preparing to leave on a mission to the south, to Uluvost. You know it, I believe." Beth's hands went cold. Yes, she knew it. She had been sent there when she was only twelve to work for the Countess Gertrudis, which her parents had thought was a plum. Beth's work consisted of carrying Gertrudis's dirty laundry personally down to the washrooms in the basements and supervising its separate and careful washing; she was admonished to never let the items leave her sight. Any imperfections on the clothes were blamed on her, which meant that the normal wear and tear Gertrudis inflicted on her garments became Beth's responsibility. What's more, Beth being in the washrooms insulted the other laundresses who assumed that she herself found them to be incompetent and untrustworthy, and therefore made her visits to the laundry an ordeal.

The coldness in Beth's hands spread to her neck. The name of Uluvost brought back the memory of the night when Gertrudis woke Beth abruptly. "This slip has a blot at the hem! You think I should wear such filth? Fix it immediately!" Beth glanced around; the windows were dark and it seemed past midnight. Beth did not bother to complain but took the garment and groggily headed for the basements, which would at least be unoccupied then. On returning an hour later, a drunken brute stopped her coming up the stairs. She was inhumanely attacked as he held his hand over her mouth so hard she couldn't scream and nearly suffocated. Afterward, gasping to breathe, she was barely able to find her way back to her room. She had come close to being strangled and so escaping with her life seemed a mercy, but just barely. When she got to her room Gertrudis was sound asleep. Very soon after that, to her great relief, Gertrudis took her and all her entourage to Wilker, Gertrudis married Gustav, and five months went quietly by. Life in Wilker was much better and it seemed her trouble was behind her. But after a while she had to confess to some of the Wilker housemaids that she was pregnant. The two women stared at her in disbelief. One finally said, "The Count won't mind but you mustn't let Gertrudis know of your condition, she will throw you into the street! From now on you must work at night and fetch the quenchers and potions she asks for; it will be dark so she won't notice your condition and then you can sleep during the day." When Beth became hugely pregnant, she was reported to have an illness. Since Gertrudis was also pregnant and deathly afraid of contagion, she did not ask for details but rather hid herself away, one of her many excuses for doing so.

On the night Beth was having her baby, Gertrudis was also busy having hers. The two nursemaids with Beth assured her it was very fortunate to have things this way. "They are occupied with Gertrudis and no one will miss us." But it also meant the most competent midwives were helping Gertrudis and not Beth, and Beth's baby did not survive its first night. Beth wept inconsolably even while the nursemaids tried to assure her it was for the best, for what did she want with a child conceived by a brute? "And how can you love such a child anyway, my dear?" But Beth protested to them,

"I do, I do love my child. He was mine, he meant everything to me. I am alone now," and she sobbed all the more, for she could not convince them that she loved, wanted and missed her child, and had separated the meanness of its father from his innocent life. The nursemaids looked at each other over Beth's wailing sobs and left her to herself. The following night, as she lay in her bed watching the sun set and wishing she would fade away with it, the nursemaids brought in a baby. At first Beth imagined it was her own; they had been terribly mistaken and it had not died. But no, this was Gertrudis's baby and she was refusing to nurse it. She had nearly refused to give birth to it, her delivery being extremely fraught with screams and threats and language so unfitting a high-born woman that those around her were nearly witless as to how to help her. Now a nursemaid sat on the edge of Beth's bed and said, "Her mother won't even hold the child and it shall not live without milk. We knew you would be able to give it this, and so take this child and nurse it as your own, for the future count is so very important, and you shall have a place of importance for such assistance."

Liesse reached out her hand and placed it on Beth's shoulder; she was deep in thought and Liesse could imagine with what. She knew the facts of Beth's early experience; she knew that while Beth cared for and nursed Dane, his own mother took little interest in him and disagreed more and more with her husband the Count. After a while Gertrudis did something so offensive that she was sent back home to Uluvost as Gustav could not stand to have her in his castle any more.

Dane was to stay, of course, he was the future Count, but no one a part of Gertrudis's original court could remain. Beth went crazy with worry; the baby was still nursing. So instead of leaving with the rest of the departing entourage, Beth hid in a closet and waited for her cousins to come to her aid, rescue her and Dane and head off to who knew where, for it was an ill-conceived plan with little definition. Trevka caught them in no time and the whole thing came to an end.

Beth shook herself out of her reverie and asked Liesse, "Why is Trevka going to Uluvost?" Liesse answered,

"He and a party of six are there to make sure the Countess is being well looked after. The Count must see it as his obligation. I myself think Gertrudis is somewhat out of her mind, and there is no help for that." They looked at each other and shook their heads sadly. "The Count is making sure she is not neglected; it seems he has little confidence in Uluvost." Just then Sparrow returned and entered the nursery, but as they didn't keep secrets from each other Liesse said immediately, "We were talking about Trevka and his trip to Uluvost. Remember Beth was there for a time." Sparrow had heard it all from Gustav, but appreciated her two friends not attempting to hide anything from her. She said to them,

"Gustav told me about it. He is thoughtful to think of Gertrudis; I know he is indebted to her for giving him an heir, which is important to him." Liesse looked to Beth hoping to roll her eyes at such undeserved largesse, but Beth was still lost in thought. Sparrow sat down next to her and took her hand. "Trevka will be all right, he's in a large party and they are on the Count's business." Beth nodded her head and tried to smile. She said,

"How long will he be gone?" Sparrow had no idea about these things and looked at Liesse. She knew it would take at least a week or two, quite easily more if the Uluvost court proved uncooperative. Liesse said blithely,

"Oh, it all depends on the weather I imagine. Good weather always makes travel faster." But Beth knew better. She said,

"They are taking him away from me because I'm not good enough. I'll never see him again." Sparrow and Liesse looked at each other and couldn't assure her one way or another. Trevka had become well regarded and it wouldn't do to have him marry someone unsuitable. Beth was, after all, a nursemaid and no more. There really wasn't much hope that she could marry anyone, let alone anyone of decent rank. She felt compelled to tell her two friends, "You know when I fell in love with Trevka? The moment I met him. I was kidnapping Dane, trotting away from the castle and he came upon us and gently stopped my horse. He could have killed me on the spot for what I was doing. But without admonition or reprimand he kindly touched my arm and turned us around. I was beginning to cry, fearful of what I had done and what they would do to me for it. But the kindness in his eyes made me give up completely and I let him lead me back to my uncertain fate."

Nobody said anything as Beth studied the three babies before them in their usual place, an area enclosed by a triangle of long sofas with a heavy wool rug in its center. Kasch and Luna were almost a year old and Kasch was putting one of Luna's feet in his mouth; Dane was trying to hit Kasch over the head with a toy but Kasch was unconcerned. Not getting attention, Dane turned around and toddled over to Beth with his arms out. She picked him up and rocked him on her lap but her thoughts were still with the party soon to be traveling away. Although she wished she could be near Trevka, she was glad not to be going with them. The idea of going to Uluvost was not something she wanted to contemplate.

3

A trip to Uluvost

Beth watched from the window of the nursery as the men and horses were assembled in the courtyard. Several horses were brought along to carry supplies and replace any that went lame. The trip would take a week at least if the party was not delayed by weather and encountered no trouble but more if they did. Much had been prepared the day before so it didn't take long for the horses to be loaded and the men to be told their riding order. Trevka was in charge of the party, of getting there safely and back, however another man, Sir Sutherland, would be the one speaking to Countess Gertrudis. He was a diplomatic man whom Gustav hoped Gertrudis didn't remember, since she disliked everyone she did remember and the feeling was mutual. Ash and Morgan would tend the horses and gear, Dr. Quillin was the accompanying physician and a large man called Brake was along for strength. As they mounted their horses and assembled into line, it began to drizzle. Sparrow and Liesse, sitting on the sofas and not wishing to watch the departure, looked up at Beth when she announced with alarm, "It's beginning to rain. Shouldn't they delay leaving?" Liesse commented quickly and without thinking,

"But it could rain for days this time of year." Beth turned back to the window and scraped the sill with her fingernails and said,

"Then the roads will be muddy, they should most definitely wait!" Liesse got up from her sofa and went over to the window. The horses were filing out of the courtyard in order. Trevka, second in line after Brake, looked back at the castle toward the nursery but didn't wave or salute. When they had cleared the gate and headed down the tree-lined road toward the village they disappeared from view and Liesse led Beth over to the sofa to sit down. Dane came over to Beth for a drink of milk. But he soon was satisfied and went back onto the floor to pursue Kasch across the rug. Even though Dane was almost a year older, they were about the same size. Beth sighed and said, "He doesn't nurse as long any more. I think one day he will just not bother." Liesse answered,

"Then he won't need it. He's weaning himself, he's growing up." Beth seemed downcast. First Trevka left and now Dane was crawling away from her. It was beginning to rain harder and she glared at the window. Liesse continued, "Now, if you want to be rid of that gloomy face before Trevka gets back, we had better start on that right now. He won't want to court, let alone marry, such a sad face." They began to gossip on the possibilities of her actually getting married and Sparrow listened with casual interest. They certainly did attach a lot of value to marriage, although to Sparrow it was just one relationship. There were so many others that she never felt lonely or sad even when Gustav was very busy with court matters. She had had a fascinating conversation with a house cat the other day, an animal she had been delighted to meet for the first time. But relating their chat might seem odd to the others and besides, the cat had sworn her to secrecy.

Along the road to Uluvost, the traveling party was encountering squalls of rain between which were bursts of sunshine competing with racing clouds. The road was familiar to all of them and they passed several small outlying villages where the people recognized the royal party, for they rode in royal livery. They stopped to water their horses at a settlement a ways from the castle and two girls came out to flirt with the party. Sir Sutherland sniffed as the girls admired both the horses and Ash and Morgan, and twittered to each other about Trevka. Trevka ignored them while watching the horse-keepers field the girls' inquiries as they checked the tack and bridles. Trevka heard Sutherland mutter discontent about the waste of time and then pipe up at Morgan about being on their way, but he interrupted before Sutherland actually articulated their destination. They remounted and continued on, eating their prepared lunch while still on horseback; the sooner they got to the first night's stop the better, as the roads were thickening with mud. They made good time and stayed at a pub the first night, one which for some travelers was the second day's lunching place.

The innkeepers there also recognized the royal livery and established the party in the private dining room, announcing to all and sundry who entered that "the room is closed due to his Augustness the Count of Wilker's men occupying the private dining room this evening. It will be closed therefore all the rest of the night." This offered little privacy to the royal party and brought forth loud, whistling intakes of breath from the patrons, whose number grew as the night wore on, and roars of assurance and delight from the innkeeper, for whom a novelty such as this was a rare advantage in revenue.

The following day it was colder and threatened to snow, but at least the roads were solid under their feet. Villages they passed through still recognized the Wilker livery but did not come out to flirt with the horsemen or the dignitaries, whether due to the icy breeze or lack of interest no one could know. As they made their way further south, mostly downhill, Trevka knew they were on the correct road and passing through the right towns, but in places the road became less familiar and he would find himself wondering if a certain landmark or valley was where it ought to be. By the end of the second day they had reached another inn and were given rooms above the stables and ate their meal there as well. Still, they were making good time and might make Uluvost in a few days total if the weather held passable.

On the third day of travel the storm that had brought spatters of rain and a few flakes of snow seemed now to be considering whether to linger or race eastward. The underbelly of a gray cloud bank hung over them as they made their way down a detour towards Uluvost. They had been warned that a bridge was out on the more-traveled valley road and they would do better to go through the hills where the river was narrower if they wanted to make good time. The air was still and quiet and Trevka listened as their horses' footfalls resounded in the closing countryside. Late in the afternoon, coming into sight of a small settlement, they decided to inquire at the largest house if they could purchase a meal and a night for men on a royal mission. The person at the door asked which royal house was on a mission and upon hearing Wilker, he merely shrugged. It appeared that whatever list of undesirables there was, Wilker was not on it. There was not a spare room for them so Trevka agreed they would stay in the stable with the horses. Sir Sutherland was less than thrilled, but to Trevka it was not surprising (but merely fortuitous) that they had acquired lodgings at all for the night. Sutherland looked around at the barn's interior and asked, "Where is a diplomat to be comfortable in this disorderly hovel?" Trevka glanced at the loft, his destination and said,

"Do you like climbing?" Sutherland looked aghast at the rickety ladder and sputtered dismay without actually saying anything. "In that case, I suggest this stall; it will be the least drafty," and he indicated a spot where Morgan was placing hay for the horses. It was dry and twiggy hay but hay nonetheless. Hoping the men would be spared another night of Sutherland's enumerations of the day's mishaps and predictions of tomorrow's follies, Trevka asked Morgan to find some dry straw for the diplomat and pointed out to Sutherland that, "This is far more suitable for a man of your rank; it would be unthinkable of me to expect you to yet again pass the night in our company." With that he climbed up the ladder, jiggling it excessively as he went.

In the loft, after eating some dried meat brought from Wilker, Dr. Quillin wondered out loud if the hill road was a shortcut or long cut compared to the valley road. "Longer, I would think," Trevka said. "Although a road to oneself is often preferable. Our host told me that the village of Stoer is within a day's ride, and that is only an hour outside Uluvost castle." Morgan said with some little confidence,

"I hope he wasn't gaming us, making us ride till midnight in ignorance."

"I paid him well enough not to be inclined to lie, and we shall be returning this same way." Trevka said. Quillin asked,

"Are we in Uluvost proper, then?" Brake and Morgan were silent and Ash waited too for an answer. Trevka shook his head and said,

"No, you can't miss it when we cross the border. Even on a lonely road as this, there will be guards."

The fourth day of their journey indeed brought them to the edge of Uluvost. A small hut slumped next to the road and a few thin and hobbled horses grazed nearby on brown stubble. It appeared to be an abandoned post, as no one emerged from the hut. Still, Trevka ordered the procession to slow to a walk and Sutherland wondered if he planned to try and sneak across. As they neared the guard house, still no one emerged. Trevka held his arm up to signal a halt and the men glanced around. Sutherland and Quillin conferred in whispers; if Trevka were planning on storming through the gates, they were not in favor of a such a plan, nor confident in their ability to join it successfully. Trevka called out in a loud voice, "Ho! We come in the name of the Count of Wilker! Greetings and hail to the County of Uluvost." A pair of men came suddenly out of the guard house with pikes in hand. One asked,

"What business have ye here? We've no expectation of your arrival and ye must therefore turn around and go back." Trevka got off his horse and walked up to the men and their pikes. One aimed his weapon at Trevka's gut but he strode right past it, pushing the tip of the spear away with his thumb.

"Gentlemen," Trevka held his hand out and shook each of their hands in turn, smiling and then bowing low. "How good of you to greet us and to guard the border with such diligence. Our dear Count Gustav knew you would welcome representatives of his court to pay a call upon the Countess Gertrudis. Her welfare, you see, is our mission and we are grateful you take the duty of guarding her borders with such fortitude. I can see this border is as secure as any on a more traveled road." He turned then and quickly introduced the men in order of rank and each one nodded in turn when Trevka blazed his eyes at them. After a series of mumbled greetings, Trevka ordered Morgan to unpack some sack, their hardest liquor, and some food from the bags and they would take a much-earned rest.

After twenty minutes the border guards were laughing and telling tales of their dull tasks with as much familiarity as if the men from Wilker visited often. After another twenty minutes the party from Wilker ambled through the gate at a leisurely stroll. Sutherland had been baffled into quietude and the guards were feeling sad to see them go. It was not until the Wilker horses walked casually over the nearest hill that they resumed their cantering pace and made for Stoer.

Installed at the Stoer inn, Trevka leaned back on a cot, one of several in their large room. Tomorrow they would arrive at Uluvost castle and Trevka pondered who had decided, and why, to send him on this errand. As usual, he questioned whether Harz and Gustav and Boris were just trying to send him off somewhere to keep him occupied. Or did they actually think he was the right man for this job? He hadn't imagined Gustav cared enough about Gertrudis to send someone to inquire after her. He wasn't looking forward to meeting the royal Uluvost family, and hopefully he wouldn't have to. Sir Sutherland was the one assigned to make all the diplomatic encounters. Trevka was only seeing to their safely getting there and back; half the job was almost done. As Trevka pondered, Brake came over and sat in a chair nearby. He said,

"These Uluvostians don't smile much, do they? How mean are they by nature?" Trevka didn't want to comment on what he'd heard and seen of the Uluvost natives. He knew they had not been kind to Beth and that was enough to make him dislike them. But he couldn't judge the whole lot by a few. He sat up and leaned against the wall of the room, faced Brake and said,

"They are pretty much like everyone else, until you cross them. Tell me, how did you get that name?"

"My mother used to spin flax with an instrument called a brake. As she watched me in my cradle, a big fat baby with swinging fists, and that machine separated the fibers from the twigs, she had a vision of me sorting out the bad lots from the good and named me Brake." Trevka smiled. "And I'm good at breaking up fights, it's true. People would rather quit fighting each other than fight with me." They heard noises and smelled food roasting and so went downstairs to wait for the meal. Ash and Morgan were in the stables watching the horses and gear and would get their food afterward.

The next morning it was clear and chilly with a crisp breeze in their faces and cold air stinging their eyes. They arrived at the gates of Uluvost and several guards kept them behind the portcullis for a while as they examined their letter of mission. Trevka studied their perusal of the document and seriously doubted that either of them could read. They looked at the signature and up at the party on horseback. They ran their hands over the horses' regalia and then conferred with each other. They spoke the same language as in Wilker but had accents and a few odd words here and there. Finally they decided to let them pass and the portcullis was pulled up and the party went through into a courtyard that was barren and soggy. It was not so much a courtyard at all; it was a narrow, winding space between stone buildings that crept with mildew.

They were escorted to the front door but were then given no introduction; the inspection at the gate was not relayed. The keeper inside the castle opened the wicket, a sliding metal panel so small it revealed only half his face. His beady eyes examined the visitors but did not voice a greeting or query. Sir Sutherland stepped up to the door and declared, "We are a diplomatic party from Wilker here to meet with the Countess Gertrudis."

"What for?" the greeter unceremoniously asked. It was insulting to be questioned by this underling doorkeeper and Sir Sutherland did not have an immediate answer. He stepped back a ways and sputtered momentarily while trying to think whether to attempt an answer or chide the man for his vulgarity. Trevka stepped into the space Sutherland had vacated and spoke threateningly to the man.

"The Countess Gertrudis herself sent word asking to see us and we have answered her summons in a most timely manner. You are delaying our mission." The man slammed the wicket shut and the double doors to Uluvost castle began to creak open. The air inside whooshed out onto the visitors as if it had been waiting to escape; it was colder and danker than the air outside. There was only darkness inside but Trevka stepped forward anyway, thinking that if he stumbled into or stepped on the doorkeeper so much the better. After everyone entered, everyone excepting Ash and Morgan who stayed outside with the horses, the door was closed and locked and the doorkeeper led them to a room down a long hall, far from the front door and hardly commodious. They were shown inside and left without a word as the door was locked behind them. After the doorkeeper had walked back down the hall, keys clanking and footfalls clapping, Brake went over to the door and checked it. Dr. Quillin and Sutherland whispered to each other and Trevka crossed his arms and examined the room, walking to the far side of it and noting that there were no other doors and the only windows were higher than could be reached by hand. Brake came over to him and asked,

"I didn't know the Countess had sent for us, that was lucky."

"She didn't send for us, but that little toad wouldn't know or have the courage to ask." He glanced around at the accommodations; only plank benches without backs and no food or drink set out, not even a table to put anything on. It looked like a room where underlings were lectured. In fifteen minutes a different man came into the room. He stood near the doorway but didn't say anything. He seemed to be looking at each of them trying to decide if they had ever met before. He seemed relieved not to recognize anyone. Sir Sutherland approached the man after a few stilted moments; it was the host's duty to greet his visitors first but he didn't appear to intend doing that. Sir Sutherland said,

"I am the right honorable Sir Sutherland, sent by the Count of Wilker to inquire after the health and well-being of the Countess Gertrudis. I do hope this does not come as an inconvenience, but with the state of the roads..." The man looked down at Sutherland as he would a spider crossing the floor. The man was thin and plain and the only thing about him that looked at all animated were his crazed eyes, which stared intently at everything. His gaze made Sutherland trail off on his explanation. Finally Sutherland asked the man, "And whom do I have the honor of addressing?"

"Malvern."

"Very good, Mr. Malvern, as I was saying, with the state of the roads it is impossible to tell when one might be able to make the trip successfully and we did come with the Countess's health in mind."

There was a long silence while Malvern gazed across the room at Trevka. Trevka met his gaze and didn't take his eyes off him which was something Malvern usually waited for. Finally Malvern said,

"The Countess is in excellent health. It is very good of you all to inquire however we cannot accommodate you. You may apply to the inn in the village, it is usually vacant." Sir Sutherland glanced at Trevka and said with some trepidation,

"We were hoping to see the Countess, to have a chance to talk to her. If it is not over a meal, that is understandable-" Suddenly Trevka broke in and declared,

"Sir Sutherland, we have inconvenienced these good people long enough. We have their assurance that the Countess is well and that is satisfactory. We must leave now if we are to secure lodging at the inn." Trevka strode over to Sutherland and took his arm while the latter continued protesting the irregularity of it all but they reached the door together with Trevka repeating in a loud voice, "Their assurance is all we need." Sutherland opened his mouth but Trevka's fingers dug into his arm and he squeaked a little before blurting out,

"Yes, quite enough," and nodded at Malvern as Trevka shoved him through the doorway. Quillin and Brake strode down the hall after the two while Trevka called out loud enough for the doorkeeper to hear,

"Mr. Malvern instructs us to be on our way. Let us not be slow in compliance." The front door opened before them and they were back in the bright morning air, Ash and Morgan turning to look at them with great surprise, for they had expected to spend the day there. They all got back on their horses and rode through the winding turns between the stone walls, each one providing a waiting spot for marksmen who would be unseen until they were right upon them. The guards at the portcullis did not open the gate but rather rose to stand shoulder to shoulder against the visitors so recently admitted; they had allowed thieves to escape in the past and were not keen to relive the punishment that had followed, and these men were in a hurry. Trevka did not wish to provide yet more excuses to them and instead tossed a coin in the air and said, "For your trouble, gentlemen, our visit was so short we must make amends for bothering you again so soon." The guard caught the coin and raised the portcullis and the six men from Wilker trotted through. Trevka led them at a brisk pace through the surrounding hutment and onto the other side, not stopping until they had reached a copse of trees where they rested the horses. If anyone had watched from the castle, it would have looked as if they were headed back to Wilker in a hurry, having turned tail and run. Finally Sir Sutherland had a chance to speak.

"Mr. Trevka," he admonished in a high-pitched tone, "I was to speak to and see the Countess, and Dr. Quillin here was to be on hand in case she had any complaints. This is not acceptable." Trevka watched the road leading up to the forest edge; no one was on it, yet at least. "We must go back at once and demand to see the Countess in person." Sutherland was quite a bit more stern with Trevka than he had been with Malvern. Trevka would have imitated Malvern's withering stare if he didn't find it so witless. He kept his eyes on the road while speaking to Sutherland in a somewhat less audible tone.

"People who could not spare a room nor even be bothered to provide a drink for the Count of Wilker's men have no intention of allowing an audience with a Countess or anyone else. The only thing they were about to spare was our time in that room and you are lucky we are not stuck the entire day there only to be turned out at dusk to fend for ourselves in a closed-up village. And my title is Squire Trevka." Sutherland considered this and said,

"But then there must be something wrong with the Countess, we must go back at once!" Sutherland certainly had more courage in the out of doors. But Trevka replied as he indicated to Ash and Morgan that they were re-mounting,

"We are not returning for at least a week, more if the weather is bad. And *you* are not returning even then. Nor you," he indicated to Quillin. Sutherland remonstrated at this apparent insult,

"We are not afraid of them, even if you are," to which Trevka replied simply,

"No, it is the fact that *they* are afraid of *you* that you shall not be visiting them again." They got back on their horses and rode back to Stoer and were reinstalled in the same rooms they had left just that morning.

The sun rose over Stoer for the fifth day of their stay and Ash and Morgan chatted with the stable-keeper, with whom they had become acquainted rather well. The cold weather had passed and the days were quiet and pleasant. They concluded their chat with the stable-keeper and bade him farewell, then strolled to the bakery and bought the items they knew the rest of the party would want. The innkeepers were not as quick to provide breakfast as everyone would like, so these trips to the bakery were happy diversions for Ash and Morgan and helped fill the days that were otherwise empty and dull. They headed up to the room that now seemed their own and entered just as a server was placing a large pot of hot cider on the table. They held the door open until she left, then settled down at the table, unwrapping their bread and butter for the morning meal.

Having idled away five days at the Inn at Stoer, Sutherland had no patience left and decided they had wasted enough time. He approached the table but didn't take a seat. Instead he declared to Trevka, "The time has come for us to revisit Uluvost. I'm sure by now they have had time to realize that we mean business and they must let us see the Countess. You may accompany me back to the castle however I shall do all the talking." Trevka sighed and appeared not to listen. He finished chewing on a piece of bread and then pulled a ring from his pocket, pushed it onto his index finger and held it out for Sutherland to examine. Harz had given him the ring before they left. Trevka asked Sutherland,

"How much would you say this is worth?" Sutherland made a sound of exasperation but looked at the ring and gasped.

"Isn't that the Count's ring? It has his insignia."

"It's one of them, I suppose," Trevka replied.

"Well then I'd say it is worth a lot." Sutherland wondered why Trevka had been entrusted with such a valuable item, (and not *him*), then glanced up at him and narrowed his eyes. "You're not thinking of pawning that to keep us here at this inn for another week, are you? This is just one big folly to you, I suppose." Trevka was not inclined to explain himself to this man who had been unhelpful from the beginning. He suggested instead,

"Sutherland, why don't you and Quillin return to Wilker. Your presence here is not needed and they will be wondering where we are. You can reassure them that we are still on our mission and completing it as well as is possible. Ash will accompany you back." Sutherland was appalled.

"I'm not leaving until I've seen and spoken to the Countess. If you are idling here to let everyone back in Wilker think you are accomplishing something, that is reprehensible. They will be thinking you are spending days and days fulfilling your mission, and here you sit doing nothing. I will not leave and abandon my duty." Trevka said,

"In that case I may *have* to pawn this ring to keep you in accommodations here. Is that what you want?" Sutherland straightened his back and declared,

"I shall pay for my own room and board." He headed for the door to seek out the proprietor. Turning before he left he poked his finger into the air and proclaimed, "I shall not slink back to Wilker without completing my mission!" And he left the room. When he was gone, Trevka muttered to himself, *Neither shall I.*

At the end of the week, having spent eight desultory days of relative good weather in Stoer, Trevka pulled Brake, Ash and Morgan aside and said to them, "I have been giving Malvern this time to work on improving whatever situation the Countess was in when we visited, my guess being it was not so great. He will calculate that we have ridden back to Wilker and informed them of our suspicions – that she is not being well cared-for, and now he will be able to prove otherwise. We are returning tomorrow morning with a message and gift from the Count, which may or may not end up in Gertrudis's hands, but either way we should at least be granted an audience with her." After considering for another moment he said to Ash, "You will stay behind and make sure that Quillin and Sutherland do not leave the inn for any reason. Tie them down if you have to." Brake asked,

"So you think they were just scared and didn't want us to see Gertrudis until they could fix things up a bit?"

"I'm hoping that's all they had to hide. But I wouldn't be surprised if they were hiding much more. I frankly wouldn't be surprised to find out she was dead."

In Wilker castle, Harz was speaking with Gustav. With Magnus away on his honeymoon and being the middle of winter at the end of the week there was not much business to be conducted. The weather had been good and so Harz was hard pressed to imagine what was keeping the party to Uluvost gone so long. He suggested to Gustav, "Perhaps we should send a messenger out to look for them." Gustav wondered how many men might wander down the road in search of the party, knowing of course that these endeavors always ran into delays and took forever. He asked his cousin,

"You're worried about them? I wonder why you sent them. It hardly matters to me how Gertrudis fares. She had her chance to escape that place and threw it away when she wouldn't adjust to life here." Harz replied,

"Nevertheless, it is a gesture of good faith to send a party to ask after her." Gustav shrugged and replied,

"The family in Uluvost won't see it that way." They were quiet a while until Gustav asked him, "What if Trevka does not prove himself well enough on this mission? Then Beth may not want to marry him after all." Harz considered but then just answered,

"It is her decision."

"Well he certainly is worthy enough already for such as her. And he might want to marry someone else. He must have at least a few women interested in him." Gustav found some little humor in the idea but Harz was more serious. He asked his cousin,

"You mean it doesn't really matter to you whom he marries? He is a squire after all." Gustav shook his head. He said,

"Oh I know that sort of thing mattered to my father very much. But look who I ended up married to." Gustav looked down at his empty hands and remembered his father's hands, so heavy with rings. He had worn a ring each for his wife, his son, his coronation and his son's investiture. As he studied his hands, Harz was still trying to find something out.

"You mean you don't care at all who he marries?" Gustav shook his head and Harz asked further, "Would it matter to you at all whom *I* might marry?" Gustav replied,

"I wish you would marry *someone*." And remembering their friend, away on his honeymoon and probably immensely enjoying it added, "Even a dairymaid makes a wife." Harz clenched his jaw and said no more. He wished he himself could ride off to Uluvost and find out what was happening; it would be preferable to this winter idleness. And it worried him they were gone so long; he'd never heard anything good about Uluvost. Trevka might be making more of it than was necessary.

Just then Sparrow walked in with Kasch in her arms. She smiled at Harz who nodded back tersely. She said, "I'm taking Kasch for a stroll by the river. It's especially slow this time of year and a good time to become acquainted." Another of her ventures into nature. "Shall you like to come with us?" she asked Gustav. Harz shook his head at the unlikeliness of that, but she did have a tendency to optimism he found amazing. Gustav replied with a gentle *No* but pulled on a bell rope. He said,

"Go with Vatra and don't let our little son fall into the river." Sparrow was still amazed by peoples' numerous, incessant fears, especially of things like drowning and falling. But then she was so sure of her body. She chimed back,

"Oh don't worry, I won't. And besides, he's going to learn to swim one day, it's quite easy." And with that she was out of the room before Gustav could protest or question her further. Harz watched her go and wondered if she had invited Beth and Dane to go with her as well. They did stay inside a lot more than Sparrow, who never let a winter cloud or a summer sun stop her from her pleasures. Just as well, for now Beth would be alone in the nursery. He considered going there, but in the end he didn't and instead sent a message to Beth that they had heard from Trevka's party and all was well, taking more time than usual, but nothing untoward. That evening he wondered at his telling such an unsubstantiated story, indeed a lie. In fact it had been Ambrose, watching Beth and knowing how concerned she was, who had put that idea into Harz's head, and he was quite pleased with his ability to influence people when they were emotional. Ambrose too was concerned as he watched the others worry about Trevka's whereabouts, who to Ambrose had been only a young page who liked to get out of work. But since it mattered to Harz, it mattered to Ambrose and he wondered if he should follow the party to Uluvost. Maybe they could use whatever help he could offer. But in the end he decided not to.

4

Return to Uluvost

Trevka, Brake and Morgan approached the Uluvost castle once again. Trevka handed the letter of mission over to the guards at the gate and hoped they did not notice it was the exact same one of last week; given their desultory attitudes, it was possible they would not. They looked up at Trevka with a bit of confusion and he leaned over his horse's pommel and said, "You gentlemen are so kind as to allow us this return visit; it seems we had forgotten some gifts the Count meant to bestow on all the helpful people of Uluvost who take a part in serving his good Countess. This," he pulled another coin from his vest, "is meant for you." They raised the portcullis and admitted the men. As they approached the front door, Morgan took their three horses and moved them to a sunny side of the castle walls. There was no stable in sight, although one couldn't see much inside the enclosing walls.

Trevka nodded to him, Morgan nodded back and then he raised the knocker on the door and waited for the beady eyes to loom from behind the wicket.

Trevka gave him the same line about forgotten gifts and the door opened. They were shown to the same room as before, not a good sign, but Malvern did appear again after a while and now had only Trevka to face. Before Malvern could say anything or begin a staring event, Trevka started right in. "Good sir, I am sorry to bother you again so soon, but upon our return to Wilker it was discovered that we had forgotten to bring some gifts intended for Uluvost. This ring in particular," Trevka pulled it from his pocket, "was to have been given to the Countess as a symbol of good will and kindness. If I were to put it into her hand, I could assure the Count that she is well indeed. And he would want to hear of her gratitude as well." Then Trevka played his strongest card by putting the ring into Malvern's hand. Malvern looked down at it in amazement. Trevka added without hurry, "Perhaps by your introducing us with this ring, she would be more amenable to seeing us this time. I know she must be a busy woman, with little time to spare some foreigners, but merely a minute of her time would be sufficient." Malvern studied Trevka for some time, studied the ring for longer, then finally said,

"I shall see if she is interested in visitors." Malvern left and closed the door. Brake and Trevka looked at each other. They knew it might be hours before they got an answer. This time however, they had brought a saddlebag full of food and ale, although some thought it contained more gifts for sycophantic Uluvostians.

After about an hour of waiting, Malvern returned and led Trevka and Brake to a different part of the castle. It was a lengthy trip, and remarkable for how few people they passed; usually castles were filled with people, servants coming and going, ladies gliding down the hallways, boys on errands. At last they came to a room and Malvern knocked three times, waited a few seconds, then opened the door. It was a decent room, though sparsely furnished. Gertrudis sat on a sofa arranged some distance from two other chairs. Malvern held his hand wide, inviting them to take a seat, however Trevka ignored this and strode over to Gertrudis, knelt down on one knee and took her hand in his to kiss it. Gertrudis was so surprised she didn't protest but rather listened to his oratory.

"Countess Gertrudis, how long it has been since we were honored to be in your presence. The time has not passed across your face but rather left you as youthful and lovely as ever." Trevka studied her face, one he well remembered. It had usually been red and twisted in contortions of anger, but now was dull. The years *had* passed across her face and left their tracks and one year appeared as five. She was also thinner and looked almost frail. On the other hand, whereas she used to hop about and flail her arms, now she sat quietly and listened. Trevka kept his gaze steady and expression calm. Having kissed her hand, he had noticed that the ring just given to Malvern was not on her finger. Brake was standing next to Trevka and when he stood up, they both stepped backward and took the seats Malvern intended for them.

Trevka asked her, "And aside from your looking well, how fares the Countess?" He glanced around the room. "You seem to have every comfort." Gertrudis cast her eyes askance at the sparse furnishings. She was unfamiliar with the room and it showed in her expression. "Tell me you are well," Trevka prompted. Finally the old voice made itself heard. Gertrudis said,

"I am well," and glanced up at Malvern, wondering if this were correct. Trevka continued,

"And how many ladies wait in attendance upon the Countess? You must keep many busy, lady of the house as you are." Gertrudis seemed too tired to count how many, or else there was nothing to count. She was not the talkative, time-wasting woman she had been in Wilker, which all in all was somewhat of an improvement, but Trevka had to admit to himself she was quite changed. She looked across at them and suddenly said,

"I remember you, you are from Wilker, aren't you?"

"The very same," Trevka replied without pause. "The Count desires to know that you fare well here at your home and want for nothing."

"Is he sending for me? Am I to return?" Gertrudis had become animated but Trevka worried about exciting her too much; he didn't think she would handle it well.

"No, no ma'am. But if you could prepare a list of items you require, I shall convey it to the Count with all speed." Now Gertrudis had a reason to detain them in the castle while she wrote out her list and Malvern would not object to having a few new items drift his way as well. Gertrudis waved her spinning hand at Malvern and squeaked,

"Get me a secretary quickly! I have a list to make." Trevka rose and faced Malvern saying,

"There is no hurry. The Countess will need time to assemble her thoughts and inventory her needs; you should be sure she leaves nothing out. You may think of something she does not. And where might my man and I stay while she ponders? Surely she will want to take a day or two, as her maids as well might have needs unspoken." Malvern considered throwing them out to the town again, but perhaps they would not return now that they had seen Gertrudis. Of course they might have no intention of delivering anything Gertrudis wrote on a list, but it was possible that the Count of Wilker was feeling guilt or following the instructions of some adviser. It was worth a gamble. He led the two to a room with only one window and no meaningful view; Trevka had little idea which part of the castle they were in at this point or where the front door might be. Before Malvern left the room,

Trevka reminded him,

"My horseman Morgan is outside; I trust he will be given accommodations and decent food for the length of our stay? The Count would of course want to remunerate such hospitality." Malvern nodded as he walked out; one more thing to see to. Trevka knew enough about propriety to know it forbade accepting payments from visiting in-laws. Malvern did not understand the difference between host and hosteler and he didn't make a good one of either. Brake looked around the room; there were straw mats on the floor and one chair, a pathetic place to put important guests. Brake asked Trevka,

"How poor are these people? I had thought they must be much richer than this, to live in the castle." Trevka just shook his head. "And where is the whole royal family? I get the idea few people inhabit this place." Trevka could only speculate,

"They may have other homes in better locations. I think I heard tell of some winter cabin on a lake farther south." Trevka went to the door and listened, then he turned the door knob and pulled. It was an old and rusted lock. He motioned Brake to come to the door and examine the lock quietly. As Brake knelt down to look through the keyhole Trevka asked him if he could break the catch or twist the knob. Brake looked up at him and smiled. He said,

"Don't have to; the man left the key in the lock; if I can't turn it from inside I can probably push it through and hope it lands on something flat we slip under the door." Trevka smiled. He said,

"Do your best then, but don't open the door, just leave it unlocked. I'm tired of being on their schedule."

To their great surprise a meal was brought by a servant and slid through an opening in the doorway. The sun was setting and the room was darkening. There were no candles or lamps in the room and so they could barely see the food before them. It did not smell inviting and they had eaten their own food an hour before. Trevka picked up a spoon-full of the stew and smelled it, then pulled away from it. His eyes lifted dubiously to Brake's who decided about the stew by putting his hand across the spoon and pushing it back down into the bowl. He then put the bowl onto the window sill, which was just an open hole in the castle wall with no shutter or curtain. They moved the straw mats to the warmest wall, sat down on them and stared into the room. It didn't seem likely they would sleep at all well.

Before midnight a waning moon had begun to rise over the silent castle. The moon-glow creeping into the room woke Brake who gazed through the window to the sky; a square of dark blue with a bowl on its sill. Then a mouse skittered across the sill; it planted its front paws on the bowl's rim and sniffed, whiskers twitching. The mouse crawled into the bowl and wee splashes and tiny scraping toenails could be heard. Brake rolled over in disgust and pulled the thin blanket over his face. He listened but did not hear any sound from Trevka; he slept very quietly or else was not asleep at all.

In the early morning, just as light was beginning to fill the sky, Brake woke up and turned again to the only thing in the room to look at; the window. Trevka was standing by it with his arms crossed considering how a mouse had been so hapless as to drown in a bowl that small. But there it lay, feet stiff and clutching the air. Was their cooking that bad? Or had the mouse died of some other cause, only to face his end in the best meal he'd seen since being born in this forsaken place? Just as Trevka decided they were leaving the castle that minute, Brake was up and on his feet. Trevka pointed to the mouse and whispered, "They are either drawing up a list or a ransom note; I'm not going to wait and find out which."

They went to the door and pushed it open. They knew which direction to head in, but the array of hallways and staircases was arcane and undistinguished by any tapestries, portraits or furniture. It was a featureless labyrinth of stone walls. They looked out every window they came upon and went down every stairway they found, but were hopelessly lost. Suddenly Trevka stopped in his tracks; he heard voices, or rather gasps and muffles. Then a man yelped as if his hand had been bitten, and a girl's voice shrieked. They both ran in the direction of the sounds and came upon a man in a stairwell assaulting a female. Trevka ran at the man and threw his fist into the man's head so that he reeled down the steps spinning. Brake flew past

Trevka to catch the man and throw him into the wall with both hands grasping his neck. He slammed the man's head into the stone wall until blood came out of his ears. He let go of the man and the body slumped down, scattering across the descending steps. The girl at the top of the stairs was pulling in air and stroking her neck. Trevka didn't know if she'd help them in her state, but he said to her, "Will you show us the way out?" The girl glanced at the body on the stairs, signaled with her hand and headed down the hallway.

Uluvost was an older castle, full of the traps and tricks used to capture enemies that had made it past the gates. For that matter, knowing the family, they might have still been in use against each other. There were a lot of stairs that led nowhere and doors that opened onto walls. The girl knew the house fairly well but had certainly never been in every room nor up every stairwell. If they were being pursued, they would have been trapped already. A stairway led down and Brake was tempted to take it. The girl shook her head and said, "That only leads to the garderobe chute." The two men shrank back and continued down the hallway. Trevka said,

"Aren't there any windows in this forsaken pile?" He would have liked to be able to look out and get an idea of where they were going for it was gloomy inside. He also would have liked to address her but didn't know her name. The girl clarified,

"I'm Cait, and the only windows are along the outer part of the castle which is lined with circular hallways; there are only a few hidden ways to get to the interior. It's how they protect themselves." It also meant there were only a few hidden ways to get *out* of the interior, obviously where they were. Trevka figured the castle had probably been a normal one at one point, but now there were halls and stairs, doors and rooms added on that just took up space and confused people. That was why the courtyard was so narrow. It was impossible to tell where they were or where they had been. Suddenly the girl stopped. If the three of them were lost they would wander around until someone found them and be thrown who knew where. The dead man on the stairwell would also be found and a casual exit would be out of the question.

Trevka waited for Cait to say something, but instead she only backed away from where they were headed. Then they all heard footsteps coming fast up the stairway. They turned and scrambled back down the hallway and each one began trying doors, looking for one that was unlocked. Just as footfalls were approaching Brake pushed open a door, Trevka grabbed Cait and all three were inside leaning against the door as the footsteps outside flew right by. They all breathed relief but the girl held out her arms to keep them from advancing into the room any further. There were windows around the small, circular room and Trevka knew if he could get to one, he would know where they were. A rope draping down from the rafters, its end fastened around a wooden cleat in the wall, seemed perfectly suited to helping them climb out. Trevka took Cait's outstretched hand and squeezed it reassuringly but froze in doing so when he heard more footsteps running down the hall. They too went past and Trevka imagined they had found the body, and the missing guests, and the hunt was on.

Trevka still wanted to get to a window or untie the rope but Cait shook her head vehemently and pointed to the rafter above them. It was dark above the small windows but Trevka saw it. Instead of being tied to the rafter, the rope draped over a groove in the beam and was tied to a mill stone. If the rope were untied, the person holding it would be yanked upward by the weight falling downward on the opposite side. At the same time, the cleat, actually a lever, would release a trap door in the center of the room. The person at the end of the rope would either slip when the rope flew out of their hands and fall into the hole or be hit by a dropping mill stone and *then* fall in. If he managed to hold on to the rope and miss the stone, he would dangle over the chasm under a rafter until he lost his grip. The body that fell would not even be retrieved, but the rope and millstone would be.

Trevka motioned for Brake to stand against the wall next to the cleat and make a foot hold and lift him up. He took out his knife and sawed through the rope above the knot while Brake tried to keep them both balanced and Cait listened fretfully at the door. The mill stone was suddenly free and so was the lever. The rope whizzed up and over the beam and both rope and stone fell into the trap door that dropped open. The trap had been dismantled, at least for now. They stared at the open hole and waited for their heartbeats to slow again. Brake was certain he'd heard skeletons snapping under the stone. The hallway was quiet, and they stepped out of the room and were back to searching for an escape.

Cait finally found the hidden door she was looking for and they followed a long stairway to a kitchen with a back door, unlocked and unguarded. When they stepped out into the morning light, Trevka could smell the stables nearby and whistled loudly. Morgan was up in a moment throwing saddles across the horses' backs. Trevka asked Cait if she wanted to leave the castle with them and she nodded her head emphatically. He mounted his horse and then pulled the girl up behind him, asking her if she knew of any exit besides the portcullis at the front gate. She shook her head in despair, Trevka told her to hang on and they headed for the front gate. As they approached the sleepy guards, Trevka took the last of his coins from his pocket. He held the bag up and told them they were departing early and the guards would get the booty meant for Malvern if they would open the portcullis. As the men rubbed their eyes, Trevka added that their other option was to have Brake beat out their spleens. Cait leaned down and implored them,

"Take it and get out of here yourselves." There was no sound of pursuit behind them, yet. It seemed there were very few people left in the castle to guard it or know what was happening. Trevka pulled the bag of coins from in front of their faces and placed it back into his vest as Brake spurred his horse into the pair of guards. They scrambled away from him and to the ropes, pulling the portcullis up. The four on horseback bolted up the hill and away from Uluvost, voices behind them yelling but no one pursuing.

They returned to Stoer and their rooms at the inn, Sutherland asking what had happened and Quillin immediately noticing that Cait was injured. Trevka put Cait in their room and ordered all the men out, to gather in the dining room. He sent the innkeeper's wife to stay with Cait and Quillin to look after her. After fifteen minutes Quillin came downstairs and reported to Trevka that Cait would be all right but that she had no desire to go back to the castle and no family to go to. They continued to linger in a private dining room downstairs all that afternoon, discussing the events of the last week and informing Sutherland of most everything, but leaving out the details of a dead man left behind. In the early evening, when Cait had rested and eaten some, the innkeeper's wife told Trevka and Brake that she desired to speak to them. They went up to her room and Trevka asked her, "Did you know the man who attacked you?" Cait replied,

"He is the youngest brother of the Countess. I was always careful around him but did not think he would be awake and about so early in the morning." Trevka thought about Beth's story, similar to this one, and wondered if it was the same man who had stopped her coming up from the basement one night. He remembered the lifeless body in the stair well and said,

"I don't think he will be up and about any more." Brake asserted,

"I killed him, I'm sure of that. If there's a punishment for it, I'd like to see the person who can prove it. He had it coming to him." Cait broke in,

"I was the only witness and shall never speak of it. You saved my life and I owe mine to you. Wherever you are going, I'd like to follow and do what I can to make repayment. I can clean and do your laundry and cook some, too. If I can work for the Countess I can obey your wives without complaints." Trevka realized that she thought they were probably merchants or tradesmen. Trevka had to correct her and said,

"We have no need of a cleaning woman or cook, even though neither of us is married. We are from Wilker castle. As a representative of the Count's, I have the right to kill anyone I witness committing a crime such as that. That is the law I obey and whatever the law is here doesn't concern me. I have no remorse." Cait leaned back and her eyes grew large.

"I had no idea that people from Wilker would ever visit." Cait felt all the worse for her slovenly appearance. Trevka studied her and wondered how she would survive in the world if not by cooking and cleaning for her rescuers. Perhaps she might find employment in the town, or perhaps the innkeepers would allow her to clean up for some food and a bed. She had courage and practicality. She was a lot like Beth that way. He turned to Brake and told him to fetch Ash. When he arrived at the door, Trevka told him to try to find a decent dress from the innkeeper's wife or perhaps in the village somewhere.

"Do you think you can find one that will fit?" Trevka asked, certain that he himself would be challenged with it. "I've spent the last of our money so you'll have to beg credit on the castle's name." Then Sir Sutherland, who was close behind, watching and listening and still not able to believe what they had seen on their return trip broke in,

"I have some money," and he took some coins from his vest pocket. "This should suffice." Ash turned and took the money, thanking him. Then Sutherland added, "In fact, I'll go with you, my wife is this girl's size and I will know what works." They left and Trevka went back over to Cait and said to her,

"You are an eyewitness to how things have been going on in Uluvost castle. Will you come back with us and give a full accounting?" Cait nodded in eagerness. Just to see Wilker castle was reward enough. Perhaps then she would know what to do with her life.

5

Harz meets some women

As the party dispatched to Uluvost trooped back into the courtyard of Wilker, a trumpeter sounded a fanfare announcing their arrival. Beth ran to the window and peered out; she had to lean to see from there but noticed right away that one of the supply horses now carried a woman. "Is that the Countess?!" she speculated. Liesse ran to the window but knew immediately by the girl's small size and tasteful dress it was not and said with relief,

"No, that's not her." Although Liesse had never met Gertrudis, a lot of trouble had come her way thanks to her scheming and selfishness and she had no desire to live in the same castle with her. Sparrow watched from the sofas the two women wondering who it might be. They could not see her well but she was escorted closely by Ash. Vatra was in the courtyard to greet them all and Harz watched from a distance, leaning against a doorway with his arms crossed. He and Gustav would hear the report after the party rested and ate. In the meantime he was left to wonder how Trevka had again managed to pry a young female out of the event. He watched Ash help her dismount and she was careful in her movements. She might have some injury, but she didn't appear shy as she looked around curiously, letting Ash wait. Her gaze finally landed on Harz and she studied him for a moment. Trevka and Vatra were discussing the events in their usual mode, which required half as many words as most people did.

That evening, the party was in the small chamber relating the tale of the expedition. There were only Gustav, Harz and Boris hearing it. Trevka was doing most of the talking while Brake and Sir Sutherland were confirming facts and not allowing Trevka to downplay his bravery and supporting his decision to stay there for so long. That he had also brought back an eyewitness to goings-on in the Uluvost castle was even more amazing. At last, Trevka said to the Count, "And I deeply regret that your ring was spent in the effort. I had to consider that Gertrudis may well have been dead or gone all together, and thought offering the ring would bring her out as nothing else. I expected her to thank me in person for the gift, but alas we never saw it again." Gustav considered and nodded; it was unfortunate but after all it had been Harz's ring and his to give, although Trevka wouldn't know it. He said,

"Yes, unfortunate. But then it sounds as if they could use it more than we. And it may be that we'll be given the opportunity to ransom the ring back at some point. Although of course, an honest house would not have taken it to begin with." They all agreed but didn't say aloud what they knew: its cash value was well short of its worth as a symbol of friendship with Wilker, yet pawning it back to Wilker some day was not out of the question. "And now, let us hear from the guest you took away from there. You say she was unhappy and asked to come with you?" Trevka nodded to refrain from explicitly lying; he was also protecting the delicate sensibilities of a lady who would not want to repeat the details regarding why she had wished to leave.

Cait came into the room and was guided to a comfortable chair while Gustav waved away the others' inclinations to hover around her. Happily for them, she was a confident woman who was glad to tell of her days at Uluvost and spoke loudly enough for everyone to hear. Gustav wanted to know how much she was aware of the Countess's situation.

"Oh she's well enough off. Malvern is a factotum who over-imagines his importance protecting her. They are in league together and no doubt if she doesn't know about the ring already, she will. She could have been with her family at their winter home further south instead of alone in the castle, but she likes to think she's queen of it, a thing she only gets away with when they are gone. They didn't much care for her coming back when she did. They are all birds of a feather, bad lots who take pleasure in making things worse for each other rather than better. That's how they spend their days." Gustav was relieved that Gertrudis had not requested anything of him, and he could leave her to her family. He didn't want to feel responsible for her happiness; she never cared for his. He asked Cait,

"And what about the cooking, I hear tell it was not very good."

"Not for guests, no. They can't employ anyone decent who will stay for very long. As to whether the meal given to the guests was poisoned or not, I can only say that it may have been, and that the incompetency of the cooking there was such that it may or may not have been deliberate, one could hardly depend upon the cooks to know the difference."

"And so you wouldn't say there is anything criminal going on there that should be attended?" Cait glanced at Trevka and Brake, her heroes. If anyone from Uluvost ever came looking for strangers who were in the house when a man was found dead in a stairwell, she would swear she had pushed him away when he tried to assault her and he had slipped and fallen backwards head first into the wall of the spiral staircase, tumbling drunk as usual. What she said now was,

"Not any more, good Count. The worst criminal elements have been eradicated by your good mens' presence. I thank you personally on behalf of all those in Uluvost for sending a party to ask after us. I'm sure it will result in an improvement as to how they treat guests in future."

"Excellent," Gustav breathed relief. He had worried that sending them at all would stir up more than it would settle, but it seemed Harz had been right and that yet again Trevka proved surprisingly capable. He glanced at Harz who was watching Cait in his usual way to detect if she were lying. When Harz didn't say anything, Gustav could assume all was well. Boris merely gazed with his jaw ajar, perhaps wondering if Trevka had indeed learned something from him. Gustav whispered something to Harz, who nodded his head and then went to a closet nearby. He came back with a sword and handed it to Gustav. They agreed that this was quite enough to merit a promotion to herald. It was not a great occasion, usually it was impromptu and unceremonious and merely a signal that a man might one day be good enough for knighthood, which required humility and this was but one reminder of the fact. If Trevka ever were knighted, *that* would be a grand celebration.

Gustav said, "Trevka," and pointed to the space in front of him with the tip of his sword. Trevka was stunned momentarily and silently aghast; he was only wearing travel clothes and didn't look at all regal! But there was no help for it. He knelt down at the appointed spot. Gustav raised the sword over his head and pronounced importantly, "For meritorious service beyond and above the call of duty, exercise of judgment and patience exceeding that of the common man, and rescuing a lady from an unwanted situation, I dub thee Trevka, Herald of the realm, keeper of the truth, servant of the crown." Trevka felt light taps as the sword touched each shoulder, and was grateful then that his heavy cape was not there to interfere.

A week later on a sunny afternoon, Trevka and Harz were at the village pub. Trevka watched through narrowed eyes as Harz casually sipped his ale whilst he carefully put his own tankard to his lips. He didn't want to take too large a swig just as Harz announced some new assignment that would make him spew his ale out. But Harz was only hoping to ascertain that being heralded had not gone to Trevka's head, at least not too much. Trevka did wonder what was in store for him now that he was a herald. Harz was plotting something, that much was evident. Heralds were expected to marry the privileged and highly regarded. Trevka suspected his promotion may have been a way of forestalling any rumors -or possibilities - about his marrying Beth. It was still not clear to him whether Harz was trying to promote or extinguish the idea. He thought to fish for a clue from the inscrutable man by saying, "That trip to Uluvost certainly was fortuitous. I had expected it to be dull and uneventful, so I was surprised to be heralded for it."

"As were we all," Harz replied, and before Trevka might take insult he quickly added, "It is not so easy to find reasons to herald young squires these days; jousts and glory in battle are hard to come by any more." Harz tipped his tankard at Trevka who merely nodded agreement. Trevka vowed not to swear the same things older people always did: *Things used to be better.* Still, thinking he couldn't be sure that things weren't better, he asked Harz,

"How did you come to be heralded? Did you kill someone?" Harz tried not to roll his eyes but said,

"No, I saved someone." That was apparently all he was going to say, but Trevka demanded to know the whole story. Harz reluctantly added, "There was a flooded river one summer and a man lost his balance near the edge. I stopped him from falling." Trevka responded that he hoped it was someone important and Harz answered, "Just the Count." Trevka stared but then spotted beyond him what looked like himself and Beth walking through the village. Of course she was with Vatra, but it was quite rare for her to go out at all. Seeing them together made him think how well she looked by his side, although it should be himself and not his twin brother with the honor. He said with a little pique,

"Well, how is it she is outside the nursery? I never see her out." Harz glanced over his shoulder at the shoppers Trevka was studying. He commented,

"Yes, she'll probably be much more out in the village soon. Dane will get a tutor and not idle away his childhood with a nanny." Harz glanced around and then raised his hand towards the barmaid and signaled for another ale, leaned back in his chair and closed his eyes, enjoying the sunshine on his face. When the barmaid brought his brew and he opened his eyes, Trevka had left.

On a day a week later when Sparrow and Kasch were visiting a rabbit warren that the gardener was complaining about, Harz knew he could go up to the nursery and find Beth with only one other person, excepting the babies of course. As he approached the open door, he made sure that his footsteps were heavy enough to be audible, but not so loud as to wake the babies from their naps. Liesse was looking towards the door and waved him in when he reached it. He greeted them but before taking a seat told Liesse that she was needed in some other part of the castle and that he would stay with Beth until she came back. When she had left he sat down.

It had been many months since she had had an audience with the Count and his cousin, and there had been no occasion to speak with either one nor become better acquainted. At least now she knew one from the other, although they almost never spoke to her, which she took as normal. She had decided the cousin was much easier to be around than the Count. He was the only man who ever noticed her, excepting Trevka of course.

Harz began, "I congratulate you on your engagement to a herald.

Trevka has proved himself well." She smiled. He didn't say anything more. He seemed to be considering her. Beth thought, *This is it. He's going to inform me that I'm not suitable and the whole thing is out of the question, I'll be sent away and* ~ Harz interrupted her thoughts by asking, "Shall you tell your parents?" Beth blinked, her thoughts interrupted. For a spell she seemed entranced with the embroidery on his jacket. Then she looked into his eyes and wondered about her family.

"No, sir." And after a bit of silence during which she figured he was awaiting an explanation she added, "They live far away."

"Where do they live?"

"Jiltradt."

"That must be very small...."

"It's a small village near Hastadt."

They were silent for a long time, but finally Harz noted,

"Still, they should be told, it is the proper thing to do."

"I do not want to trouble the court. I'm sure they do not care." Harz gazed at her a while. Beth realized she had not made it clear that she thought her *parents* didn't care; she had not meant to say she thought the *Court* did not care. Harz said at last, "You are too young to be married without the knowledge of your parents." Beth nodded agreeably but her eyes were glassy. *Yes, he's going to find something objectionable about my parents, and that will cause the wedding to be canceled. He will have no trouble finding objectionable things about my parents.* She gave the name and address of her home in a whisper and prayed silently that he wouldn't find it. Perhaps they have died; that would be convenient.

A week later Harz was riding alone towards Hastadt. It would take only a day to get there, but it could have been in another world. The countryside was like an ocean surrounding small islands and most inhabitants of these little hamlets spent their entire lives within them. He inquired as to the location of Jiltradt, which was described as just a few houses around a mill by a stream. He headed in the direction given. It was a lonely road and he passed only a few people, remembering that traveling at leisure was both a prerogative and a danger. He was fortunate that he could go where he pleased without giving an explanation. He made inquiries and found the house with the sign in front saying merely *Carpenter*. He stood in front of the door and studied it a long time. Finally a woman came out and asked him if was needing carpentry work done. The woman began to explain that her husband was out just now but if he wanted to inquire-. Harz said plainly,

"No, I have news about your daughter."

"Are you the school master? If she's in trouble again I-"

"I am not the school master. I am cousin to the Count of Wilker and am here on official business. May I come in?" He dismounted and tied his horse to the front post as the woman straightened her apron and stepped into her home with Harz following.

The dwelling was slightly below street level, small and cluttered. Harz squinted against the smokey air and crude surroundings. He took a seat at the only table and waited silently as the woman busied herself boiling water for tea, whispering that she did have some very good herbs somewhere, yes there it was and it would be ready in very short order and yes he would have the finest cup although the best one had broken a while back. She was very nervous now and continued muttering to herself. While she rummaged for the finest tea cup, Harz stopped listening and closed his eyes again. He did not open them until he heard the clink of the cup being set on the table in front of him.

The woman, still waiting for the water to boil, said in a quiet tone, "Now, you inquired about my daughter being in service at the castle?" Harz lifted his eyes to the woman. She had changed in fifteen years but this *was* the woman he had married those many years ago.

"Madam, I am not here to hire anyone. I am here to tell you that your daughter is to be married to a herald of the court this spring."

"*My* daughter?" she blurted out, disbelieving. Harz wondered how many daughters she might have.

"Beth. Whom I believe is *our* daughter."

The woman sat down slowly across the table from Harz. She murmured the name Beth several times, her chin heavy on her palm. The light slanting through the window fell onto her face as she gazed into the past, into a time far away. Harz looked steadily at his bride, with whom he had spent only one night. He was going to know instantly if she tried to lie. He said,

"Beth is my daughter, isn't she?" The woman repeated the murmuring of Beth's name as she nodded her head. Her hand closed into a fist and her face slid down against her wrist, obscured behind her arm. Harz reached over and held the arm she hid behind until she opened her eyes and looked at him. "Why did you leave me?" She composed herself, putting her hands into her lap and began,

"The morning after our elopement I woke up and was filled with such amazement at my bravery for defying my family that I wanted right then to tell them I'd gotten married and was no longer their servant. I took our marriage certificate and went home to wave it in my father's face and prove that I didn't belong to him any more. I was going to tell them the news, enjoy their blanks stares and be back in five minutes. I'd never defied them till then. But father threw the certificate into the stove without even hearing me and threw me and my things into the wagon. He was in a rage about my brother, who had been in a knife fight and had killed a man in a drunken state. We were leaving town that morning and he was so anxious to get away and furious when I made to run off that he actually tied me to the wagon. I began screaming and then he hit me so hard I must have passed out, because when I woke up we were in a town I'd never seen before." Harz gazed off into the room, dumbstruck. He had imagined that what happened all those years ago was Robyn waking up horrified at defying her family and running back to them to be spirited away for safekeeping. He had searched for the family but never found a trace of them, had imagined her laughing at their impulsive marriage. He had cursed a thousand times the hour he slept while she was gone. He shook his head against this new image of her bravely facing her father only to be struck by him and practically kidnapped. He wondered,

"In all those fifteen years you never tried to come back to me." Robyn clutched herself and said miserably,

"I couldn't leave, I had no means. Father had to sell the horse and wagon as soon as we got here. We were terribly poor. I didn't know where I was or how to get back to you and I had no one to take me in any event. I had no proof we had been married and my father would hit me again whenever I tried to say so. And I was sick, too, every day since we arrived. First it was because of what had happened, but later I couldn't keep food down at all and was flat in bed unable to even stand up without crumpling. Months went by and I finally got a little better but by then the fact that I was pregnant had become obvious. Whenever I told them it was yours they scolded me and said I was a lunatic if I thought I was going back to Wilker claiming that my bastard belonged to a nephew of the Count." Robyn let her head fall onto her crossed arms and whispered to herself again her frustration at not being able to send a letter, for although she could read a very little bit, she could not write and there was no one to deliver a letter anyway. How was it fifteen years could fly by so quickly?

Harz heard the water boiling and since Robyn ignored it, he got up and made the cup of tea meant for himself and slid it across the table to her. She looked at the cup but didn't drink. "Yes, Beth is ours. She was so like you, too. She took care of me and loved me, just as you had promised you would. My husband, the carpenter, sent Beth away as soon as she was old enough because he never accepted her, always resented her, even though she was the best child I ever brought into this world." Harz glanced out the window, hoping this husband would come through the door so that he could personally beat him senseless. He asked Robyn,

"And where is this husband now?"

"In the woods gathering timber with our sons. He's teaching them the trade."

She looked up at Harz. "My parents made me marry him, and he has taken care of me but I hated him when he sent Beth away, she was too young and that Lady Gertrudis, I was afraid she might not be good to her. Is Beth all right? Is she to marry someone good?" Harz put his hands over her clenched fists now planted on the table. He nodded and closed his eyes, swallowing hard.

"She's going to marry a much-regarded herald, and will have a home in the castle the rest of her life." They held hands across the table. The tea grew cold, untouched. The light faded slowly, ten minutes went silently by and finally Harz said to her, "Do you want to live in Wilker? I could try to find something for you in the village, at least you would be close by." For a moment Robyn's eyes lit up, but she knew it would be impossible. She drifted in thought for a while, letting the possibility exist. Then her eyes fell on the crib in the corner, her youngest baby sleeping quietly and she said,

"You are too generous. But my home is here. My husband's business is here and I have – much time to myself. And I do not believe Beth would want me nearby. I have failed her too many times." Harz couldn't make her move and wasn't sure she ought to. At least now Robyn knew where her daughter was and that she would be safe. He stood up to leave and she followed him out. When he was outside and mounted on his horse he said to her,

"I'll watch over her, and so will her husband. We both have been doing so since setting eyes on her." Robyn looked up at him and smiled. She longed to go with him but thought it likely he had married someone else. He turned his horse and it slowly walked away. Robyn watched him go.

When Harz returned to Wilker he again caught Beth on her own in the nursery, sending Liesse on an errand. Liesse walked down the hall away from the nursery slowly, hoping to hear some of what Harz had to say. She would hear it all from Beth herself, but it would be fun to hear Harz tell it. He was very protective of Beth, unlike the Count. Harz spoke pleasantries until Liesse was out of earshot, but this took a while for she knew that Beth was worried about this meeting.

"Your parents have no objections to your marrying, I am glad to report." Beth smiled and marveled that he was still being kind to her; her parents were so far beneath him. Harz straightened his back and tugged on his jacket. "Unfortunately, your father is away and unable to attend your upcoming wedding." This was a relief to Beth. Harz thought for a moment before proceeding. "It would look so much more acceptable, that is, your marriage would be more highly regarded, if you were to have someone to walk you down the aisle at your wedding." Beth had wondered about this. She was not comfortable in crowds, and cowered at the idea of all eyes turned upon her, even if she were wearing a magnificent gown. Some of those eyes would certainly belong to women who had fancied Trevka for themselves. Some would be the eyes of those who saw her as only a servant, or worse yet, a thief. She didn't need Harz to remind her of the dread she felt about this solitary ambulation. "If you would find it helpful, I can accompany you down the aisle, as the Count's closest relative." Beth could not imagine how she had earned such a privilege. Perhaps he was under some delusion, but she wasn't going to turn down this offer. She looked him straight in the eyes and said, "Sir, I most gratefully accept."

"Good," said Harz. "Now tell me about little Dane here. How does he do?" They spoke for quite a while and Harz, being thorough and diligent, asked as well about Beth and whether she had everything she needed. After all, she could not care for a child properly if she herself were not receiving the best of everything. Liesse returned and Harz left them soon after. Liesse waited for the news from Beth, and then dropped her jaw at the thought of Harz and Beth walking down the aisle; *she* had not had such an honor. But it seemed right.

6

Gowns and dressmakers

Sparrow was in her room looking out over the courtyard, the setting sun casting different hues of blue over the castle walls. Gustav came in and sat down in a favorite chair and gazed over at her. He asked her, "Did you hear that Harz has offered to walk Beth down the aisle at her wedding?" Sparrow nodded her head. Gustav rested his head onto the chair back. He sighed and mumbled,

"Of course you know." She had spent another day with a family of rabbits discussing the raiding of the kitchen garden and yet had received this news. She knew all the gossip, and was in this regard like his uncle Ambrose, who had spent his days fraternizing with everyone at court. Sparrow knew hardly anyone and spent her days outside the castle walls, yet the gossip still found her. Gustav held out his hand to Sparrow and she left the window to join him on the chair, plenty large enough for both of them. She looked sad, and Gustav was afraid he knew why, and also knew there was nothing he could do about it. He told her, "Don't regret not having a huge wedding for yourself, they are overwhelming, tiresome affairs." Sparrow looked at him anew to study him, then smiled.

"My darling, I don't. I'll love you and stay with you until I die. No ceremony changes that." Gustav stroked her face and smiled. Sparrow's look of concern returned though. "I am thinking of Beth. That girl has nothing, certainly not the means to acquire a dress suitable to the occasion. I don't think she realizes how big this is becoming. For some reason people think it's going to be the wedding of the century!" What people, Gustav wondered, did Sparrow know? And how did she know what they were anticipating for a wedding they were not officially invited to? As to a new dress, Gustav figured it was another non-problem, easily solved. He said to Sparrow,

"We can buy her a dress, have one made. Where is the problem in that?" Sparrow knew he wouldn't understand. How to explain this to a man, for whom attire barely differed? She began:

"Well, Beth is not inclined to accept kindness from others, especially you. She is scrupulous not to take any more of your largesse, beyond what she has already accepted by your kindly letting her stay here and look after Dane. She already feels so beholden to you and despises the idea of feeling more so. She is quite determined to fend for herself. Besides, you know how Trevka likes to dress, so flamboyant and beyond the pale. Imagine how he will look at his own wedding" Gustav slapped his forehead, then made a huge gesture with his hand sweeping out, mocking his own ignorance and Trevka at the same time. Gustav said,

"Yes, there is a great risk that Trevka will be even more spectacular than the bride."

"And she doesn't need another reason to feel inferior or out of place. A brand new dress will only reinforce the impression that she is new and different from us. I wish I had my own dress to give her to wear. She would like something as simple as what I would have." Suddenly Gustav interrupted her musing with a declaration.

"That's it! You are in dire need of your own lady's maid. Someone to sew your clothes especially for you and see that they fit and then help you dress, even do fancy things with your hair. You shouldn't be seen any more in unflattering hand-downs. As it happens, this lady Cait that they took from Uluvost said she could sew and so has been mending clothes in the laundry basement, but I would prefer that if she has any gossip it goes to you first of all, and only to you. She seems very keen and capable, not one to waste on dirty laundry. Isn't that a marvelous match-up?" Sparrow could only blink and wonder what extravagance he would think of next. Surely women were capable of dressing themselves and Gustav was just hoping that Sparrow would keep an eye on this Cait because he was suspicious of her. Sparrow asked,

"Do all women have lady's maids?" Gustav was quick to answer,

"All the important ones do. And you are most important. We can arrange a meeting and if you don't like her, it's back to the basement with her. If she can't make you look and feel like a queen, then we shall find someone else." Sparrow was still contemplating this new distraction. "Have her make you a gown for the upcoming masquerade and see if she is qualified." Sparrow couldn't imagine how to refuse the offer so she nodded her head and shrugged her shoulders. It was then she sensed that Uncle Ambrose was nearby. He was lingering in the hallway outside their door, listening to their conversation. He had followed Gustav up the steps to his room, knowing he had the news of Beth's wedding on his mind. Sparrow glanced at the door and wondered what his interest in this might be while Gustav mused about the masquerade and postulated,

"If she can't sew one in time, there must be gowns in the attics somewhere, if they can be found. Although if Gertrudis left any of hers behind, they will be too big to fit little Beth." Now it was Sparrow who interrupted his drifting thoughts with excitement,

"You mean we can search through the attics for a wedding gown for

Beth? That would be perfect, something older, with history, something ancestral!" Sparrow imagined finding something beyond description, something to give Beth the confidence and luster she lacked. Gustav sat up a little straighter, wondering how his wonderful idea had been supplanted by another. He cautioned her,

"There are as many attics as there are bedrooms, my dear. Heaven knows how many dressers and dilapidated trunks you'll have to search through." But Sparrow was undaunted, so Gustav figured he'd have to recommend some help, and at least an escort because who knew what dangers lurked in the rotting timbers of the attics? "All right, if you really want to go. But take Trevka with you, he must have played in those attics more than any boy." Sparrow was a little amazed,

"We can't take Trevka and risk his seeing the dress! It's bad luck and besides, he might then out-do her with his own costume."

"Then take Vatra, since he and his brother went everywhere together."

"We don't need an escort, certainly not a male one." Then to soften the slight insult, she began to nibble on Gustav's ear and in the hallway, Ambrose moved off with a purpose which included not wanting to hear love making that was not his own. He headed for the attic in the oldest part of the castle to try to figure out where the clothes might be.

"This castle has ghosts," Beth said to her betrothed the next morning in the nursery.

"I know that," Trevka said as he worked on fixing a toy that Dane had thrown against a wall and broken. He turned the parts over and over and couldn't see how they had gone together. "In fact, you used to be one of them." He looked up at her and smiled. He could tease her because she wasn't afflicted with excessive pride. She smiled back and said,

"So you know how to deal with ghosts, very commendable. Now tell me what I'm going to wear at our wedding." Trevka thought about this as he held two pieces of the toy side by side. He wasn't sure he wanted her to look better than him, but she mustn't look worse, either. He supposed he would have to arrange for a dressmaker from the village to come in and design something special. Just then Sparrow walked in with Liesse, now a party to the scheme and both of them were eager to begin it. Liesse said breathlessly,

"We know exactly where to find you the perfect dress," and they took her hand and led her out of the nursery, leaving Trevka with a broken toy and three drowsy babies. When Genivee ambled in a minute later, she was not surprised to see the four of them each entirely occupied with their own thoughts and objects on the floor and making not a sound, some near sleep. Trevka looked up and half rose to bow but Genivee waved him back to the floor and his task. She wouldn't have

Trevka bow to her just because she was married. Trevka nodded to her instead and thought to himself that she didn't look very pregnant. He sat back down and returned to the toy; the pieces were not fitting and he suspected there was something missing. Genivee dropped onto a sofa and exhaled heavily. The stair climbing was becoming more tiresome. She put her hand over her stomach and tried to soothe it, hoping she wouldn't feel the urge to heave in front of Trevka. Her head rolled back onto the sofa as beads of sweat tickled her forehead. Trevka glanced up at her, wondered if she was going to be sick. She used to talk a lot more but perhaps this was one result of pregnancy. He went back to studying the toy. Genivee moaned at the heat in the room and Trevka asked,

"Can I help?" She raised her head and smiled at him. He now asked the question with complete earnestness, whereas in the past he would ask just so that she would have to look at him and say something. Since men could only rightly interfere in a woman's activity by sincerely offering help, they often were quick and repetitive in offering it. But Trevka now waited until help might truly be needed.

"No," she answered but with a smile of recollection on her face. Trevka would only rarely come to the nursery after he was married. More nausea came over her, possibly from lifting her head up too suddenly. "Some water would be nice," she said. He put down the toy and went to the pitcher nearby, giving Genivee what water there was in the room. He pulled on a rope and when a servant came he told the boy to fetch water from the well in the courtyard and reminded him to put some stones in the bucket first so the water would be taken from below the surface and fresh. Then as an afterthought he told the boy to stop by the kitchen and pick up a few pretzels with extra salt. He then went back to reconstructing Dane's toy. After a time, he got up to check under the furniture where the toy had hit the wall; he searched around and finally found another missing piece, rather far from the site of demolition. Genivee belched, covered her mouth and then smiled at Trevka. He renewed his efforts to reconstruct the toy.

When the water came, (the pretzels were still baking), the babies had begun to rouse themselves from napping and started to wonder where their nannies were. Genivee was still sprawled on the sofa close to fainting and Trevka figured if one of the babies began to cry, there would soon be full-out wailing and possibly barfing, so he decided to tell a story to distract everyone, as they seemed in need of it.

Still sitting on the floor, he leaned against a sofa and faced the four captives. Without speaking, he slowly pulled a strip of leather from his jacket. He always had it on him, for in his mind it was still his duty to find the user of it even though it had been some time since that duty had been given to him. What's more, he had had exceeding good luck ever since it was handed to him. The babies gazed at the brown leather strip and Dane reached out a chubby fist towards it. Genivee lifted one eyelid. Trevka put his finger to his lips, not that anyone had made a sound, and began to tell his tale.

"This strip of leather, yes this very one, was at one time wrapped around an eagle's foot." The babies of course had no idea what he was saying but knew when a good story was being told and their eyes were wide. "An imperial eagle, no less, in the Count's realm. The very bird that *is* vision, power, and soaring to great heights. These three things should always go together. *Someone*," he looked at each of the babies with scrutiny, "someone used this strap to catch an imperial eagle. Hoping, no doubt, to capture power for themselves." He leaned back; these suspects were in the clear. "But it didn't work," he concluded simply, swinging the strap in front of them. "A certain person, who shall remain nameless, rescued the bird trapped in this noose. Take no heed that it was seventy feet up in the air at the top of a tree!" Genivee knew the tree was perhaps fifty feet high at best and so muttered *Trevka*... "Yes, that was his name! Bravely he climbed up to the eagle and her two little chicks in a nest nearby. If the eagle should be lost, then so too would be her chicks. A triple death in the realm, which as you know foretells disaster. This brave lad, whose name has been mentioned, calmly cut the noose and freed the eagle." Trevka's tone became thoughtful. "And now it is left only to find the culprit, or culprits," he glanced over at the babies again, "who were responsible for this terrible act of treachery, larceny and banditry." With that he tucked the leather strip back into the secret recesses of his jacket pocket and the servant came with the pretzels. Genivee had been sipping her water with apparent good results. She gazed with hungry eyes at the salty pretzel, fat and warm from the oven and now in Trevka's hand. Trevka, eager to bite into it and forestall any divisions, instead saw the look on Genivee's face and handed it to her. She smiled and took it, pulled off one loop, then handed the rest back to her old friend who sat down next to her and they both ate their pretzel together. When they had finished, she picked crystals of salt off her lap and ate them too.

To the attics above Countess Gertrudis's old quarters, Sparrow, Liesse and Beth were climbing the creaking wooden stairs. A door at the top might have been locked but instead opened with a little shoving and the upsetting of much dust. The room was an open expanse filled with trunks, furniture and objects covered with dust cloth, making it a sea of strange and lumpy shapes that Liesse was sure included semi-animated creatures about to be roused by the entry of three curious, living women. She bravely squinted into the shadows for movement. Beth was overwhelmed by the number of possible places to search and Sparrow was transfixed by the figure of Ambrose sitting comfortably on a trunk at the far end of the attic. Sparrow was turning to leave, her eyes casting dismissive glances at the objects all around them, but when she turned her gaze on the stairwell, Ambrose was instantly there blocking any retreat. "This way," Sparrow chirped out loudly as she spun again and led them away from the ghost on the stairs and into the depths of stored objects.

Beth was asking meekly if they shouldn't stop and glance into this trunk or that bureau, Liesse followed silently, glancing at the cast-aside portraits leaning against the furniture. Some of them watched her pass, others were draped in more dust cloth, leaving her to wonder how wretched was the ancestor who must be covered. Sparrow led them purposefully to the trunk where Ambrose had been sitting while also retreating from his sudden appearance on the stairwell. She was heading to what he obviously wanted them to examine. She also hoped there was another stairwell at the other end of the attic. They arrived at the trunk and Sparrow hesitated to open it and placed her hand on it instead. Feelings of long-ago happiness came through the wood and she reverently opened the trunk, not locked or even creaking with age. Inside they removed several layers of fluffed fabric, meant to protect what was below. Under these lay a wedding gown the likes of which Sparrow had never seen before, and she didn't know what to make of it or what Beth would think. It was surely as regal as they came, for Sparrow could not imagine a more elaborate one. Liesse finally made a sound, a long drifting expression of wonder as she reached her hands in to pick up the dress.

She lifted it gently, worried it might disintegrate from age, but it was sturdy fabric in fine shape. She held the dress up and studied the sleeves sculpted of ruffled silk and the lace cascading down the bodice. Behind her Beth gazed at the dress in awe and admiration; it was a work of art that showed what finery there was to be had here, and hoped there would be other dresses to choose from better suited to her, as this one would certainly be remembered by older folks who would be appalled to see it on someone who had not properly inherited it, but merely found it in a trunk. Still, it was beautiful to look at.

Liesse, instead of turning the dress to show the others, turned herself and placed the dress against Beth's shoulders and assessed the size. Beth looked down at the dress curiously. Liesse said finally, "This dress was made for you, it is just your size."

"But much too formal," Beth said simply. Liesse shook her head slowly while Sparrow looked around the rest of the room and Liesse said,

"I don't think you know how much Trevka's status has increased of late. You must wear a dress like this to marry a herald who will one day be a knight, no doubt." Liesse turned the dress over and studied the back, then told Beth to turn around and held it up to her shoulders again, assessing the length. "Yes, perfect," she concluded as Beth gazed into the open trunk and wondered about the rest of the contents. There would be other dresses; perhaps those for the bridesmaids or flower girls; this bride had indeed been small and so would her entourage have been. But when they examined the rest of the trunk there were only other elements of the bridal costume; huge ruffled skirts to wear underneath and make the gown voluminous, a veil with a train they could not fully unfold in the confined space, gloves and shoes. The shoes, unfortunately, had not survived the test of time very well. They were in fact terribly worn as if the bride (or some thief thereof), had fled the country and returned again, all in rain and snow, and then hid the shoes in the trunk. "What happened to these?!" Liesse exclaimed as she held them up to the faint light. Ambrose could have answered that although the dress and shoes had been put away and preserved, the shoes had stayed on the bride's feet in a spiritual sense. She was happily married for decades, and with each one, the shoes in the trunk aged and grew old, but never wore out. Odd how someone could affect a physical object which remained locked in a trunk. Beth would not wear these, but another pair all her own, and she too would have many happily married years. Ambrose smiled at the thought.

Liesse sniffed her disgust at the shoes and put them back in the trunk. She was about to close it when Beth noticed something else at the bottom. It was a leather pouch with a necklace inside; pearls on a strand that would go perfectly with the dress. As she ran the necklace across her fingers she imagined the pearls falling off the thread and scattering across the floor, but they too were well-made and holding fast. She had been on the verge of saying they must look for other possible dresses when Liesse took the necklace from her hands and said, "That will go perfectly, and you will look stunning." Beth wasn't sure how comfortable she would feel stunning people, although the pearls were gorgeous and she did admire them. She still wanted to protest and look for other possibilities, but Sparrow interrupted and stated they should get the dress downstairs and have it dusted off and fitted. Ambrose, though no longer visible in the stairwell, was not the only ghost in the attic and Sparrow did not wish to linger with any of them. Animals were easy to talk to, but ghosts did not seem very able, or willing, to talk. They mostly gazed and wondered at the living, and this was disturbing to Sparrow.

The women left the attic by the stairway they had used earlier, now empty. Liesse chattered on happily about making the dress fit while Beth wondered if they could de-emphasize it somehow; perhaps wear it without all the fully ruffled underskirts, maybe shorten the yards-long train. Liesse wasn't listening to a word of it however, and they were both still talking when they got to the sewing room where they would ready the dress for the wedding. Sparrow finally silenced them both by saying, "You mustn't change the dress at all; wear it as it is, as it was worn before, or you risk offending the other brides who have worn it." The idea that it was not her dress alone and would be likely worn again some day finally quieted Beth and she happily took off her frock as Liesse had been urging so she could try on her wedding gown.

7

Masquerade and Wedding

In a room near her bedroom that had mostly gone unused, Sparrow now had a formal dressing room. At first she had seen this as extravagant and vain, but eventually Liesse had convinced her that to not have a lady-in-waiting and seamstress both taking pains with her appearance (and appearances) might not be fitting for the Count of Wilker's right hand. Not that her appearance lacked in anything of propriety or beauty. In fact, her unique reputation as a woman completely different from others made her an object of interest and curiosity in the village as well as around the castle. If for no other reason, Sparrow decided there would be advantages to blending in with other women more, for drawing attention to herself was never her desire. So she consented to have Cait, a lady she found to be creative and strong-minded, serve as both her seamstress and lady-in-waiting. One morning soon thereafter, she was casting her eyes upon a dress Cait had made for her, her first that was not borrowed from the closets of Wilker. Sparrow felt amazed that she had constructed a garment both unusual and in keeping with castle fashion. Cait explained,

"The colors of the forest, browns and greens, express your connection with it. I didn't use bright blues and reds; those are for court ladies who want to draw attention to themselves. However, I've added some embellishments unlike the ones they choose. Instead of a low neckline, I've made yours of sheer fabric that is overlain with small beads for both modesty and interest."

"It reminds me of the sun filtering through the trees," Sparrow commented.

"Yes, just so. I also put these embroidered silk leaves randomly at the hem instead of a sharp band of lace or ruched fabric, something popular with the well-off who can afford expense on unnecessary excess. These leaves can be made with the smallest scraps of fabric."

"That appeals to a woman who is still somewhat surprised to be spending anything at all, let alone on clothes she used to make for herself." Cait began gathering up the dress to put it over Sparrow's head and fit it on her.

"What did your clothes look like?" Cait asked as she threaded Sparrow's hands through the sleeves.

"They were mostly feathers and vines woven together; in the cold I would wear furs my father had trapped that I brushed with twigs to keep tidy, although I only did that when it was too cold to do anything else." Cait was tying the laces that fitted the dress tightly to Sparrow's body. She still found these castle clothes binding and uncomfortable. Sparrow imagined Gustav preferred her old dresses, easily removed, to these complicated ones that took so much work to put on and take off. He said he liked them both but alas, the castle called for formal ones. Satisfied for a start, Cait turned her lady around so that she could see herself in the full-length mirror. Sparrow, prepared to dislike the look of anything that would draw attention to herself, was instead amazed at how well the dress not only fit (she had been making do with dresses made for larger bodies) but how much it reflected what Sparrow felt inside. It was more than well-made; it was well-suited. Cait continued to adjust and inspect the smallest details of her creation while Sparrow turned slightly to see the sides and study the full effect. She muttered, "This is amazing."

"How do you feel in it? Tell me what is nagging to be fixed." Sparrow turned again to view the other side. Finally she said,

"It is perfect as I didn't think a garment made here could be. I've spent nearly a year in this castle thinking something was wrong with this environment, that it didn't suit me. Now I see I was in the wrong clothes, trying to look like something I wasn't. I belong in this dress, and for the first time, somehow also look as if I belong in a castle." Cait looked at her creation, then its reflection in the mirror. She said,

"Of course, this is just for ambling around. For special occasions, I shall have to begin working on something much more inventive. Something from deeper within the forest..." Cait tapped her chin as she thought about it.

"But this is perfect!" Sparrow protested.

"Yes, I believe it is. But you can't wear it every day, and certainly not to the masquerade coming up. For that, you shall have to look more like a queen." Sparrow just nodded; protesting was counter-productive. They talked about shoes and slippers then and at one point Sparrow asked what Cait herself was going to wear to the masquerade. Cait paused before answering and said, "I'm not invited. Dressmakers don't go to the events they help create." Sparrow felt her usual dismay at castle etiquette, which excluded and selected capriciously.

"I will never make sense of these rules." Cait held up swatches of fabric to Sparrow's dress to find one good for slippers. She went through a dozen, then narrowed the selection to three, then gave turns to each of those before settling on one. When Cait remained silent,

Sparrow added, "I think you should go anyway. It's a masquerade, so who will know who you are? That makes more sense than only having people there everyone expects and knows already. Where is the interest in that?" Cait looked up at her and asked,

"So all the important, well-known people will be there?"

"I'm sure," Sparrow exhaled with a sigh of boredom.

"Including Harz?"

"Oh, yes," Sparrow answered, "Unless he is too busy checking the doors and gates for spies. But perhaps he will leave that to someone else for a change."

"Shouldn't he stay with his wife?"

"He's doesn't have one." Cait nodded. Sparrow was kind not to ply her with questions. Liesse might know more, but she also talked more. Sparrow just gazed at her reflection and mused at the fabric samples. She had been trying not to delve into Cait's obvious (to Sparrow anyway) interest in Harz whenever his name came up. Besides, Sparrow wouldn't have much advice for her friend; a subversive invitation to crash the gates was all she could manage. She hadn't exactly played coy with Gustav and didn't know the finer points of making a man notice her. If Cait went to the ball and Harz was there, he would notice her. And he would be there; Sparrow only hoped he did not keep himself too busy with vigilant eyes on the entrances and exits.

By the night of the masquerade, Cait had managed to make for herself a dress she had never been seen in, which wasn't difficult as she only had two, one of which was given to her in Stoer. Personal dressmakers were allowed to make use of fabrics that were left over from other things, as long as they never resembled the original. To make sure of this, high-born ladies often purchased the bare minimum fabric necessary for their gowns, which made the task of construction more difficult for the seamstress and left precious little for anything else. These apparently thrifty practices were usually followed by complaints that the dress was still not elaborate enough nor sported the requisite train or excessive sleeve, a debate common at many a fitting. If there were leftover fabric, it might be appended to the dress just to use it up, rarely improving the design. But Sparrow was generous in her allowance at the haberdasher's shop and in fact instructed Cait to purchase extra, knowing she would make use of it and not wanting to impose a restriction on her creativity. Because of that, Cait now had a gown that would not look at all like the ones she had made for Sparrow, and certainly not the one she had made for her masquerade debut. True to her word, she had made Sparrow appear as queen of the forest in a gown trimmed with the narrowest bands of fox fur that draped over her shoulders and ran to each hem, front and back in undulating, body-hugging stripes It was both prim and arresting, brave and sly. It was much too fun a dress for Sparrow to protest about, and besides, she could not disappoint Cait by refusing to wear it.

In a further effort to keep Cait from being disappointed, Sparrow spotted Harz at the masquerade early and approached him before he could set off to do anything other than take part in the dancing. She implored of him, "Dear cousin, help me prevent embarrassing Gustav by letting me practice before the dancing begins proper. I'm not used to this enormous dress." Harz could do nothing but agree, so he led her to the floor where the dancing was still just warming up for the real festivities. Harz noticed how this new gown fit Sparrow so well and was so unlike the old dresses she had been wearing. It was rather surprising in fact that Gustav had put up with her donning those old things for nearly a year when she had such a beautiful figure to adorn. After one dance, Harz declared to her,

"Your gracefulness cannot be improved, certainly not by me. You carry yourself and your gown beautifully." His eyes followed a stripe of fur down her dress and then up again.

"Too kind, I'm sure. But let me try one more dance, for this music is so lilting I fear I will simply drift away in it." Harz took her hand again and pulled her back into the next dance. He glanced around the room and commented at the same time,

"You need never doubt your success at dancing if the music inspires you." Sparrow finally spotted Cait and declared she felt dizzy and needed to rest. Harz looked at her directly and sighed, led her to a chair where she sat, but didn't release his hand, and thus he was obliged to stay by her side.

"I'm fine," she said suddenly and Harz kissed her hand, turned to leave and found himself face to face with someone else in a much simpler gown, but equally as well-made. She stopped him from moving away by curtsying low right in front of him and saying,

"Honorable sir, I beg to express a sentiment of gratitude to you." Harz felt the eyes of those around him and although he could have done without any expressions of gratitude, he could do even less with having others overhear them. To get away from them, he took her hand and led her to the middle of the floor, dancing a third when he had planned none at all. He said,

"Madam, are you sure you have the right man? I don't recall your name."

"Perhaps not, but you should know a person whose life you saved, even if it was inadvertent." Now Harz remembered her from the time Gustav was interviewing her after returning from Uluvost. "Trevka told me of how the trip, which turned out so advantageously for me, was on your directive. I therefore wish to thank you in person for your ken and command."

"Thank Trevka," Harz said as he studied her green eyes, hidden behind the mask and looking at him intently. He was trying to guess her age but thought whatever it was she was beautiful.

"I have thanked Trevka, and Brake and all of them many times. But I know it would not have happened without your ordering it. I believe you have perception beyond what you think." If that were true, he would know a lot more about her. He said,

"Cait, I believe?" she nodded. "It is we at the court who have gained so greatly from the venture." He paused a bit before adding, "I believe Sparrow is much at an advantage for having you as her lady-in-waiting. The gown you made for her tonight shows clear mastery of your craft." He glimpsed Sparrow dancing now with Trevka and her gown flowed out and around her in flawless orchestration. Suddenly Cait noticed what Harz was wearing, which was remarkable in that it was completely unremarkable.

"But why are you not in a costume? This is a masquerade, we are supposed to disguise ourselves." Harz didn't answer her. It might seem impolite to remind her that he had had no intention of dancing or taking part in the festivities, especially since he was now enjoying them. She scrutinized his expression and asked with slightly narrowed eyes, "You aren't going to wear this same thing to Beth's wedding? Walking down the aisle with such a bride as she will be requires more formality than this. Especially with Trevka as the groom." Was there any gossip girls, even new ones, didn't know? Harz was beginning to think he should spend his days indoors and learn more. Or just have someone like Cait to relate all the information to him. He asked a bit sternly,

"And I suppose you know what Trevka will be wearing as well?"

"Oh yes, for he dresses well even when rescuing ladies from castles." But she wasn't thinking about that, but rather studying Harz's dimensions in a seamstress's way. As the dance ended she stood back and regarded him as if seeing a new suit on him and assessing how it fit. "I should like to sew for you something to wear at the wedding, if you would permit me. My debt of gratitude might then be somewhat satisfied, at least for a while." Harz just wagged his head from side to side. She was planning something, but it wasn't dishonest or contrary. He dismissed the idea by saying,

"I'm much too busy on the Count's business for such frivolity." He smiled, though, and bowed slightly to show his own gratitude. But Cait was not easily put off. She clutched his arm and countered seriously,

"This *is* the Count's business. You will represent him and his sentiments at that wedding and must not look ordinary. Besides, you wouldn't want to embarrass the bride, would you?" Harz's smile faded. But looking at Cait, he knew she wasn't wise to the truth about

Beth being his daughter, and what's more, she was entirely right. So he nodded and said,

"Very well, a gift for the bride, then." Cait continued to study his dimensions up and down and concluded,

"I'll be attending in my sewing room, come whenever you like but make it soon for there is much to do."

He almost didn't go at all, but every time he dismissed the idea of having some special clothing made for him the words came back, *you wouldn't want to embarrass the bride*, and so he found himself climbing the stairs to Cait's sewing room. The door was wide open to a large, two-room suite with a curtain closing off the view of what was likely her own apartment, a luxury for anyone who worked in the castle. Cait was bent over some fabric with a needle and thread but looked up at Harz as he stood in the doorway surveying the room. "And none too soon," she said. She took his hand and led him over to the window. She took a fabric tape measure from her pocket and began measuring his body. She stood behind him, raised his arm and measured it, measured his back from neck to waist and the span from shoulder to shoulder. The light from the window illuminated her work and Harz was left to gaze across the room and all the various fabrics and boxes lying about, a lot of materials but organized and all of them off the floor. Cait then turned Harz around to face her and the window, and he noticed a view of the courtyard he had never quite seen before. It framed the archway of an interior passage between some tree limbs; that archway led through a secret passageway to the outside of the castle that few knew about and no one used, except for Harz on the yearly trip to inspect it. Cait was making measurements and taking notes with a stick of chalk. He looked down at it and asked, "Don't you have a better writing tool than that?" Cait shook her head and then wrapped the tape around his neck. She read the number and said,

"This is fine, it works." It seemed she was going to measure every length and breadth on his body and wondering how exacting she might be, he suggested,

"Couldn't you just take the measurements from clothes I have?" Cait stood back and replied,

"You'd have to take them off." Harz folded his arms across his chest and submitted to the rest of the measuring without comment. When she was done, she stood back and took in the whole effect. Harz gazed down on her with a skeptical glare. She took his wrists and unfolded his arms, held them and stepped back a pace, then let them go and watched to see if they folded back up again. Instead he just put his hands on his hips and continued to stare. "Yes, I know what would look good on you. I'd make a sketch but I haven't the materials for that. Sparrow doesn't insist on them, so I sew from the idea in my head and memories of other things I've seen. Is that satisfactory or do you require a sketch?" Harz considered it. She could be trusted to sew well, but then he didn't want to end up in something absurd. Finally he said,

"You should have drawing materials. It would be best. Buy them when you are in the village at the haberdasher's, in my name." Cait nodded and said,

"I should have something for you to try on in a week. Come back whenever you can." She smiled at him and added, "Or sooner if you'd like to see the sketch. That way you can stop me if you don't like the design." Harz considered again, saying

"No whatever you have in mind will be fine."

A week later Cait was in her room sewing Harz's jacket. She had considered jacquard or brocade, but thought each one would be too showy for him even if she made the style plain. In the end she chose black velvet because at a distance it would simply appear as a plain black jacket, but up close it was rich, with thin gold silk trim outlining it and resembling gold dust shimmering at the bottom of a stream. She had been both anxious to get the jacket ready but also wishing to linger over it, for when it was finished there would be little chance to see Harz again. She almost considered sewing in some mistake so that she would have to fix it and have him return again to re-fit it, but she didn't do this as she wanted the fabric to be undamaged and she didn't want Harz to think her incompetent, especially after all those detailed measurements, some of which she hadn't used.

She sighed as she glanced up from her work to rest her eyes. She looked out the window and watched people cross the courtyard, somewhat envious that their jobs took them out and about more than hers. Still, she enjoyed going to the village and buying whatever she needed at the stores there. She now had a colored wax pencil and a smooth slate board to make sketches on. It was easier than trying to remember every design detail in her head or sketch with a blunt chalk. As she watched another worker cross the courtyard, this time with a heavy load that threatened to topple, she realized she did not envy them so much, but it would be nice to have more companionship. Her sewing room was a solitary place, which did suit her, but being a widow was lonely. She didn't expect Harz would want to marry her, and she had considered that she could be reducing his chances of finding someone suitable, but Sparrow seemed to think he had remained unmarried for some particular reason she couldn't name. She genuinely liked Harz, an intelligent man who didn't chatter on and on, wasn't full of himself nor inclined to great drink or loose women. Well, Cait smiled, perhaps he might find interest in one almost loose woman. She tied a knot in the thread and held the jacket up for inspection. She had taken great care with it and was quite pleased. She laid it on her bed and admired it. That night she slept with it over her, the window curtain open as a cool breeze drifted in, the jacket keeping her warm and snug.

A few days later Harz, having put off the whole day going for his fitting, finally ascended the stairs to the sewing room. He imagined being greatly embarrassed at whatever she had created, it being too ridiculous or unacceptable somehow. He imagined her only completing half the job and making him return again and again with one limp excuse after another. If so, he would resolve to not go at all; he would wear what he usually did. Then he would hear her words, *you don't want to embarrass the bride*, and finally he was at the sewing room door, which as usual was open and Cait was inside humming a tune. She smiled when she saw him at the door, not fully inside the room, and said to him,

"I'm just finishing with something. Come in, sit down." Harz went to the window and sat. He knew it was where she worked but he didn't want to sit in the other seat, a sofa large enough for two. Who furnished these rooms? Cait was busy folding fabric and putting odds and ends away. Sewing was a messy business but she seemed to have a system, arcane and scrupulous, but a system nonetheless and she sorted and arranged with nimble hands. When the room was somewhat more organized, she smiled and said to him, "Now, let's have a look at this jacket. It's been hanging for several days, you have to do that to make the fabric relax into its new form." She went to a wardrobe and pulled out the jacket, holding it up and then hanging it above the full-length mirror. Harz blinked at it. He got up and walked over to it. At first it had just looked like an unusually long jacket, with a hem around the thighs. The lines of the lapels and long sleeve holes were trimmed with a very thin line of gold and a broad collar was enhanced with a voluminous hood that ran in layers down the back and added a breadth to the shoulders that was impressive. She had somehow managed to take everything that Trevka sought in his outlandish style and condensed it into its most essential form; he would at once be less flashy and more stunning than Trevka had ever been. There was a pleated white shirt for underneath and between the tops of the tall boots and the hem of the jacket, a short gap would reveal a pair of black velvet pants. "Want to try it on?" she asked. Harz shook his head and said softly,

"No, I'm sure it's just fine. Isn't it bad luck or something?" Cait chortled and said sympathetically,

"Well, perhaps. But at least put on the jacket, I want to make sure it is right." She took the jacket off its hanger and draped it over Harz's shoulders. It was loose-fitting but had a tie in front to keep it in place. She came around to stand in front of him and tied the tie, which was then hidden under more lapels, and tugged at each shoulder until she was satisfied with it. She ran her hands down the lapels and over the trim. The shirt he had on wasn't the one she had made but she examined the sleeves of it and imagined her own shirt there, the cuffs tied smartly with cuff strings made of fine leather that would hang down. He took her hand and lifted it to his lips and kissed the back of it.

"It's perfect," he said, and turned her hand over and kissed the palm of it, the capable palm that had worked to create it all for him. She pressed her palm to his face and stood on her tip toes and kissed him lightly on the cheek. She had expected to rock back on her heels and bid Harz farewell, but her feet never got back to the floor as she was grabbed up in his arms and kissed rightly.

Early June came around and on the morning of Beth and Trevka's wedding, Cait and Harz were in her room, where she had insisted on keeping Harz's new outfit so that she could see him into it properly. "The only reward I insist upon for having made it but not seeing it in use inside the church," she said. Harz replied to her, a bit abashed at the fact that she was not invited,

"You can be there, no one will notice. It seems everyone is planning to be there, regardless of the official guest list." Cait shook her head; she genuinely didn't want to fight the crowds, but she did want to see Harz in her entire creation and so helped him get dressed in it. She put the shirt on him and gazed at his fine figure and said,

"I like you this way; informal and dashing and almost topless." She giggled and hummed. Being able to touch him so freely was still a treat. Harz said in reply,

"If I'm ever to be called dashing, it is only thanks to these clothes." Cait pulled herself away from him and tied the cuffs of the shirtsleeves with the leather strings; the ends of them collided playfully. She put the jacket over his shoulders and tied it again; doing so would always remind her of their first night together and she wondered how many there would be. Harz held her face and kissed her tenderly before leaving. "I'll be back," he said.

At the same time, Liesse and Genivee were helping Beth into her wedding dress while Sparrow gazed out the window listening to all the animals chattering about the upcoming activity. These were the village animals: rabbits, squirrels, birds. They must have sensed that everyone was going to be gathering in one place and they themselves were planning to stay out of the way but nevertheless catch a glimpse of the event. Sparrow did not mention this to Beth as she was already nervous about having to make such an ostentatious public appearance. Knowing that even the animals would be watching would not lessen her self-consciousness. Liesse and Genivee made sure her dress and veil were perfectly arranged and complimented her on her appearance, which Beth acknowledged with nods and smiles, unable to speak. A young boy delivered the bridal bouquet and Beth was not sure whether she was grateful for the large object as something to hide behind or ungrateful that it was another grand thing she would have to carry off. She gazed at the gardenias in the bouquet, wondering where such flowers had come from, and the scent wafted up and comforted her. She had never held gardenias before and knew forever after that the scent would always remind her of this moment. Liesse and Genivee had stopped talking and Beth looked up to see Harz standing in the doorway looking at her. He was usually dressed so plainly that she was taken aback by his formal, imposing outfit. Heaven knew what Trevka would be wearing. Her gaze came up again and Harz was smiling and holding out his arm for her. It couldn't be time to leave already, but since he was here she guessed she had better go with him.

They rode to the village in a carriage pulled by the whitest horses the royal stable had, caparisoned and with manes braided. As they left the courtyard no one seemed to be about, a great relief to Beth. Apparently everyone still had jobs to do and things to take care of. However as they approached the village, people were lined up by the road to see the carriage pass and at first Beth gazed at them in amazement, only to hear them cheer louder when the bride looked on. Beth turned away to the only refuge there was, Harz's arm, but he put his hand on her chin and said to her, "I think they're right." As Beth looked past him to the crowd on the other side, also waving and calling good luck, she raised her hand and waved back and they cheered even more, making her chuckle at the sway it held.

The carriage reached its destination and Beth was smiling as she walked on Harz's arm up the path past the last crowds of the people for whom there was no more room inside. Bride and escort waited in the vestibule inside the front door while the bridesmaids caught up to them. Liesse and Genivee arrived but had lost their giggling excitement, alone themselves now and nervous about their own procession up the aisle. There was silence as the four of them waited together, Liesse busily checking her own gown, Beth peeking out into the church between the crack in the double doors and Harz and Genivee looking at each other across the short expanse. Organ music began with such a sudden loudness that Beth pulled herself back upright away from her spying and Liesse took a deep breath as the doors were opened from within by two ushers and she stepped out into the church and began walking up the aisle, followed after a pace by Genivee and then Harz and Beth, whereupon the entire crowd rose as one at the sight of the bride and made such a loud whoosh that Beth was thereafter in a bit of a trance.

In the front row, Gustav and Sparrow watched. He still worried that she wished she could have a big ceremony, for the other women must gossip about weddings a lot. Sparrow watched the bride and groom and felt happiness for them. Just to see such a grand wedding was quite enough for her, for she had sworn herself to Gustav with such vows as these long ago. Her mother had told her about grand weddings, but not with envy, even though she herself had never been married. In the forest, ceremony happened every day if one bothered to watch.

Beside Beth, off to the side, Liesse relished the lavish beauty of it all. She had imagined once that Trevka favored her. No, more than imagined, he had been sweet on her. She had thought him rather immature and unpromising. Now she was at his wedding and it was far grander than her own had been, but still she was sure Boris was better for her. She might have trampled all over Trevka with her wants and needs. That didn't happen with Boris. Next to her, Genivee wished the muttering and music would end. She felt hot and dizzy and wished she could sit. It was all too bizarre. Harz giving the bride away; Trevka, a herald. She had imagined her and Harz's wedding once. Inside her, a baby wriggled around and reminded her of the realities. She covered her mouth but thankfully just to hiccup, quietly, in the grand hall filled with people.

Beth awakened from the dream she was in when someone asked her if she would take this man and she looked up, saw Trevka looking at her hopefully, and she said yes in a brave voice. There was further ceremony and music and proceeding down the aisle and when they emerged out of the church, the crowds were still there, even larger, and now they threw flower petals and pine sprigs in the air as they all cheered and Beth wondered at their great enthusiasm. She and Trevka made their way to the carriage and climbed in to be carried back to the castle. It made slow progress past the crowds now wishing for a glimpse of the couple; there were even more people lining the roads than before the ceremony and so the horse-drawn carriage moved only at a walk up to the castle, fading away from the church.

The guests inside the church filtered out. Those who were invited to the reception at the castle followed on their own horses or on foot. Others lingered about and chatted until making their way back to their homes in the village. Inside, Robyn was sitting alone, still watching the activity at the front of the church from a seat along the far side; altar boys blew out candles and folded altar cloths. At last she grasped the pew in front of her and stood, then made her way out of the church.

Outside, Harz was standing on the church steps watching the bridal carriage make its way to the castle. He didn't take his eyes off the road but his thumb made a reflexive twitch, aware again of the absence of the ring gone from his finger; it was somewhere in Uluvost instead. It had paid for the proof that Trevka was worthy of his daughter. Much as he valued it, that was more important. He had not been able to give her anything while she grew up, but that one ring was as costly as a whole upbringing. He turned then as Robyn emerged at the door beside him. She shaded her eyes against the noontime sun and didn't notice he was there. Harz said to her, "I hope you were able to see the ceremony from where you were sitting." She blinked and tried to see who it was in the dazzling light and answered,

"Yes, thank you. Good enough." Harz glanced around at the still-milling crowds and assemblage of horses and carriages. She should have guessed she couldn't attend the wedding completely unnoticed.

"Did you arrive here by your own conveyance?" he asked her. Robyn watched the carriage with the bride and groom making its way slowly over the bridge and begin to climb the hill to the castle; soon it would be out of view behind trees and turns.

"Public coach," she answered. She imagined the group she had traveled with the previous day would likely remain in town to enjoy the festivities around the village if not the actual reception at the castle. But she had no friends in Wilker and nothing to keep her here; Beth had not even known that her mother had been at the wedding, so in actual fact, Robyn supposed she too was one of the gate crashers that had so swelled the church to capacity. She had never received an official invitation. "I was surprised when I saw you walk the bride down the aisle," she started to say. But Harz clarified,

"That was to serve as a representative for the Count. Circumstances about Beth's being here were rather...unofficial...but he wanted to make it clear that he approved of the marriage. She looks after the Count's son in his mother's absence." So the Count made clear only what he wanted to make clear. Perhaps that was all he knew clearly. Robyn said,

"I'm to be on the public coach this afternoon. I don't imagine it will be too full." Harz glanced at the wedding carriage until it disappeared behind a turn in the road, then looked towards the public inn and stables where the coach back to Jiltradt would be waiting. He turned to Robyn and said,

"Let me escort you to the inn then. This crowd is rather rowdy."

"No, you must be expected somewhere else." She said, "I'll be leaving today. I have another daughter barely one year old waiting at home for me." And with that Robyn began to walk towards the inn, which would be busy with customers but not overrun. There were many people selling food in the market this day and to eat an ordinary meal inside the inn would not be the choice for everyone wishing to enjoy good weather and gossip about their view of events. She might in fact enjoy a solitary meal. Harz watched her fade into the crowd. Ash, coming from a private stable, made his way over to Harz with both their horses and waited. Although he very much wanted to glance in the direction of Harz's intent watchfulness, he also very much wanted to advance to squire some day so he kept his gaze to himself. Finally Harz took the reins from Ash and they walked their horses out of the village, for it was too crowded to mount and ride: there was a hazard that the horses might be spooked. And anyway, Harz preferred not to be noticed just then.

Inside the church, the two altar boys had finished their tasks and were heading back to a side room to store the items special for weddings. "Glad that's over with," one said as he yanked his robe off over his head and rolled it up into a wad. "What a bother, getting married. *I'm never going through it.*" His companion felt obliged to agree in some way and said,

"*I'd* run off and elope." Just then the door to the supply room creaked on its hinge. The two boys spun around, certain the curate was about to berate them for dawdling and blaspheming. But no one was there, although the door continued to creak closed. The two boys gazed at each other, their previous affirmations about the church being haunted now coming to life, and ran to the door before it closed entirely and most certainly locked them in. They burst out of the store room and sped clamorously down the aisle, arms cartwheeling and voices howling. The curate saw them go and tut-tutted them, in too good a mood to chastise them and instead yelled after them, "Girls after ye, lads?"

Outside the storage room, Ambrose watched them go, hoping they would never speak so unkindly of a marriage ceremony again. It had been his greatest joy to see his own granddaughter married in such high fashion. He had had every front row seat there was. There was no need to follow Harz or Beth or Sparrow around any more, it all seemed settled now. He would stop frightening and confusing people. The church began to fade from his sight and instead he saw in the distance someone he recognized. He began moving towards her.

Part II

Fifteen years later

8

A Birthday Festival

A raven landed on the dead limb of a tree in a field on the outskirts of the village of Wilker. Below him everyone from neighboring villages around were gathered and long tables of food and drink were laid out for the celebration of Count Gustav's 50th birthday. The raven eyed some colorful and flashy decorations, as well as the food. Too many people to grab anything now, though. The raven hopped twice, flapped its wings and took flight over the crowd. As he headed away, he swooped over the grandstand where the Count and his entourage were watching the equestrian competitions. The competitors were mostly peasants, but members of the castle were allowed to compete as long as they designated their winnings to charity.

When the call came to assemble for the first event, a round of tent-pegging, Dane and Kasch mounted their horses and joined the others on the field. As the seventeen-year-old Viscount, Dane had several pages under him while Kasch, a year younger, had only one. "Where's my page?" Dane called out loudly. Kasch ambled his horse to the back of the line and Dane followed, hoping he had spotted their pages. They arrived at the end of the line and Kasch commented on the competition, several good riders from the village and a few from outside of it. Dane continued to glance around while Kasch's page approached on the other side with a water bag and Kasch took a drink from it. He handed the bag back to his page and gave him a casual salute.

"You shouldn't reward him for doing his job," Dane scoffed but Kasch just shrugged. Dane's pages finally arrived with a water bag and some food from the table. Dane took both items and was going to say something to them but as his hands were as full as his mouth, they escaped before he could. The tent-pegging began and the first contestant ran the course, which consisted of galloping through the field and finding a half dozen cow pies (there were plenty) to either spear, slice or swat into the air. Whichever method of pegging they chose, they had to use it on all six of their targets. The more targets that were sliced or divided by spearing, the smaller were the targets left for later contestants, who often chose to swat their targets into the air. Being smaller this was easier, but still the most difficult choice as the lance they used had to just graze the ground enough to hit the object, but not enough to catch the ground and lose momentum; targets that were swatted had to be lifted at least as high as the horse's chest to count.

The first contestant sliced his targets and made his way to the exit with polite applause. He had accomplished his trek in good time and a score was tallied for him. A perfect score went to someone who not only pegged all targets, but did so with an economy of movement that suggested foreknowledge of each peg and perfectly spaced journeys between them. Riders who trotted around sizing up pegs to poke were considered dull and fussy, and jeers from the crowd were often their reward. The next rider chose to spear his targets; he had the choice of either keeping them on his lance or flicking them off before spearing the next. Usually spear-peggers did not prefer to keep pies on their lance as it not only weighed down the weapon but they tended to break apart, often falling on the rider in chunks. There was no loss of score if they did fall off, but riders who speared six cow pies on one lance were rewarded with applause for doing so, and sometimes with laughter for a last-second failure of the pies to stay on. This materials failure was not unusual with a jolting horse ride and the poor integrity of the pies to begin with. The current contestant flicked the pies off his lance as soon as he had speared them, but first tossed them over to the other side of his horse to prove that he had control of them.

Several more contestants followed, the last one giving an unrewarded showing by his apparent inability to find the right pies; either they were too big for swatting or too small for spearing or slicing. He could go farther afield, but then any successes would be hard to see at such a distance. Dane muttered that he knew the field would be deteriorated after so many contestants, but Kasch remarked it gave them a better chance to excel. When there were only the two of them left in the waiting area, Kasch bowed his head to his half brother and Dane spurred his horse into a startled entry onto the field. Dane flew at the first target he saw and sliced through it with a vengeance, his lance gashing the ground. With such a late arrival on the playing field, the targets were now reduced to bits and dregs and spearing them was nearly impossible. Swatting them would be easier – if one's aim were up to it. Dane dashed from one target to another, slashing and splashing bits of mud and cow pie into the air, it was hard to tell one from the other. He then sprinted to the exit and there was excited cheering from the band of girls gathered to watch and support him.

In the waiting area, Kasch was distracting his twitchy horse by moving the reins back and forth across its neck and walking him in slow figure eights. When the crowd had quieted down and the scorers had had enough time to make a mark, all eyes turned to see when Kasch would finally enter the field. When he had spotted a row of targets and his horse again faced forward, he gave his horse a kick and they headed off into the arena. With such small targets, there was not much left to do other than swat them into the air. He sought out the likeliest pieces and took aim, turning his horse just as his lance made contact so that the bit of pie would fly into the air and be visible as his horse veered away as if offended by bovine effluvia. For a moment it would seem as if he were giving up on a target, and then it would fly into the air and people would sigh with approval. After five such successful motions, each one more entertaining to the crowd than the last, Kasch could see no more pieces large enough to swat at that weren't a ridiculous distance away. Instead of losing the crowd, although it meant losing the contest, he headed for the exit and tossed his lance into the air and caught it again just as he crossed the finish line. Much to the relief of Sparrow, watching in the stands, he caught it on the handle and not the blade.

The results of the score were announced and neither Dane nor Kasch won, but the cheers for having competed were worth the effort, at least to Kasch. "Next time, I'm getting to the front of the line," Dane remarked with disgust. Kasch shook his head, knowing the others would give way without protest. On foot now, they led their horses with Dane still swatting targets and causing his horse to flinch as they walked around to the next event.

In the pause between events, two girls on the sidelines were watching from the front row of the grandstand, well below the adults who might overhear their gossip. One of the girls was Luna, now 16 and brunette like her mother and watching Kasch make his way across the field. He saw her and bowed, having lagged behind Dane so the bow would be private. He so loved her rounded face and big brown eyes. Next to Luna was Minka, Genivee and Magnus's 15-year-old daughter who was blonde like her mother, but whose green eyes were narrower and were like sharp slits across her face from which her eyes hid but never stopped observing. She had a complexion like a porcelain doll, with a broad expanse of pale cheek accented by a tiny nose and cupid's bow lips. Her mother was in the stands above, keeping her own keen eyes on her daughter, born too canny and cunning for her liking. She would wonder if her child had been switched at birth if she did not resemble her. Minka smiled smoothly and watched as Luna blushed under Kasch's attentiveness. "You're a silly girl," she said, "to so obviously favor him. And anyway he's plain and not noble enough." Luna perhaps stopped blushing then but kept her eyes on Kasch nevertheless. Minka preferred someone with real rank and she watched Dane cross the field, then scanned to the left for whatever his attention had turned to, it had better not be another girl. When the two were out of sight, Luna turned to Minka and remarked,

"You do enough of your own staring, dearest. And don't you think that hat will be interfering with spectators' views behind us?" Minka stretched her lips into a falsely sympathetic smile but did not remove her hat. They sat down again and waited for the next event. Genivee shook her head vaguely as the girls behind her daughter shifted their gaze to see around the cone with fluttering veil that was Minka's millinery masterpiece. Nothing she said influenced her Minka other than perhaps to make her do the opposite. Next time she would have to remark that the hat was too plain and perhaps she would choose not to wear it. Next to her Magnus touched her elbow and smiled at her.

He knew she was not looking forward to being left at home alone, but the upcoming trip to his homeland was rather important to Gustav and Wilker in general, and he did not want to delay it again. Genivee would have accompanied him, but her health was delicate and it was better that she did not travel. Finally Gustav had agreed that enough revenue had been raised to spend on a bridge across the river that divided Wilker from lands beyond, including eventually, Magnus's homeland. He was traveling there to hire an engineer to plan the bridge and obtain information on workers capable of the job. It was something he had been advocating for years, and now finally Gustav had agreed to it.

On the other side of Gustav and Sparrow, who remarked to each other the fine showmanship of both sons, Trevka and Beth were also watching the events. Trevka had been knighted three years after the title of herald had been bestowed for his many accomplishments, and had then busied himself with fatherhood as one child after another were born to the happy couple. They were all running about somewhere amidst the activity, too lively to just sit and watch. Their first child, Leopold, was now 14 and was a page to Kasch, who wouldn't normally have his own page except that he was the Count's son, albeit illegitimate. Leopold kept a watchful eye on all his younger siblings as much as he could while still keeping Kasch supplied with water and making sure his horse was tended between events.

The next event was quintain in which the contestants charged at a post with a cross beam. On one end of the beam was a target that had to be struck with a lance and on the other was a sack of sand that swung around when the target was hit. The player had to hit the target hard enough to make the crossbeam swing around – the faster the better – but also had to duck quickly to avoid being smacked in the head by the sack of sand. Hitting the target so lightly that the contestant avoided being whacked resulted in a low score and was a sign of either bad aim or timidity.

For this event, the order of play was less important but Dane went to the head of the line nevertheless and was first. He hit the target well but instead of ducking he swung his lance around and slashed the bag of sand so that all of it poured out. There was a mixed reaction from the crowd as some found it innovative and dashing (mostly the female crowd members) while others found it an annoying delay of the game. The officiants found another sack and re-assembled the quintain. When it was Kasch's turn, he hit the quintain but then immediately swung his horse away, barely missing being hit but displaying again his close understanding of his animal. The scorers didn't know how to assess the nontraditional players and in the end awarded the prize to someone from the village who had played the standard way and done well.

Trevka and Beth left the grandstand and went to the refreshment area and sat at a table under the trees. They had just finished their food when a little boy came up to their table and sat down as if he were rejoining them. Trevka figured this was one of their childrens' friends, although it was a little odd to show up without them. But Beth noticed that he was rather dirty and undernourished; he was probably going to beg them for some food, not knowing he could take what he wanted. Then a loud voice could be heard declaring,

"Thief! Stop that thief!" The boy put a foot out as if to make off as fast as he had arrived, but he reconsidered as Trevka narrowed his eyes and stared at the boy, fixing him to the spot. Trevka glanced at the man who had shouted thief; he was joined by another man who spoke in his ear and they walked away without any further declarations. Trevka watched them blend back into the crowd and wondered about them. Beth asked if he knew them but Trevka just shook his head. He then turned back to the boy and said,

"Perhaps we should investigate this young man's hands." The boy turned in his chair as if to bolt again, but when Trevka's arm shot out to stop him, he turned back and slowly brought both hands over the edge of the table and spread out two grubby, empty palms. Trevka put his own hand over the little palms while reaching into the boy's shirt and pulling out a short leather strap that was trying to hide. He examined it and said to the boy in a serious tone, "I won't ask the Count to press charges against you if you agree to cooperate with the authorities."

"All *four* T's?" the boy asked, dismayed.

"*Authorities*," Trevka replied, "And that means me and you'd better tell the truth."

"Awe right," he answered, figuring it was better than a trial with four judges.

"Very well then," Trevka began his official interrogation. "From whom did you acquire this piece of evidence?"

"Evidence?" the boy said, confused.

"This leather switch, where did you get it?"

"That man in the street, he was just carrying it around and he off and pelted me backside with it, so I yanked it from him and ran off with it. He put it up to me body so I figure it's mine now."

"Describe this man," Trevka instructed. The boy thought intently for a few moments; how to describe one man? They all looked alike. Finally he concluded,

"He had a gap between his front teeth."

"Many men do," Trevka observed, wondering if the boy were making things up. But the boy added,

"He was mean-looking. And I'd remember him if I saw him again, he looked at me real mean-like when I grabbed this from him."

"Have you ever seen him before, does he live in this village?" The boy shrugged. "Where do you live?" Trevka asked, wanting to be able to question the boy again in the future. But the boy refused to tell them where he lived, claiming he had stowed away in a wagon headed to the celebration and now he didn't know how to get back home. He said his name was Tag and Trevka decided to take him back to the castle to spend the night. It was likely that some parent would come looking for their lost child and go to the castle to do so. They left together and when they arrived at the castle, Trevka put Tag in the blacksmith's quarters and told him to sleep on the floor and not make trouble.

9

A small smith

Harz stood in the doorway of the blacksmith's shop studying Tag, who was poking at the fire and adding one small log after another. The blacksmith, a large man with a black beard, was sitting in the corner scratching his chin and drinking hot cider. He answered with shrugs and open hands to each of Harz's questions. Finally Trevka appeared in the doorway behind Harz, who turned to him and said, "It appears the knight Trevka has a new page." To this, Tag came over to Trevka, put one knee on the ground and asked if there were anything he could get his knight. Knowing full well Tag had no knowledge or means of acquiring anything in a castle where he was a stranger he responded,

"Not for right now." Tag nodded and went back to the fire, brushing off the two ashes that had fallen onto the hearth since he'd left it. Harz motioned for Trevka to follow him outside while the blacksmith pointed to the broom Tag seemed to be looking for.

"Somewhere someone is worried about this child, so we must find them," Harz said as he glanced around the courtyard, expecting some half-crazed mother to be scurrying about yelling for her boy. Trevka replied,

"He told me his mother died a year ago and his father drinks and beats him. He doesn't want to go back home and he won't tell me where that is, only that he hitched a ride on a wagon already full of people to get here." Harz sighed. Trevka already knew what he was thinking and added, "He says he's nine." They both knew that meant the boy was free to work for whomever he could as long as he didn't get into trouble. Harz glanced inside and watched as Tag swept the floor while the smith raised his feet and balanced his mug as the broom whisked underneath. Harz said,

"He does have some bruises on his neck. I wonder how hard a father who beats him will go in search of him. He's your page now so keep him well as you see fit." Harz was about to go back to his breakfast when Trevka interrupted him by taking a switch of leather from his jacket. Harz looked at it and remarked, "Great gods, Trevka you don't need to tell that story to every child in the realm just because he hasn't

152

heard it a dozen times already." Trevka shook his head and said, "But I got this from Tag, he took it from someone at the celebration yesterday." Harz looked at it carefully. He hadn't really examined the original in many years but this one looked just like the one Trevka carried around and was always telling his story about. It seemed to be Trevka's good luck charm, the noose of leather he had freed an eagle from, the thing that fell to the ground instead of his own self from the top of a tree and the charm Count Gustav had given him, albeit quite casually, with a charge to find its owner and tell the tale to his children. Although he had not intended to take the instruction so seriously, over the years he had held onto the bit of leather as a talisman. Now it appeared he had found its twin. He brought out the piece he had carried with him for sixteen years and the two men looked at them side by side. They both had wear marks in the same crisscrossing pattern and on the back, at the bottom, if the third piece of the braid were there, a maker's mark would come together to form the letter W; only a caret was missing from the center of it. Trevka pointed out a slash on the leather. "I always thought this scratch was made by the eagle's talon, but it couldn't have been because it lines up with the scratch on the second piece; it must have been scratched when the pieces were all together." Harz just nodded. It looked to be from a horse harness originally. He asked Trevka,

"Can Tag identify the person he took this from?"

"Maybe, but I'm not sure I'd trust to a 9-year-old's memory."

"Let me know if anyone comes to claim him." Harz glanced one more time into the smithy and instructed the smith to show Tag around and tell him where he could eat meals. The smith bowed his head and set down his mug; he had needed a helper.

At breakfast in another part of the castle, Gustav was congratulating Dane on his successes at the jousting games of the day before. "Unusual methods can sometimes win the day." It was milder praise than Dane would have liked to hear but his father was usually circumspect in such things. He changed the subject and said,

"Now that that is out of the way, when can we plan my investiture?" Sparrow seemed uncomfortable in her chair while her breakfast began to go cold. Gustav was slow to answer, as usual, which always annoyed Dane who liked to settle things quickly and make certain what was what. Finally he said,

"In the spring is a good time for such celebrations. We wouldn't want people to still be tired out from yesterday's activities." Sparrow rested her forehead onto her palm and Gustav watched her. While Dane was on the verge of protesting how many months were between then and now, Gustav waved off further discussion and Dane pushed back his chair and rose to leave. Two pages followed him out while the third stayed behind for now. Kasch watched him go and then returned to eating, nodding when his page brought more ale. He always marveled at Dane's impatience. Spending many summer days in the forest with his mother waiting for some animal or sign to appear had taught him acceptance of any pace, including those that seemed to take forever. Gustav asked Sparrow, "Are you unwell, my dear?" Sparrow smiled weakly and replied,

"Perhaps I got too much sun yesterday, I feel queasy." Gustav had waited fifteen years for her to have another child, and even though it had never happened he still imagined signs such as these to be hopeful portends. He replied,

"Then maybe you should rest inside today, there was a lot of activity yesterday." Sparrow nodded but did not want to stay inside. Instead she said she would prefer to go on a short excursion to a nice shady forest with Kasch, perhaps for the last time now that he was getting to be a man. "Well all right, but keep a close eye on her," Gustav instructed his other son. Kasch nodded and didn't complain, even though he had other plans. He felt slightly incommoded when his mother wanted to take him into nature, ever since the activities and people inside the castle walls had begun to gain his attention. But he never failed to learn something new and he wondered about his mother's apparent delicate condition. She never felt unwell and if she were pregnant, as he suspected his father was hoping, Kasch wasn't entirely sure she would survive a second such event after so many years. Kasch, having grown up his whole life as a member of the castle, felt as at home there as Gustav. Sparrow however, always missed her original home in the forest in some ways, especially when the trees changed color she longed to be there and watch the dried leaves drift to earth for the winter, a settling of the energies that comforted her.

Later that mid-morning in the forest, while several pages stayed behind with the horses they had ridden in on, Kasch and Sparrow took a walk to a favorite spot on a rocky ledge and surveyed the countryside below them. Sparrow sat down with relief and wiped the perspiration off her forehead. Kasch handed her the water bag he had brought and she drank a few sips and then looked out to enjoy the view. The breeze was cool and she felt better, she thought. She had had the feeling that this would be her and Kasch's last visit to the forest together. She had tried to teach him as much as she knew herself about conversing with the animals, reading the signs for rain, snow, wind. She concluded that it was this feeling that soon he would be married and leading his own life that made her feel agitated. She knew he was meant for Luna, had known it from the day they were both born under the same star, and that there was little reason not to get married if that was what they wanted. She hoped to impart any last wisdom that perhaps she had missed over the years, although she couldn't imagine what it was. A breeze swept over them and she turned to her son and said,

"You know, you can do more than just listen to the animals. You can ask for their help. I know I've told you about the time when you were so very little – we still lived alone in the forest then, and suddenly I sensed two very bad men were bearing down on us both. They would have killed us, eventually." She tried not to recall the images she had of what would have happened before that. "But I called on the animals nearby, some deer and some birds. They made a ruckus that frightened them so badly the men not only left us alone, they left the forest for good soon after that." Sparrow tried to laugh but the memory seemed too fresh, even though it was many years ago. It had been so close to turning out differently. She swallowed and put her hand on Kasch's as he listened closely and watched her face. "They are willing to help you if they know you are a friend and your cause is just." She couldn't say any more. The feeling that he was leaving her came over her and so she just smiled and enjoyed being on the ledge with him. He smiled back at her, his dear mother. How mothers worried about their children. But he wasn't a child any more and his thoughts went back to Luna, back in the castle. He hoped he could persuade her to come out to the forest with him some day soon. He had never had the desire like his half brother to seduce every female in the village, he only ever wanted Luna. Kasch could have competed strongly with Dane for the attention of the castle's younger women, for half of them were in love with him already. He was the more handsome and the more confident, although Dane would always have the advantage of being Viscount, heir to the throne.

Kasch put his arm around Sparrow who seemed to be shivering even under the warm sun. He wasn't about to leave her and go off somewhere; the castle and the forest were his home and he would spend the rest of his life in them. "Don't worry, mother," he said. He was in fact more worried about her; she was never nervous like this. Maybe she was pregnant.

Back inside the castle, Dane had decided he was not satisfied to wait 6 or 8 months for his investiture and was going to approach Gustav after lunch about the matter. He had decided he needed another champion on his side and could think of no one else with any more influence in the matter than his own mother, his *natural* mother. Wouldn't she be indignant to find out her son of sixteen had not yet had his investiture? From what little he knew of her, indignation was one of her strong points. They rarely spoke of the Countess Gertrudis, but it had been made clear to him that the kind little woman who raised him, Beth, was not his real mother. He was the son of a Count and Countess and was the Viscount and he wanted it made official. When Gustav had seen the last of the supplicants for the day, Dane approached him with more patience and deference than was usual. Gustav knew he was in for a bit of drama and it was rather all too similar to the discourses he had endured with Gertrudis. It was an unpleasant coincidence when Dane brought up that very name.

"There is something I wish to discuss with my mother, my real mother, and I would like a visit arranged for that." Dane stood his ground in front of Gustav but didn't look him in the eye; instead he fidgeted with the sleeve of his jacket while Boris, Harz, Magnus and Gustav glanced at each other in wonderment. They knew, as Dane didn't, that discussion with his mother would not be the trade of agreeable pleasantries or productive exchange he might imagine. Yet none of them could think of a single reason why it should or could not be allowed, other than that Gertrudis herself might refuse it. Nevertheless, Gustav indicated to one of the heralds to send a message to Uluvost requesting a visit by the Viscount of Wilker to call upon the Countess Gertrudis at her convenience and to please say a date when it could be arranged. Gustav and Dane then looked at each other. Gustav said,

"I'll let you know when we have heard back from them. It might take several weeks." Dane nodded and turned on his heel to leave. He never bowed and Gustav didn't insist on it, but he should have done so. Gustav had always known this day would come, that he would not be satisfied with simply being told about his mother, that he would insist upon seeing her. Gustav was not concerned with divided loyalty but rather with Dane's disappointment. Gertrudis was nothing if not disappointing. How he would love news of a new baby to create a happy distraction to all of this old business.

Having the room to themselves now, Magnus turned to Gustav and remarked, "And I too shall be leaving soon myself, although in the opposite direction. I'm off to find an engineer who can design and build a bridge that will join our countries with a trade route that will shorten the distance between us by nearly half. It will benefit both economies." Magnus often had ideas for economic improvement –

and they were usually of some success. While they discussed the various details of his entourage, Harz studied Magnus. He never seemed to change from one event to the next, always steady and the same. Marriage to Genivee had not changed him into a blushing bridegroom, the birth of a daughter had not turned him into a chattering papa and now even a trip home after many years away seemed only to mildly interest him. For how long would he be away, neglecting Genivee?

Genivee had gathered all the things she thought her husband would need for his trip and was asking him about a few remaining items, to which he would answer with a short yes or no. He was watching her carefully, wishing she would change her mind and go with him. But she always insisted that Minka could not be left alone. He tried one more time to convince her. "Minka is old enough to look after herself." Genivee shook her head quietly and said,

"And shall we have the fox look after the chickens too, while we are gone?" She held up a spare jacket, wondering if there would be room for it and if it would be that much colder where Magnus was going. She asked,

"Does it snow in Brylle?" Magnus shook his head and tried to hide a smile.

"Not at this time of year," he answered. Genivee put the jacket down and sat next to him. He was kind to hide his little smiles but she knew what he thought of her education nonetheless. She said,

"It will be so wonderful for you to be among people more like you." She looked into his eyes. "I'm sorry I'm not more bright." It wasn't the first time Magnus had heard this sentiment. He put his arm around her.

"You are the brightest lady I've ever known and should come with me so that I can show everyone in Brylle what a luminous wife I have. No one will believe me if I simply tell them so."

"Because they are skeptical and question everything. Is that what makes them superior?" Genivee wouldn't dream of trying to hold her own in a country like Brylle. She was comfortable in Wilker, which was plenty enough for her. Magnus answered,

"They are not superior. Well, perhaps there are more inventions there. But with everyone's nose in a book they all become near-sighted and squint when they look at you; you my dear, still have the same soft and open eyes as the day I met you." Genivee took the compliment and just smiled. Even though she hadn't the courage to go traveling with her husband, she wished she did. A part of her wasn't sure he would ever return from this trip. But if he did, she might have more faith in his kind words than before.

10

Dane Spars

Cait was in the village at the haberdasher's shopping for fabric, ribbon and buttons. The knight with her, Vatra, had stepped outside to wait for her and noticed the two men he'd seen earlier and whom he did not recognize. If they were travelers they would be buying supplies for a journey but instead they were idling about as if looking for something not for sale. As constable, he could certainly detain them or question them, but instead of sitting on the bench outside the haberdasher's shop to watch them, he headed down the street away from the shop, turned a corner and walked out of sight in the direction of the stables where their horses were.

Inside, Cait picked out several bolts of fabric while the two strangers watched from across the way. It was a quiet day, with not many people were about. As the strangers drew closer to the shop, Vatra entered it through a back door. He was immediately recognized by the owner who was there looking for a special item Cait had asked about. He began to speak, ready to ask if there were a problem but Vatra put his finger to his lips and shushed him, asking

"Those two men outside, do you know who they are?" The owner shook his head and replied,

"They've been hanging around the last couple of days. They seem to feel right at home but no one knows them. Looks to me like they're planning something and my guess is it isn't something good." The owner had found what he was looking for, a bolt of gold velvet he only sold to the royal family and didn't keep out in the shop on display. Vatra asked the owner to distract Cait in a corner of the shop away from his cash box while Vatra kept an eye on things from the back room. The owner walked back into the shop and said, "Mistress Cait, I want you to see these buckles I have over here," and the two of them conferred with their backs to the front door. The strangers had skulked across the street and now glanced inside the shop, then around the street. They were skinny and in need of better clothes, but did not appear to have the means to get them honestly. Their vests were made of fur and probably too hot for such a day, but they were probably wearing them to hide their shabby shirts. The men seemed to think it over, then suddenly disappeared. Vatra came out from the store room and opened the front door to look for them but they had left. While

Cait compared buttons, Vatra told the shopkeeper to let him know if the men returned or he saw them again anywhere else. Vatra would be assigning some of the castle's lawmen to spend extra time in the tavern so that if anything came up, they would be close at hand.

It wasn't long before Vatra had spoken to his twin brother Trevka, who then relayed the information to Harz, and the three of them were plotting if they could get Tag to possibly identify the man he had encountered at the festival. The twins exchanged coats and Vatra went to check on "his" page. Inside the blacksmith shop, the smith was pounding a red-hot iron while Tag stood on a box and watched. The smith said very little as he poked the iron into the fire, took it out and pounded, turned the object for Tag to inspect, then buried the iron back into the red coals. Tag was spellbound by the process and tried to lean closer, but the smith placed his hand on the boy's chest and put him back. When Vatra appeared in the doorway, Tag jumped off his box and went over to him to bend on one knee and ask if there were anything he could get his knight, to which Vatra answered that they would be going on a tour of the castle later and he should eat a good lunch so he was ready. Tag nodded his head eagerly. Vatra took Tag's elbow and made him stand up while kneeling himself to look straight into Tag's eyes. He said,

"For right now, I want you to remember the other day when you were at the festival. A man hit you with a leather strap and you took it from him." Tag's eyes grew wide and he said,

"I wasn't trying to steal from him but he kept hitting me with it, he'd stumbled over me and was mad." Vatra quickly tried to calm him down by saying,

"That was the right thing to do, Tag, so don't worry about that. I want you to think back to when you took it from him. Did you see his face?" Tag seemed blank for a bit. Vatra stood up and asked him, "Was he as tall as me or taller?"

"About as tall," Tag replied.

"What color was his hair?" Tag thought a minute.

"Dirty," he answered.

"What kind of shirt or jacket did he have on?" Again Tag screwed his face into remembering.

"Raggedy." Vatra looked over at the blacksmith who had been watching the exchange with interest. It wasn't much of a description to match what wasn't much detail of what he had seen through the window of the haberdasher's, but it wasn't far off the mark. He indicated Tag should go back to his spot next to the blacksmith and then asked the smith,

"Is he demonstrating good manners and behaving?" The blacksmith nodded and replied that his new apprentice knew where most things were now and ate his meals with the other pages-in-training. "Good," Vatra replied and smiled at the boy and then left.

Near the castle, Dane and Kasch were sparring in a field. Their fencing master was an older man who knew his art, but teaching these impulsive boys was tiring. He stood between them as their foils rested across his making a three-pointed star; he flicked his lance into the air and stepped back to judge. When Dane struck at his opponent's arm the master called out, "Off target." The two fencers stepped back, then leaned forward with foils at the ready. "Again," the master said. As they continued, Minka stood along the sidelines and watched. She had been invited by her father to accompany him on his trip to Brylle, but had been reluctant to go as there seemed little promise of anything interesting to it. When Dane made another hit with the side of the blade, the instructor called out "not valid!" and they kept on fencing. Kasch made several hits which the master awarded with a call. Finally Dane had a valid, on-target hit and the master called it out. Minka cheered from the sideline and the two glanced at her while the fencing master barked at the young men, "No distraction!" and they turned back to each other to continue the lesson.

When it was over, the two of them left the field and having no way to avoid Minka, greeted her as they approached the exit. "That was marvelous!" she gushed and since neither knew which one she was gushing over, they both bowed to convey their thanks. "I'm just so sad I won't be able to watch for the next three months as my father needs me to accompany him on his trip to Brylle." Kasch bowed to her again, wished her a good journey and continued to remove his gloves and jacket as he headed for dinner. Dane stopped and said to her,

"You'll miss my investiture, that's not very good of you." Minka smiled and said to him,

"Oh well, if it's going to be that soon, then I shall have to cancel going with my father. I can't miss the most important celebration of your life." Dane poked the point of his foil in her face and corrected her saying,

"When I am crowned Count of Wilker, that will be the most important day of my life, or of anyone else's for that matter."

"Of course," Minka corrected. She knew the Count would want his son to be married well before such a day, and in fact was probably impatient for him to marry as soon as possible. Counts were like that, wanting children to carry on the line and all. She wished she knew just how picky Dane was going to be on that topic. He didn't seem to show much interest in it, although he had enough interest in his investiture and becoming Count. He'd better hurry up and realize that becoming a husband and father was an important part of that. "Will I have a place near you at the banquet afterward?" Minka inclined her face and smiled over at him. Dane didn't concern himself with seating arrangements and merely mused,

"That isn't up to me, I'm sure. But you're invited, no doubt." It was hardly an endorsement of his desire to have her nearby. Maybe she would go to Brylle with her father just to peeve him and make him search around for her. But it might not be safe to leave him to the mercy of all the other ladies who would be there and certainly have their hungry eyes on him.

"Whether I'm invited or not, I may not be able to attend," Minka sniffed. "My father does so depend on me to see after him when he is away from home. He's quite lost without a female companion." Dane lifted his eyebrows at this, since he had never seen Magnus in the light of neediness about anything, least of all a silly girl, but then since he cared not at all and did care about dinner, followed his brother to the castle hall. Alone now outside the fencing field, Minka gripped the rail behind her and leaned outwards as she watched the retreating men. Her lips pursed with annoyance and she finally ambled to her own lunch where, instead of eating heartily like her friends, she would pick at the food as if it weren't quite good enough for her.

Sitting next to her, Magnus finally said, "Have you decided whether or not you're coming with me to Brylle? It's quite the trip and we're sure to see lots of interesting sights, not to mention the young people you'll meet and make friends with." Minka wondered if he meant male or female friends, and knowing he likely meant both, decided she had already made up her mind about what friends she wanted and said,

"Daddy, I don't think I can miss the investiture, it's going to be soon." Magnus looked askance and replied,

"I don't know about that. It's hardly begun to be planned."

"Well I don't want to miss it, and besides mother can hardly take care of herself so I should stay."

"Your mother is quite capable and you'd enjoy a trip away. I'm sure the investiture won't take place for many months, perhaps not until next spring." Minka looked at her father intently, adding him to the list of people who annoyed her. She asked him,

"Why did you marry a dairy maid? There must have been precious few choices." Magnus ignored her presumption and made no reply. She had always seemed to bear a grudge against her mother for not being more high born and lofty, whereas he had always admired her for those very qualities which kept her both earthy and elegant in equal and honest measure. Magnus knew why she thought it so important to be at the investiture and said to his daughter,

"My dear, being royal consists largely of listening to people and waiting. I don't think you're suited to it." Minka pretended to need the attention of some servant and looked away from her father. Magnus shook his head, which Minka knew meant the end of the discussion. He got up to leave but she remained to pick at her food and watch the others file out while servants began to clean up. When one walked by her with his arms full of dishes she pointed out to him that she was finished also and watched as he piled one more plate onto the stack. He made it into the kitchen without dropping so much as a fork and Minka finally got up to leave.

A reply from Uluvost had arrived much sooner than Gustav had ever expected; apparently the messenger had waited at the door to the castle for five minutes and then instead of being invited in, had simply received a note saying, *Viscount Dane may visit as he pleases*. No time or date was specified and since the messenger had returned safely, Gustav had no choice but to convey the message to his son. Dane looked at the note and remarked, "Well, perhaps now there will no more faltering about setting a date for my investiture. Mother will certainly want to attend and the sooner the better, no doubt." Gustav had long ago ceased to worry about Gertrudis's influence in his life. He didn't know to what extent she would try to influence her only son, but since she had shown so little interest in him from the very day he was born, Gustav felt more despair for Dane that suspicion. He was certain he was headed for disappointment, as Gertrudis had never once sent messages of inquiry into her son's health or well-being, never once remembered his birthday or asked to see him. He was a mere detail in her life and Dane hadn't quite yet grasped this truth. Gustav asked Dane flatly,

"When would you like arrangements for travel to be made?"

"Immediately!" Dane said loudly. He certainly knew how to rush headlong into uncertainty. Gustav nodded and at the table by the window, a scribe noted the order. After Dane had left, Gustav gazed absently into the room. After several silent minutes, the scribe came over with a page of instructions, Gustav glanced at it and scribbled his initials, and the scribe handed it to the page who would commence the proceedings. The page stepped forward and knelt before the Count, waiting for him to assign someone to the task of conducting a party to Uluvost and back.

"Sir Sutherland shall be in charge of the party going to Uluvost," Gustav declared and the page bowed and left. Gustav wondered if it would be a similar debacle to the trip of 15 years previous.

Early one morning a few days later, Magnus was readying to leave. Everything had been prepared in the days before, so there was little to do but eat breakfast in his room and say his farewells to his family. Minka was still fast asleep in her own room but Genivee sat across the table from him and said,

"It's a pity Minka chose not to go with you; I think it would be good for her." Magnus shrugged his shoulders; they both knew how likely she was to make the least wise choice in any matter. Only rarely could they deceive her into making the choice they secretly preferred. Magnus said to her,

"I wish *you* were coming with me. Minka is old enough to be left alone." Genivee raised her eyebrows and gave a wry smile.

"Perhaps," she answered. "But anyway do you really want a woman along on a trip to find engineers and workers? I would be of no help." Magnus stopped eating and took both her hands in his and said,

"You would be of immense comfort and delight is what you would be. My dear, you are a support in ways you still don't see. I didn't think myself that having a woman around was something I needed. *The world's problems can be solved logically,* that was my motto. But one must also think with their heart as well as their head. That is what you are good at, thinking with your heart." He kissed her hands and put them back on the table, then got up to put the extra rations into a saddlebag. Everything else would be waiting for him in the courtyard with the readied horses. "Coming with me to the courtyard?" he asked. But she shook her head. She stood up and put her arms around his neck and kissed him as if he had just returned, hoping he would tease her about needing to stay just a little longer. He did chuckle at her attempt and kissed her back, then took up his travel bags, touched her cheek and left. Hours later, when Minka woke and rose to take some breakfast, she complained that her father had left and without saying good bye to her.

"It was early," was all Genivee said.

"Well I might have wanted to go with him, he could have asked." Genivee shook her head. She knew when to quit with Minka and sooner was better than later. Instead she just reminded her,

"Don't be late for your deportment lesson," and she rose to leave the room. Sometimes she wished she still had cows to milk early in the morning and could idle in the buttery for a while.

As Minka walked along the corridor with Luna to deportment lessons, they noticed the horses gathering in the courtyard for another departure, this one by Dane and his entourage headed for Uluvost. Minka clutched Luna's wrist and said, "Oh we have to see them off!" Minka stopped to lean out over the half wall that overlooked the courtyard and called out, "Ho, there!" But Luna pulled her onward and said,

"They don't need our help, dear." Minka cast a glare from the horses and men to Luna, who quickly added, "I mean it is no help for us to remind them how much they are already missing our company. It will only delay them and you know they dislike that." Minka shrugged herself out of Luna's hand and they walked onward. But near the deportment lesson, Luna suddenly clutched her abdomen and groaned, leaning on the half wall and then sliding onto a bench. "Oh, Minka, I fear today is one of those days. I'll never manage a book on my head. I thought the pain would pass with a short walk but it's no better, I'll have to go back to my room and lie down." Only steps from the door, Minka was a bit annoyed.

"There's no time to walk you back, Luna, we're late already."

"I know, I know. I'll find a page to help me back to my room, there are plenty about. You go on ahead, I'll be fine." Minka turned to the doorway and went through. When the door had closed, Luna leaped up from her bench and ran off.

Kasch had been in the courtyard overseeing the readying of Dane's horses. There were six horses and four men and Kasch watched as supplies were loaded and discussions were finalized. Soon Dane urged them all to be on their way and Kasch watched them trot off. He went back to the stable and glanced at the groom, now eating his breakfast. Instead of interrupting the man's meal, he simply smiled and said, "We need two more horses but I'll get them." Kasch saddled up two compatible horses and led them out, the groom finishing his meal and wondering where Kasch was going.

Once a year Harz would make an early morning trek from the castle gates and around the whole of the structure to a secret entrance on the far side. There he would open a hidden door and enter one storage room after another until he emerged into an interior portion of the courtyard where extra wagons and equipment were stored. He would then watch from the courtyard archway as people began to rise and would eventually make his way to breakfast, satisfied that the door still worked and no one was hiding out in one of the many places where vagabonds or vagrants might keep themselves. But this was not Harz's day for that and he was nowhere in sight as Luna waited in the passageway and saw Kasch approaching walking two horses. She walked with him through the passageway storage area, and with no one about they quietly walked into the darkness and eventually made their way to the open countryside. They were the third party to leave that morning, but unlike the other two, they escaped unnoticed.

11

Trips abroad

Kasch and Luna galloped away from the castle, through the trees and out to the meadow above, then continued on to the forest at the other end of the meadow and stopped. They laughed as they got down off their horses and Luna asked, "Aren't you going to be missed?" Kasch shook his head and replied,

"I told them I was going to walk half the day with Dane and then return, how about you?"

"Minka thinks I'm sick in bed and that will keep her away. Mother will think I'm in deportment." Kasch muttered bewildered disgust at the mention of deportment.

"How do you stand that?" he asked her.

"Minka loves it. She'll bore our teacher to death balancing a book on her head, parading like a queen in her *process* and *egress*. Then she'll make him watch her rise and fall into a chair and make him critique that until she is perfect."

"Who runs the class?" They smiled at each other. Luna looked up into the treetops and said,

"Isn't this where Trevka says he saved an eagle, its nest and all her chicks?" Kasch nodded but Luna shook her head. "I always knew it couldn't be true. No one could climb a tree that tall without falling to their death." Kasch just spread his arms out and shrugged, then took her hand and they strolled the edge of the meadow while the horses grazed. "How far from here is the hunting lodge?"

"A few hours," Kasch said.

"Do you think you'll finally be included in the next hunting trip? They don't allow *children*, as I understand." Again Kasch just shrugged and smiled. Then he remarked,

"They are fond of making children there, as I understand. It doesn't matter, I've already seen it."

"You haven't!" Luna exclaimed. It was an exclusive retreat, meant only for the Count and his best and closest friends and a few lucky servants.

"I've seen everything in the forest and know every inch of it, although of course my mother never showed me the lodge. Just as her parents forbade her from it as a place where trouble began and even spells were cast, she said I'd get to go soon enough and until then we'd stay away. But I went anyway once, when they thought I was in bed." Luna wagged her head. Kasch added, "It's very secluded and romantic." He pulled her close and wrapped his arms around her. Some day he would have to become serious with her, a serious romantic suitor. Not that he thought he had any competition, but before it arrived he wanted her to know that he didn't just think of her as a childhood companion, but as the loveliest and liveliest lady he knew, the only woman he could imagine spending his life with. But he wasn't sure if she might still think of him as an immature boy, so he waited.

A bird called out overhead and they watched it fly into the treetops. "There's Trevka's eagle," Kasch said, "Some fairy tales are true." But the bird disappeared and did not re-emerge. There was only silence from the top of the tree and the whole of the forest. A chill of loneliness overcame him and he dropped down on one knee and looked up at Luna, clutched her hands and said, "You will marry me one day, won't you? You won't fly off and never see me again, fall in love with someone else and live in a big castle all by yourself with some black-hearted husband?" Luna kissed his forehead and said with as much seriousness as she could muster in the face of such melodrama,

"I promise to marry only you and no one else." Kasch gazed back at her, but appeared to be watching something much farther away. "I promise," she added. Her face came back into view and he smiled, then he pulled her down next to him and kissed her, the first time he had ever kissed her sincerely. They had to head back to the castle soon enough, but he would have preferred to ride on into the forest, up to the hunting lodge to show her the bedrooms. He offered to do either one but she declined both ideas. Instead, they stayed at the edge of the forest for most of the afternoon, satisfying their curiosity about what it would be like to *be* blissfully married.

When they returned via the castle gate later that day, Leopold was waiting and watching. After Luna had been left by the door to her apartments inside, he came up to Kasch walking the horses and said, "How can I be a good and right page if I don't know where you are or what danger you might be in?" Kasch gave the reins to Leopold and replied,

"There you are, my good page. As you see I am fine and well, no need to explain your absence."

"Explain *my* absence? You said you'd be practicing your fencing and then I hear you have gone off with the party headed to Uluvost. I caught up with them only to find you not there. Then I thought you had gone with Magnus instead and left me to rot!"

"I would not leave you to rot," they reached the corral and Leopold gave the reins over to the boy inside. Kasch sat down in the shelter of the stable and glanced around. Leopold got him a cup of water and waited on one knee. Instead of dismissing him, Kasch pulled another footstool beside him and motioned for Leopold to sit next to him. "It never feels right, your waiting on me. I should be waiting on you." Leopold, still feeling anger and consternation, just shook his head. Finally he said,

"I only thank the gods they didn't make me a page to the Viscount." Kasch chuckled and ruffled his page's scraggly head of hair. "Will you please at least tell me where you are going even if you won't let me follow?"

"Leopold, I've been in the forest my whole life. To tell the truth, there is more danger here in the castle than out there."

"I don't doubt that," Leopold replied. He rubbed his forehead, worried and waited. It seemed to Kasch that Leopold had been born old and was more mature than many adults he knew. Kasch downed the last of the water in the cup and then handed it to Leopold and said,

"Get some for yourself." But Leopold just shook his head and looked at Kasch bewildered. "Or maybe we should get something stronger for you," Kasch suggested. They smiled at each other and headed off to the banquet hall for some dinner, Kasch insisting as usual that Leopold walk beside him and not behind and Leopold protesting it should not be so. Kasch remarked, "I think you are growing so fast that by tomorrow you shall be as tall as I." Leopold looked around to see if anyone had noticed a page walking next to his captain. "And I won't have a taller man in my shadow."

A week later, the party from Wilker rode out of Stoer and toward the castle of Uluvost. There was a steady rain as the full entourage approached the gates. It was the same dark, unadorned pile of stones that Sutherland had visited so many years ago and that his party had barely escaped from. A dark fungus crept up the walls and although it was early fall, the cold rain made them shiver. They waited endlessly for the doors to open so they could escape the elements. Once inside, it struck Dane as a place that was still and silent and at the same time not at all peaceful. Noises came suddenly and then vanished. Doors slammed, voices barked and there were no aromas of food or wood smoke. A messenger had been sent ahead of them so they were expected. However little ceremony and only stark civility greeted them. Dane consoled himself that he was being spared endless introductions to his long-lost relatives. Instead he was led to a small, enclosed balcony that overlooked another room from behind a screen.

He was in what was called a nanny nook: a place where adults could watch over children without the children knowing. He was left in this nook with only his own attendants, whom he quickly ordered to leave. He wanted any conversation with his mother to be private. He seated himself and waited for her to arrive. It was an odd place to wait, but he assumed she must be a busy woman and this was the most convenient location for her to meet him and at least it was private. In the room below a woman was seated at a mirror strung with shawls and scarves; he wondered how she even saw her reflection. But she studied it intently nevertheless. Next to the woman were two other ladies who handed her various objects by turns; a hairbrush, a bottle of perfume, pieces of jewelry that were tried and then discarded. Dane tired quickly of the scene and went to the door of the nook and signaled to his Uluvost escort, asking,

"When will the Countess Gertrudis be joining me here?" The escort remained silent, as if deaf. Repeating himself with much annoyance, Dane said, "When -" The escort broke in,

"She is here, Sir. Seated at the mirror. Sir." Dane began to protest, but his fellow countrymen were within earshot. He retreated back into the nook so they wouldn't see his disbelief.

Dane sat down, feeling imprisoned in his chair. Gertrudis did not rise to greet Dane; she in fact appeared not to know or care that he was there. The ladies waiting on her might have informed her of the visitor, but it was impossible to know for sure, for when they did lean close to her to say a word or two, the words were private and inaudible. The attending ladies acted kindly, although perhaps seemed a bit bored. As the woman at the mirror brushed her hair – could this really be the Countess? - the brush encountered a knot in her hair and flipped over and out of her hand before she could stop it. It hit the floor and upset a neatly laid pair of slippers. Gertrudis turned suddenly and pointed with deep concern and the lady next to her rescued the slippers as if they were an injured pet, making a great show of gathering them together, brushing them off, arranging them carefully again at their place on the floor, retrieving the hairbrush and returning to her station. Dane focused on the rest of the room. It was well-appointed and orderly, almost rich. A lit fireplace blazed with warmth and the dampness was at bay. There was a gentle giggle from all three of them. The Uluvost attendant quietly entered the nook and sat silently next to Dane, who turned to gaze at the man who dared to merely sit next to him without being invited. Dane studied him, anything for a distraction. The man had a slim, unimpressed smile and said,

"So you are the Viscount from Wilker, hmm? My, my aren't we important." Dane was shocked at the man's disrespect. He responded flatly,

"I am the heir of Wilker castle. And you are insubordinate." Yet, he could not accuse the man, or anyone, of mistreatment of his mother.

She was well cared-for, in apparent good health and smiling. She was well-fed, but not overly so. Her hair and clothes were neat and clean. The room smelled fragrant. He struggled for something of which to accuse this awful man beside him. "When does the Countess receive visitors? Hasn't she been informed that her only son is here?" The man's expression didn't change, his smugness in place.

"She has been informed. She did not say she cared to receive you. She did not send you away. She did not express an opinion about you in any wise." Dane took a reluctant look toward the be-decked mirror. The woman, his mother, gazed into it with her head cocked to one side, slowly brushing her hair and that of her fur-collared robe. One of her attendants sat next to her, the other one reached for a lute and strummed softly while the others listened. Dane was going to say something but wedged his thumbnail into his teeth and fumed. Then the Uluvost man leaned in, speaking quietly and sympathetically. He said,

"Take heart, Viscount. That silly woman, she is not your mother. Her child was stillborn, such a disaster. But we were lucky; we traded her poor babe with that little chambermaid's. *She* is your mother. What was her name? Beth?" The man leaned back in his chair and exhaled long and slow, then added, "I don't know what ever happened to her." Eventually he got up and left. Soon after, the party from Wilker trotted away from the Uluvost castle, and now the rain fell in heavy splats like frogs being pelted at them from above.

As they made their way over four days back to Wilker, Dane had only one thought consuming him: He was not really the Viscount. He was some bastard belonging to a woman now married to someone else, who was clearly not his father. As the worry of this overtook him, he made himself repeat over and over again, *no one knows, no one can tell. I am the Viscount, I will be the Count.* On the last day of the trip, his silent demeanor vanished and he was suddenly very talkative, exclaiming to Sir Sutherland, "My mother made it very clear that I should be crowned right away. Any delay is unacceptable to her. I'm seventeen after all. She was shocked I had not come with the news of it's already having happened this summer!" He went on and on and Sir Sutherland did not care or bother to ask for anything written by the Countess; it was not for him to demand such proof. He was getting old and could only hope that future trips on this muddy road were assigned to someone else.

Upon their return, Dane burst into the audience hall where Gustav was, quite fortunately, not engaged in any business other than conversing with Boris and laughing over his recounting of a tale from his youth. Harz was there also, enjoying the entertainment. Magnus was still away of course. "Mother sends her greetings!" Dane declared, to which the three men who had been acquainted with her just pondered in mild surprise. Dane quickly took in the looks on their faces and added, "And she was quite dismayed that I have not been crowned officially as Viscount, heir apparent, and insists the ceremony take place immediately." That was more like the Gertrudis they remembered. Gustav, a bit weary of celebrations and looking forward to a quiet season, sighed and shifted in his chair. *Soon* was obviously a priority for Dane; how *much* pomp was expected was still in question. He said to his son,

"We won't be able to arrange as large an affair if we have it right away." To this Dane waved his hands in dismissal.

"Not important." There was a moment of silence, then he added, "As long as it is a loud affair, with everyone in the village crowded into the courtyard and a formal crowning ceremony that all can see." Harz walked away from his place at the buffet table and took out a sheet of paper to write down notes. Gustav wondered, then asked,

"You want to be crowned in the courtyard, not the royal hall?" Dane crossed his eyebrows.

"Well, no. The royal hall will do for the official ceremony. After that I wave to the crowd and then there is a huge feast. That's all we need." As the word *we* hung in the air and on everyone's mind, Harz scribbled notes and Boris examined a pork rib bone. Gustav waited patiently until Harz came over with the sheet of paper, perused it, then consulted the list of dates that were available for such an affair. Finally he said,

"The diocesan will be leaving in two weeks, then won't return until a month after that. I think that puts us at two months from now. That should be enough time to plan something grand enough to suit you." But Dane protested,

"We must do it in two weeks then, before he leaves!"

"Dane there isn't time, he's a busy man. We should be lucky to find that he can perform the ceremony in two months time, let alone two weeks." They all waited for Dane to say something. Gustav was no longer going to dismiss him or his demands; they would have to come to a compromise together. But he knew of no other alternative and thought the circumstances would dictate the event's timing.

"Then we can have the dean perform the ceremony. He is always here, he should be allowed such privileges." This seemed perfectly fine to Dane; what was the difference between one religious leader and another? What did it matter as long as the ceremony were performed? Gustav just blinked. It wasn't like Dane to scrimp on officiousness. Finally he said,

"You really want a dean to perform your investiture?" Dane replied,

"It will still be legal, won't it?" Boris glanced over the top of a loaf of fragrant bread at Dane.

"It is a formality and will be legal even if the servants perform it, but I didn't think you'd want that."

"No, the dean will be fine, but not the servants."

"No, not the servants," Gustav repeated and waited for Dane to change his mind. When it appeared he was happy with the arrangement, Harz scribble the details, certain they would be changed, perhaps by tomorrow.

12

Injured Parties

Beth was walking down the long corridors of the castle on her way to Cait's sewing rooms with a page accompanying and two of her little girls skipping along beside. She didn't really need or want a ladies' maid of her own, but rather enjoyed visiting while Cait stitched and the children dressed themselves up in lengths of fabric from Cait's vast collection. With the upcoming investiture of the new Viscount, and Beth being the wife of a knight prominent in the court, having a new gown to wear to the event was appropriate. Beth wasn't ostentatious, but she didn't want to attend in something old for an occasion that was to mark a new beginning; that would not portend good luck. She still loved the boy she had raised as if he were her own, even if he himself seemed to have forgotten her. She arrived at Cait's who asked the page to fetch refreshments, leaving the two women to sit and peruse the drawings Cait had made for Beth's new dress.

Beth held up one drawing and remarked to Cait, "Now I don't want to compete with my dashing husband; he's the famous one and I'm just along for the food." Cait snatched her lovely drawing back and made a good-hearted sniff. Beth smiled and waited to be shown other dress ideas. Cait didn't want to draw only simple dresses and have her friend think that *she* thought of her as plain, even if Beth would always be convinced of it.

"You're famous enough," Cait remarked. She continued sketching and then asked, "How is Trevka?"

"He's fine. Greatly enjoying this new twist in his on-going investigation of the still-at-large eagle snatchers. He's quite certain that the strap that set their trap was once braided to the one little Tag found, stole actually, at the birthday celebration. How this helps him find who used it sixteen years ago escapes me." Cait just lifted her eyebrows and wondered herself. She handed a sketch to Beth and remarked,

"I could add a trim around the hem of this one that would look formal yet understated. You don't always have to be in Trevka's shadow." Beth thought to herself that Cait certainly understood that sentiment. In all the years she had been friends with her, she had never asked her why she and Harz had never gotten married, never had children, never set themselves apart from this simple sewing room and instead lived their lives in surreptitious seclusion. Having married up in a way she never thought possible, Beth knew she was a hopeless matchmaker but in this case she had long ago given up. It wasn't a secret that Cait was Harz's steadfast companion. Gustav had suggested that Harz marry Cait, hopeful for a short spell when Sparrow informed him of the partnership between them. But Harz had just declined the generous idea, shaking his head and not giving any explanation. Gustav suspected his cousin set too high a standard for the woman he would marry because being his cousin, such a woman should have a distinctive rank and breeding. Gustav tried to deny his having this prejudice, but his cousin only shook his head again and Gustav gave up. Sparrow was right, Harz and Cait were in love, but for whatever reason, he wasn't going to marry her and Cait didn't seem to care so there was nothing for it.

Cait alone knew the truth and was perfectly content the way things were. Perhaps being taken into Harz's confidence was enough for her. She knew that Beth was actually his daughter, something Beth herself did not know. She also knew that Harz would have married her in a second if he weren't already married. It would have been an invalid marriage with Robyn still alive, which she was, and any children he had with Cait would not have been recognized as legitimate heirs of royalty. Of course no one but Harz and Cait knew of Robyn's existence, and he might have merely tossed the fact aside, married Cait and carried on. Hadn't Robyn done as much? Although Robyn wasn't likely to come forward and make any claims, Harz wasn't willing to take any risks. He had made one impulsive, secretive move in his life and wasn't going to make another. It never mattered anyway, as Cait never did have any children. With every year that passed, Harz felt it was less and less important to be married and have children. There was a legitimate heir to the throne, soon to be formally recognized, and Dane had all the arrogance men usually had when they were going to spend the next fifty years ruling over others.

Beth finally handed the simplest design over to Cait and declared it would be fine, especially if she could remove the extra beads around the neckline. This Cait refused to do and in fact proceeded to remark on all the other embellishments she was going to add and that by the morning of the investiture, Beth would not be able to remove them all. The page arrived with tea and cake, nearly losing the tray as he wove his way around Beth's madly dashing girls, now chasing each other around the room.

The knight Trevka was occupied that morning with taking his newest page around the town. If Tag were from out of town as he claimed, he should become acquainted with the marketplace. But if Tag had lied and already knew the village, Trevka would detect this. No one had come forward looking for him so his story might be true; he might have a father who truly did not care about him. As they crossed the bridge and approached the village, Trevka waved at Tag who walked a few steps behind, to come forward and walk alongside him. "I must stay behind," Tag said. Trevka corrected him saying,

"Not when I want to talk to you; then you walk beside me." Trevka wondered how best to render any confessions out of Tag. "Let's sit outside at the tavern first and have some drinks." Tag remained silent as they made their way over to a table. It was a busy day with many people walking by and going in and out of stores. Tag studied Trevka as the latter perused the street for worried parents or bird-toting brigands. Trevka, knowing he was being examined, finally looked over at Tag and said, "It's not right for a page to stare at his knight unless he is in dire need of saying something the knight should know." The two glared at each other, Trevka trying to be intimidating and Tag trying not to say something. A barmaid brought ale for Trevka and root beer for Tag, setting the drinks down slowly between the two men locked in a strange staring contest. When she had left, Tag finally said,

"That man you are looking for is over there." Trevka swung around in his chair. The common area between the tavern and wherever *there* was was knotted with people and Trevka did not know where *that man* was. Trevka grabbed Tag's hand as it was just about to tip the root beer to his mouth and said,

"Show me where." Tag dropped his drink and ran into the crowd. He wove his way through the crowd while Trevka endeavored to keep up. Tag had the advantage of being able to squeeze between people and of not caring if he was impolite, but Trevka managed to keep up with him. They got to the pig pens and Tag searched around expectantly. There was no one in sight and only the sounds of oinking. Then there were shouts coming out of the stables nearby as a groom was chasing two men making off on stolen horses. Trevka ran to the stable and shouted for a horse. The groom had just one left and as Trevka grabbed its mane and pulled himself on, Tag was running after him yelling,

"I have to stay with you!" but there was no saddle and no time to pull Tag up; the two men were trotting off towards the woods. With the sound of Tag's voice fading behind him, Trevka headed after the escapees. Even riding bare back he stayed close behind them, following the path of beaten- down grass they left in their wake. He had heard them yelling to each other but couldn't make out what they said, then they made the edge of the forest and disappeared in the trees. As he reached the forest himself, Trevka spun his horse to check the path around him when he was suddenly hit on the head and knocked off his horse. He heard men's voices and Tag's yelling and pigs oinking all at once while his head spun with pain. He tried to stand up to fight back but he fell over immediately for lack of balance and temporary blindness. Then he heard Tag bellowing out with frightening screams and he thought the men had captured him and were hitting him over the head too. But it was only Tag riding towards them on an enormous sow at top speed, her extreme annoyance filling the air with porcine expletives and Tag adding to the noise as he tried to stay on the pig's back as it trotted madly towards the three men in a zigzagging pattern that defied Tag to stay on top of the beast. If the boy had been any taller he would have toppled over, but he hunkered down over the pig's back with arms wrapped around her face so that she trotted with blind rage trying to get away from the little pack rat stowed away on her back. His feet scattered over the ground behind him, now and then bonking the pigs' feet and startling her on to even greater annoyance and speed. The two men gazed dumbfounded at the spectacle while Trevka swung out both arms to grab at least one of them. His hand brushed against something but they were both still mounted and quickly kicked their horses and fled into the woods. Close after them Tag tottered into range and jumped off the sow, who ran two enormous, curse-filled circles around them just to show her displeasure and then headed back to her piglets.

Tag ran to Trevka and told him to sit down, for the fearful streak of blood running down Trevka's forehead and into his eyes made Tag shake with anxiety. He mopped at the blood with his shirt sleeve and was relieved to see that there was intact flesh beneath it. When the light filtered back into Trevka's eyes Tag's face came into view. Trevka tried to reassure him that he wasn't that badly hurt and could he see the horse thieves any more? Tag shook his head and wondered why catching them could matter so much, or be worth this kind of danger. When Trevka was able to stand, Tag took his hand and led him back to the stable where Trevka's horse had wandered back to. Tag took it upon himself to say to the bewildered groom, "Saddle that horse and be quick, the knight Trevka is injured and must return to the castle at once." When the horse was ready, Tag and the groom helped a still-dizzy Trevka onto its back and Tag climbed on in front of him, took the reins and led them back to the castle at a steady walk. By then Trevka's head had stopped bleeding but it had not stopped spinning. He finally rested his chin on Tag's shoulder and thus they arrived at the gates of the castle with Tag calling out loudly that Trevka was injured.

The next morning as Trevka was recovering from his adventure, his son Leopold was sitting next to him. Beth had gone off to the kitchen to strictly oversee the broth for his breakfast and had told Leopold to watch his father carefully and not let him move from his bed. The two men reflected on her orders and listened to her footsteps fade down the hallway, then studied each other. Leopold said to him, "Why do you do these things, father?" Trevka just shook his head and tried to smile. Then he started to speak but Leopold stopped him. "I know, I know. The Count told you to find them." He shook his head too, then and reflected that, "I guess we do want to keep his orders, don't we?" Trevka asked him about his own responsibility:

"How is Kasch? He isn't feeling left out with all these plans going on for Dane's investiture is he?"

"Of course not. But he is still making it hard for me to keep my eyes on him. He's at fencing right now, but I'd better get over there before he makes off to somewhere else. He's free spirited, like his mother."

As soon as Beth returned Leopold relinquished his seat to her and she held out the tray of light food as she sat down next to Trevka. "Is the knight hungry?" she asked. Trevka nodded and Beth added, "That's our good knight." Leopold smiled at them and said,

"He's all right, mother," and went to the door. Trevka said to him before he left,

"Go to the smithy and tell Tag how well he did yesterday. Tell the smith he's to have a day away from his work for his bravery and then teach him what you know about being a page." Leopold smiled, bowed to them both with affective formality and then left. Beth and Trevka looked at each other and sighed.

"Is he really only fourteen?" Trevka asked. Beth nodded and confirmed,

"Yes, I was there. And he didn't give me any trouble then, either."

After a fortnight of hurried preparation, the investiture ceremony for Dane was finally taking place, and at long last he breathed a sigh of relief on that bright Saturday morning. The sun rose through a few wisps of cloud, then shone overhead much to Dane's relief; he did not want to toast the crowd and be cheered in anything less than a fully shining sun. On the western horizon, obscured behind the treetops, there were gray clouds but they remained low and out of sight. It was a formal occasion celebrating the fact that he was the recognized heir to the throne of Wilker and would succeed his father when the time came. Villagers and commoners filled the courtyard (one of the very few occasions on which they were allowed to do so), and waited for the official ceremony to be over so they could wave and cheer to their future Count, set to appear on a balcony far above them.

The ceremonial room was filled with attendees humming with anticipation. There was limited seating, but Minka, who was not officially invited to this part, cajoled an acquaintance sitting on the aisle toward the back to give up his seat for her, in return for a whispered favor to be delivered at a later time. She sat down quickly and looked about, studying the scene carefully, willing that one day it would be *herself* at the center of attention, that *she* would be the one honored and be-royaled. She noted the details and harrumphed that her ceremony would have more ribbons and banners, louder trumpets, and more servants scurrying around. A hush fell over the crowd and a processional fanfare began. As Dane made his way down a center aisle, Minka noted carefully the fur-lined cape, the gold medallion, the gold chains of his costume as he walked stiffly by. She had a sly wink in store for him, but he did not turn his head or even seem to notice her and she wanted to reach out her foot and tap his trailing cape as he glided past her, but resisted.

After what seemed like much muttering and promising and tedious declaring, finally Dane stood with a small crown now on his head and everyone applauded and cheered while Minka plotted her wink for his return trip down the aisle. She had had time to surmise that he did not see her while walking up the aisle because her back was to him. The return would be different.

In fact is was very different. He did not walk back down the aisle at all, but instead everyone on the dais in front moved into an adjoining room and took seats for a formal feast. Minka was fuming in her chair when its original occupant made his way back to her to inquire as to her enjoyment of the ceremony and when exactly the favor of an aisle view would be repaid. Simultaneously, Genivee (who did have an official invitation), noticed her daughter in the back and wove her way against the tide of the moving crowd to approach her. The would-be favored gentleman noticed her and left the room abruptly.

Her mother did not even question her out loud. Instead she took Minka's arm and waited for the pouting eyes to look at her. Minka finally shrugged and mumbled she had wanted to see the ceremony. Genivee was about to warn her not to gate crash the dinner as well, but Minka wrested her arm from her mother's grasp and spun on her heels and left out the back door. Genivee watched until she was out the door and apparently gone for good. She turned slowly and watched the crowd gather into the banquet hall. Magnus was still away and instead of taking part in the celebration, she decided to go back to her room alone.

Minka ran outside, against the crowd that waited for Dane to appear on an upper balcony. She was both jealous and scornful of them. What was so special about one man that they should all squander a good morning just to wave at him? She imagined the day the crowd would gather to look up at the *two* of them, newly married, she the stunningly beautiful blond by his side, he the unbelievable lucky groom who was her husband. Secretly, everyone would find her more interesting than him. She moved against the direction on which their attention was fixed and found herself headed for the dairy where, she imagined, her disadvantages of birth had some of their beginnings.

The milking parlor was nearly deserted, but one lonely cow was licking the last bits of hay off the dirt floor and seemed forlorn that there was no one around to notice her or give her more of what she wanted. With a sudden and fierce hatred, Minka picked up a short shovel, the one the boy used to gather the manure, and lunged towards the passive creature. She raised the shovel and took a swing at the beast but a rail of the milking stall blocked an otherwise good blow. Even more angry now, she ducked under the rail and raised the shovel again but the cow casually shifted and Minka was now trapped between a half-ton cow and a stout wooden post. The cow continued to munch, indifferent to Minka's presence or distress. She gasped for air as the cow rubbed against the vertical object to scratch its side. This cow was in fact very pregnant, probably why its appetite was so hearty, and the added girth was at the perfect height to press into Minka's own womb like a flower smashed in a bible. Minka tried to scream, but there was no air in her lungs. The shovel had fallen from her hands and she slapped at the animal with the effect of two flies. The cow swished her tail and bits of manure flicked into the air. No one was around to help, they were all in the courtyard waiting for Dane to appear. Just when Minka thought she would die and had ceased to struggle for air or space, the cow once again shifted its weight and Minka collapsed in a heap on the slimy floor.

Outside, the crowd cheered; Dane appeared on the balcony and waved to the attendees. A squire brought a glass of wine on a silver tray and Dane picked it up, raising it in a toast to the commoners. They all cheered again, this time because they knew that a swig of ale would now be dispensed at the gates to every guest when they departed the festive occasion. The sun was still shining with a dazzling metallic brilliance. Dane retreated from the glare to the interior of the castle. He took his place at the head of the table, toasted again to his favored guests, and everyone began to eat.

When the meal was ended and after the guests had dispersed (for they did not dance on what was a solemn occasion), Gustav was able to talk to his son for a moment before he surely dashed off. Hopefully it was not already too late for Dane to listen to his father. Gustav said to him, "Now you can relax, it is official. One day you will be Count and I am required to give you one piece of advice at this point which you are obliged to hear." There was a long silence. Gustav wanted to impart at least ten points of advice to his son, but he knew that Dane would hear very little, so he chose carefully. "Dane, never let it be said you owe a favor back to any woman who gives favors. Paying them can take a lifetime." Another silence as Gustav remembered. "There is very little joy in such a relationship." This completely quashed Dane's hopes of being a free-spirited and highly satisfied young Viscount who had the favor of *many* women. Well, it was only advice, he needn't follow it.

Thunder was beginning to rumble over the sky and the cows were stamping to get into their feeding stalls. The pregnant cow had finished its snack and was placidly chewing its cud while the cows still outside bellowed for a meal. The dairy mistress Marta entered the milking parlor and the whole herd followed her happily in. When Marta spotted Minka in a pile on the floor, it was all she could do to direct the beasts away from the unconscious girl and into another area. Alarmed and tipping the girl's face up, Marta feared perhaps an assault by an attacker as Minka was lying in a pool of blood. Soon she had Minka carried to the infirmary and Quilin immediately attended to her. The thunder continued all evening as the sky grew dark, both from thick clouds and the setting sun. It began raining as Genivee arrived and took up a vigil at her daughter's side. For two days and nights it rained slowly and ceaselessly while Minka went in and out of awareness. Those nursing her put broth into her mouth and since she swallowed them, they had hope that she would recover. On the third day Minka woke up enough to ask why she was being held in the infirmary. Genivee told her to lie still and try to remember, asking her what had happened. Minka just blinked. Then it came to her: Dane ignoring her, the crowd not cheering her and that damn cow. She wanted to pick up the shovel again and take aim, but her gut was torn apart and she winced and moaned. "Did someone attack you?" her mother said. Minka considered her options. This could work in her favor. She answered,

"Yes, someone attacked me." Genivee waited for more details. "Someone grabbed my wrists – hard - and then my throat and knocked me down. He hit me and nearly choked the life out of me, you have to find him!" Minka had begun to yell and Quilin, hearing the account, came over and put some drops in her mouth and pressed her forehead down onto the bed. Away from the sleeping patient, Genivee and Liesse nervously prompted Quilin that they needed to begin searching for a perpetrator, but he was not convinced. He was shaking his head and holding Genivee's arm to keep her calm. He said in a quiet voice,

"Ladies, her account does not match the marks on her body, of which there are none. She doesn't have bruises either on her wrists or throat, she doesn't even have a bump on her head where she might have fallen or been slammed into a post. It appears she laid down and bled." They silently shook their heads in confusion. Quilin voiced what he had suspected from the beginning, "She may have had a miscarriage." They all looked at each other. Genivee had firmly believed her daughter to be a virgin, but with an inner resignation, knew this might not be true. Quilin knew Genivee would be worried about her daughter's future and put his hand on her shoulder and said, "Women survive these things and live to have babies later on. I'm sure Minka will recover and have new chances again." Genivee didn't know what to say so Liesse thanked Quilin for his attentions and put her arm around her friend's shoulder and led her back to her room. There wasn't much to say. They would have to hope Quilin was right and not just comforting them.

Minka remained for a week in the infirmary hoping to receive visitors, but it was a lonely recovery. She had expected, then hoped, then despaired that Dane or Kasch would visit her. However they reacted the way many do when someone they don't particularly care for is injured; they pretend they haven't heard the news. Dane was suspicious of a girl who could not conduct herself safely through a milking parlor and scorned her for not being in the courtyard with all the others, raising a glass to him. He felt an obligation to be more picky about the company he kept now that he had a crown on his head and she was beneath him in class, and apparently in common sense as well. Luna came and sympathized but since Minka didn't seem to take much comfort from it, she didn't visit again. After a week during which Quilin was never asked by Minka if she would ever be able to have children, she left the infirmary with a noticeable lack of gratitude and much to the relief of those who worked there.

13

A Fateful Day

Minka was recovering although she still felt weak and dizzy much of the time, but then she never knew how much blood she had lost. Having been taken unconscious from the barn, she was never told by her alarmed elders of the condition they found her in; that would require discussing the matter and none of them cared to do it. She hated playing the part of an invalid though and so sallied forth, pretending all was normal. In spite of this, she was not rewarded with the admiration she thought brave actors deserved. She still reserved hope that Dane would show some concern for her, at least as one of his future subjects, wasn't it his duty? Then again, perhaps that was what Dane was so busy with now: official business. Perhaps his father was acquainting him with a Count's duties. She thought back to a few months ago, which now seemed like years, to her brief tryst with Dane. It was before all that 50th birthday celebration preparation nonsense. Dane was feeling left out and so Minka decided to make him feel appreciated. And what was her reward? He didn't seem to want more trysts with her nor was he curious if he had made her pregnant. In truth, Minka wasn't sure herself. As far as anyone knew, she'd been attacked, not leaned on by a cow. They said no attacker had ever been found nor evidence there had been one. Didn't anyone care about her? Well she would confront Dane today, no more waiting for things to improve on their own: she was pregnant and he was the father.

She had intended to watch the royal sons' fencing lesson again but halfway there could walk no farther. She waited near the stables but when a young man did emerge from there it was not Dane but Kasch. Well, that might work just as well. She called out his name urgently. He glanced at her and nodded his head but didn't change the direction of his horse. She called again and waved him over. Reluctantly, he turned his horse towards her. She waited to speak until he was right next to her, which was annoying for him as he was headed somewhere and wanted to get there, not linger around here with her. Finally she asked him,

"Do you have a minute for a lady?" Kasch wondered to himself which lady, but that was unchivalrous. Instead he perked up his brows and looked steadily into her eyes, but he didn't get off his horse.

"How can I help a lady," he asked. She paused and looked around, and although no one was nearby she whispered softly,

"It's not for all ears." With barely concealed impatience, Kasch dismounted and stood beside her while his mare stamped her hooves, annoyed. It seemed the horse wanted to get away as well.

"My ears are listening," he prompted when she was not quick to explain herself.

"Well, I was wondering if I might join you." Kasch looked at her sideways, waiting for anything important to be said. When nothing was, he got promptly back on his horse and shouted down to her,

"It's been raining for a week and I want to see what the falls below the headwaters look like, you are free to join me." Minka pushed out her lower lip and wagged her head slightly. "Good day then," Kasch said as he turned his horse and left.

Minka stood for some time and looked around hoping to see Dane. Of course he was no where in sight. Petulantly, she turned and headed for the royal apartments. She had never approached them before and was not a little put off about asking to see the heir apparent, but eventually was able to convey a message through channels that she wanted to speak to him. Much to her delight, he chose to go out to the hallway where she waited so they could talk in private. His greeting, however, was not impassioned but impatient. In fact he seemed rather indifferent, so she employed her meaner alternative.

"I've just been talking to Kasch." Dane was still indifferent. "He was most peculiar. I think he was trying to...seduce me. He asked me to go with him to the waterfall at the headwaters." Dane seemed more dubious than jealous. But Minka pressed on. "He said something about what a good pair we would make, me being the daughter of the Count's most important advisor and him being, well the *favored* son of the Count." Dane showed no reaction but felt rising anger. "It seems to me he has some idea of taking your place. After all, I'm pregnant and although it is yours, I could just as easily say it is his. Then he would be the son with a firstborn." Dane crossed his brows and thought: how many men did she sleep with? He had ceased to think about their encounter, but the idea of Kasch claiming a more legal right to the throne had gnawed at his conscience ever since visiting Gertrudis, even after the investiture. Then Minka added, "So I guess it's up to you to say who's it is." With that she turned to walk away from him, swishing her rear end as she went. She glanced over her shoulder, expecting to see his eyes focused on the moving object, but instead his eyes were fixed on hers.

Up in the mountains, steady rain had filled the mountain meadow lake above and now the usually calm stream below was a bounding flume.

There was a waterfall along the stream and right above it was a pond with boulders around the edge. In most years it was a gentle place to swim and relax; the fall over the edge was a trickle. Now waves raced over the rim of the pond, the depth of which could not be discerned. In dry years a person could cross the stream here by hopping from rock to rock; now one could only glimpse those stepping stones as gray apparitions fluttering in the depths.

Kasch stood above the torrent and studied it. It was an unusual occurrence to flow this fully and he had thought of visiting here as the rainy week wore on, each storm adding more and more to the font that fed the flood. He took note of the trees at the stream's edge, now flooded at their base. Their branches swayed with the passing gusts of air created by the racing waves. It was a powerful event, and he would have to make another trip up here when the flow was low again, and take note of how the flood had changed things.

The stream roared loudly as it sped down the mountain. Above him, a hawk soared past screeching out, but Kasch couldn't hear it and didn't notice. Neither was he aware of the approach of Dane who had come after him, although with much less speed. Dane was amazed at his brother's strength and somewhat disgusted with himself for not being able to match his pace. Apparently, his summers in the forest with his mother had taught him how to climb a mountain without flagging or pausing. Dane finally had Kasch in his view and stopped to catch his breath before climbing the last bit up to the stream's edge.

When he did, Kasch had found a place to sit and watch the stream. Two feet below him the water was a roiling blackness, entrancing in its ever-changing form and motion. His eyes were fixed on the water and what lay below when a shadow fell over his view. It was a cloudless day and he turned with surprise to the figure dark in shadow looming above him with the sun blindingly bright behind him.

Even in darkness, he recognized Dane and turned back to studying the water. He could easily predict that Dane, once satisfied with knowing what Kasch found interesting and he found boring, would tire of watching the water and go back down the mountain. Dane said something but the roar was so loud it was muffled and garbled. Kasch was hardly interested in knowing anyway. But Dane repeated himself louder. Without bothering to stand, Kasch twisted around and looked at him annoyed and said,

"What?" Dane planted his hands on his knees and leaned close, saying,

"What did she say to you?"

"Who?"

"Minka." Dane was yelling and not entirely because it was difficult to be heard.

"Same as always, nonsense." Kasch replied.

"Didn't you ask her to come up here with you?" Dane realized, and not for the first time, that women probably found his brother handsome, much more so than himself. He was also taller and smarter and would make a better leader, and the only thing keeping him from it was a quirk of birth. "Aren't you waiting for her now? What else would you be here for?"

Bored and disgusted, Kasch stood up intending to hike further up the stream side, hoping to lose Dane to fatigue in the process. He spoke close and loud in Dane's face before leaving,

"I can't stand Minka and if you had any sense, you wouldn't either. She'll ruin you if you aren't careful," and with that he moved forward but Dane stopped him with a fist in his elbow, saying,

"But ruining me would make her tolerable?"

Kasch would never understand his brother's insecurity. There was simply no question he was next in line and Kasch was no where in line. Why was this so easy for Kasch and so hard for Dane to grasp? He shrugged off the hold on his arm and took several leaps up the rocky slope until he stood on a boulder by the churning pond. Dane followed, unsteady on his sore feet. He had to know, so he asked,

"Did she tell you she was pregnant?" Kasch stared, dumbfounded. He was worried about his brother. Oddly, Dane was also worried for Kasch.

They stood in silence for a moment; each one seemed to be realizing something. Kasch almost chuckled as he said, "Well it's not mine; *it can't be*," and spread his arms out wide, declaring it to the world. A wave of water washed over the rock and their feet. It was enough to take them by surprise and as Kasch's arms went wide, Dane's grabbed hold of one and they lost their balance.

From far below, Minka looked up, finally spotting them. A sheet of water splashed over the rock they stood on. She saw Kasch's arms spread wide, Dane take hold of one of them, then she saw them fall backward into the water. She didn't even know if they had seen her. She watched the horizon for their bodies to reappear, but she finally had to give up when the sun glinted off the rock shelf they had stood on and stung her eyes. She had only seen them for a second; maybe she hadn't seen them at all. Maybe they had never been there. She clutched her aching belly, turned and headed back down to her waiting horse.

Were they drowned? No, that's ridiculous. They had seen her and were playing a game. Would her plans be destroyed? As she rode slowly back down the mountain, she began to perceive that not all might be lost. She had hoped to get pregnant and claim it was Dane's so that she would be the next Countess. She'd make a better one than that Gertrudis everyone spoke ill of and no one ever saw, and better than that humble little Sparrow whom everyone seemed to love and no one ever saw. She would be a much-seen Countess and well-regarded by all. It had been her dream since she learned that the word *Countess* meant a woman to be respected and bowed down to. It had never ceased to stick in her mind that somehow that title must come to *her*.

But who would be the wiser if she simply came up pregnant and she claimed the father was Dane, now temporarily missing? Things might be decided before they dragged themselves home, if they ever did. How convenient that neither one was here to deny it. She almost smiled to herself, but stopped; still it appeared they had fallen into the river and were lost. Having only a verbal claim on a royal was not quite as secure as having one of them actually to be married to. And certainly Dane would have married her, or at the very least been forced to. Gustav was just that determined to go by the book.

That evening Sparrow went through her dinner with increasing unease. Although it was not uncommon for Kasch to arrive late for a meal, it was very unusual for him to miss it entirely. But since Dane was also gone, they all suspected that the two of them were on some extended exploration and would return later in the evening, bedraggled but with another tale of misadventure. Gustav ordered that the guards at the front gates were to inform him the moment they arrived and reassured Sparrow that if they just went to bed, they would be awoken at some wee hour with the news of their arrival. But after a night of fitful dreams, Sparrow saw light on the horizon and her dread returned. She sat up in bed and worried. She had forgotten that on occasion, people could talk to each other even with great distances between them, as when she had called out into the forest and the old lady Mona, now dead, had heard her and spoken a few words. But in her present state of agitation, such communication would have been totally unreliable. She wanted so much to talk to Kasch, to know he was all right, that that desire alone would make anything she thought she heard from him utterly unreliable.

The members of the castle spent an uneasy day going about their business with everyone careful not to mention that surely the young men would be returning any minute, and when they thought no one else was looking, glanced toward the gates or into the courtyard, hopeful that they would be the first to spot them and make the delighted announcement that of course all was well.

But all was not well and at the end of the second day, with 30 hours gone by since anyone had seen either of them, Luna came to Sparrow after the evening meal and sat down next to her. She put her hand over Sparrow's and they sat silently while others tried to carry on conversations having nothing to do with the missing men.

On the third day of their disappearance, search parties were sent out in all directions. Minka stayed very quiet on the topic, for it was she alone who knew where they had last been and had sent Dane to that very place. She might be blamed for something, and did not want to be in the spotlight as the last person to have seen them alive. Given the claims she was on the verge of making, she did not want to look guilty of anything.

But in order for her claim of being pregnant to be legitimate, she had to become pregnant again as soon as possible. While she slowly regained her strength, she stayed in bed late into the morning, claiming to have morning sickness and telling her mother that she must be expecting. Genivee only smiled wanly. She must be fantasizing, unable to face the likelihood of having lost a child. How like Minka to wish she were the center of attention amidst this terrible time of uncertainty. Genivee gazed down at her daughter lying abed with the sun full up, remembering when morning sickness had struck *her* down when *she* was pregnant. She had been laid so low she couldn't keep food down and there was Minka, resting comfortably, not even a drop of sweat on her forehead. Genivee wondered what she was pretending or hiding. She asked Minka, "What would make you feel better?" But when Minka just shook her head, Genivee left her to herself.

After being abandoned by her unsympathetic mother, Minka set off in the direction of the sheep stables whilst most everyone else was involved with searching or was off in distant villages to glean information. The sheep were still in their corral eating their grain rations for the morning. The shepherd who would eventually take them into the field to nibble grass and clover was propped in a corner snoring. Minka hoped to wake him slowly and so began to pick some wildflowers, although this was challenging as the sheep had already taken the best of everything. She finally yelped out an *ouch* (in response to an imaginary thorn) to awaken the lazy shepherd, whose name, oddly enough, was Thorn. Finally his eyes blinked. She pretended not to notice.

Thorn, however, noticed she had not put on an undergarment and not only was her cleavage rather visible without a slip-dress to conceal it, (and she was bending over at a very viewable angle) but the dress was rather thin and threadbare. The sun was shining through it and as she bent over to pick – weeds? - her legs were planted rather far apart and the scene was most intriguing. He was disinclined to interrupt her, so he watched rather some time before she finally looked up and noticed him, and walked over to him rather fast, as if something were the matter. Thorn sat up abruptly, straightened his shirt and blinked his eyes fully open.

Minka pretended to notice a cut on Thorn's face. This strategy was more effective (and less painful), than actually cutting herself and then hoping for sympathy afterward. It didn't matter the unlikelihood of his having cut himself while napping, Thorn had no inclination to retreat from female concern. So he played along with her ruse and when she suggested they go to the well so that she could dab the supposed wound with cool water, he agreed out of curiosity.

There were three wells to choose from, and of course she chose the one near the edge of the woods. Unfortunately and quite by plan, the well was dry and so Minka resorted to taking the hem of her dress, dragging it slowly and thoughtfully across her tongue, then wiping Thorn's cheek with careful slowness. After this effusive show of much concern over a non-existent cut, and a gentle kiss to ensure a charmed healing process, it was not long before they had maneuvered each other into the edge of the woods and onto the fallen leaves where some actual cuts from some actual thorns came to be inflicted on the smug but uncomfortable Minka. Thorn was simply amazed. Who had known it could be so easy? His luck was certainly changing this day and when he stood up to return to his flock, (for it wouldn't do to take too much time with this) he was actually unconcerned whether he saw this sudden partner again or not. Minka felt exactly the same.

When Minka sauntered back into her home her mother was there. She noticed the dirt and bits of grass on Minka's clothes and remarked to her daughter in an impatient voice, "You could at least get dressed before you go out. Where have you been?"

"I told you, I'm sick. I went outside to be sick, there was no time to dress."

"Suppose someone saw you like that, they'd think you're a trollop.

Now bathe and dress properly, it looks as if you slipped and fell." It seemed her daughter couldn't keep herself upright any more. Minka just shrugged and pulled on a bell rope to order hot water for a bath. This would take all morning, which suited her fine.

14

Explorations & Revelations

Three weeks had passed since Dane and Kasch had disappeared after their fencing lesson. Where at first the castle gossip had been restrained and positive it was now wildly conjectural and grim. Kidnappers had struck, they said, but then no ransom note came. Thieving murderers were on the loose, but no one else had disappeared before or since. Then tales even more ridiculous spun about; they had been snatched by witches, were at this moment having their guts torn apart and auctioned off at a witches' coven of commerce. They had been entranced by malevolent spirits and were wandering the woods aimlessly unaware of their starvation into perdition. Then the truly dangerous theories began to fly: They had entered into a mutual suicide pact because the truth of it was that the whole kingdom was doomed and they knew it and the only thing left for anyone to do was make similar pacts with each other.

Minka remained unconcerned. While it was unfortunate that everyone seemed so upset by the recent developments, for her it was actually a time when she could recoup her losses and regroup. Although it might be too soon to play her last card, she was too impatient to wait any longer and decided to make her move and secure her place in the royal hierarchy. She'd be pregnant now or later, so she'd better make her claim right away. When her mother returned from wherever she had been, *what did she do all morning?,* Minka stood up erectly and looked at her.

"What is it, child?" Genivee asked with exasperation. Minka bristled at the appellation, but that only made her straighten her back and speak.

"Mother, you will have to come with me when I ask for an audience with the Count on a very important matter." Genivee turned to Minka and stared at her.

"Speak to the Count?" Genivee was almost horrified. "About what? What can you possibly have to say to him?" Then her eyes lit up for a moment. "Do you know something, where the boys are?" Genivee took a few steps towards her daughter but Minka shook her head violently.

220

"No mother, it's not that. I have news of my own and the Count must listen." Genivee exhaled with sadness and sat down, saying in a tired voice,

"No, that's ridiculous. You shall not be bothering the Count and I shall most certainly not accompany you." But Minka pressed on.

"Oh yes I must speak to him and you must be there to support me. You see, I am pregnant with the Count's grandchild and demand recognition. It is most important now that the heirs have disappeared. He will be needing an heir and I imagine should be very relieved to hear my story."

Your story, Genivee muttered to herself. "Whose heir, whose child?" Genivee demanded. Minka wondered which name would sound more believable. She decided to go with the more legitimate name.

"It is Dane's. I saw him in the stables as he was preparing to leave that day. He – cornered me. Being the heir, an important man, I didn't say no. And now I am pregnant. He always had his eye on me." She added the last sentence because once, long ago, it may have been true. Now her mother's eye was upon her and she squirmed.

There was heavy silence in the air, then Genivee grabbed her daughter's arm, and practically dragged her to the infirmary.

Once there, she found Quilin and went straight to him. He was not ministering to anyone unwell, but rather at his desk talking to Tag about a metal object the boy had just delivered. She interrupted abruptly and asked for him to speak with them as soon as possible, then sat herself and her daughter down on a nearby bedside. Quilin told Tag to sit and wait a moment and went over to the two ladies. Tag focused all his attention on the metal in his hands and tried not to overhear the conversation, but that was impossible given the raised voices. He heard Quilin say, "I don't think that's probable, nor even possible for you to know. Even I cannot know so soon, it would be weeks yet until the signs were reliable."

There was a long silence. Minka was losing this argument. Finally she declared, loudly and desperately, "But I am pregnant, I must be, I know it. It must be acknowledged, for if not-" at this Minka began to choke and sob, burying her head in her hands, sounding like a wronged woman who was on the verge of being further wronged. Tag felt for her and wanted to help, so he rose and approached the group, speaking quietly to avoid anyone else overhearing. He said,

"Then excuse me, my lady. But I can help you for I can swear that Thorn is responsible. I know because I saw." Three sets of eyes turned to him, amazed. "I'll swear to it. I saw them together, not long ago, by the old well. I go there to toss the ash from the smithy, it's a dry well after all and that's a safe place for ashes. I can swear it was him, you shan't be wronged, my lady. I'll swear he is the one to be held responsible." Genivee didn't know whom to stare at with more shock. She managed to blurt out to the little boy,

"He attacked her? And you did nothing, alerted no one?" Tag was suddenly terrified that his effort to help was being torn apart as untruthful.

"Oh no, my lady, I saw her take his hand and lead him into the forest; she didn't scream or call for help, I'd have gotten help for sure, I swear. She was laughing, saying to him real nice things like -" Suddenly Genivee put her hand over Tag's mouth and said quietly that he didn't need to recount any more details. Tag looked downcast and frightened but Quilin whispered in his ear to go back to his desk and wait a minute. Tag slunk away and everyone's eyes seem to drift in different directions, but Tag had truly wanted to help and thought the blonde girl wanted to get married. It *was* the truth and he was even familiar with Thorn, for they said hello as he came and went to dump the ashes. Quilin felt he could add no more and so got up and went back to his desk to finish discussing the new instrument Tag had delivered. Genivee stood up and pulled Minka up after her. They left the infirmary in silence.

Luna came to visit Sparrow and offer her company. In truth her body had just informed her that she was not pregnant as a result of her one afternoon with Kasch when they had escaped and been together at the edge of the forest. It had been a hope she held out when he disappeared; that a part of him was yet with her and he would indeed return to marry her and see it born. But alas, this hope too had slipped away and while she held hands with Sparrow, she didn't know that the older woman also had her own similar sadness to bear. These months when she thought that she too might be pregnant had just come to an end and now it seemed clear to her that all the nausea and uncertainty she had felt were not the signs of another child beginning but for the impending loss of her precious and only one. She could not bring herself to tell Gustav this news. It would bring nothing but further sadness. He mourned not only the disappearance of the two liveliest young men in the court, his precious sons, but the fact that now there was no one to succeed him, and this weighed heavily on his mind. The throne would go to Harz and after that, who knew.

After a lunch served in Sparrow's room which was barely touched, Luna wandered back to her own rooms next to her parents' apartment. Sparrow had spoken off and on about how the animals in the forest knew her and Kasch and that they were surely now busy helping him find his way home, the reason why none of them had time to chat with Sparrow. Luna only half believed any of it, because while it was evident that Kasch had always enjoyed his numerous trips to the forest with his mother, he never bragged or demonstrated any ability to talk with animals or shared any wisdom of theirs with anyone. Her own personal theory was that he had had some kind of disagreement with Dane, who was entirely too full of himself and was becoming exasperating about his ascension to the throne – an event that could be decades off. And so they were both hiding out, or fighting among themselves or proving their manhood until they had settled their status with each other. This was her theory. She decided to write him a letter; it was her only means of communicating with him.

My Dearest Kasch;

I know you are on important business, otherwise you would not leave us all to wonder about your well-being, which I know in your eyes is unassailable. So I will not worry about you and instead will tell you of my own dear regard and hope it will compel you to return to me all the sooner.

I have loved you since ever I remember knowing you. Your soft green eyes are the deepest this kingdom has ever known. Some eyes are shallow and see very little; they barely look beyond their own nose. But your eyes look deeply into all that is around you, and so deeply into another's soul that they feel they have met with someone who truly sees them. Or is it just that you look at me alone that way? I shall not flatter myself to think I am reserved for that special treatment, as I believe you do see truly into others' souls and do not judge. Yet you do see the faults in others, for you see truly and truthfully. Perhaps you saw faults in your brother that gave you pause; we know he is the next Count and yet we wonder if he shall have enough humility to make it a success. He does not yet realize that to lead does not mean to hoard and loaf while everyone else wanders in confusion. As you once told me, to be a good leader one must think of himself only as much as necessary and then direct his attention to all the others who so depend on him to set an example, to lead with courage where they are too fearful to go alone and to never give in to despair. Well I shall follow your advice and not give in to despair, though many about me have done so. I shall trust in wherever you have gone. I shall take this letter to our spot at the edge of the forest where it meets the meadow, where eagles nest and nurture their young and send them out into the world to find their own life. You too are on that quest and I can wait until it is finished. I will leave my letter for you in case you are too busy to come see me, but I'll return with other letters and hope you find time to meet me. Your dear father the Count does so wish to hear you are well. How I would love to convey that message to him.

Your dear devoted love,

Luna

Luna melted some wax and sealed her letter with her own signet ring. She tucked it into her dress and resolved to pack some food and water and take a trip into the meadow where she would lie in the last warmth of the sun for this year and leave her letter in a vessel for Kasch to find. Soon enough, the days as well as nights would be cold and venturing out would become arduous. Briefly, the thought of Kasch in such conditions worried her, but then she reassured herself that if anyone could survive it in, it was Kasch.

At mid morning, Gustav stood at the window of his royal antechamber and gazed out. Two women below him chattered excitedly to each other with their hands next to their mouths, guarding their words from traveling about. Their faces were red and their words were black and when they departed each others' company it was with fretful feet and fluttering eyes. Didn't they even have the decency to gossip out of earshot? Gustav sighed heavily. Could he order everyone to stop talking about his two sons? The worst of it was that Sparrow was beside herself with distress. She headed out several times into the woods herself to look for them. If only she could get to the forest and talk to the animals, they would all be involved in the search. But these forays came to nothing as she was too distressed to draw the animals near her; they scattered from the aura of fear and worry that the search parties exuded. Sparrow would return with head cast down, knowing she could never succeed in this way but having nothing else to try.

Harz was leaning against the wall under the archway that led to the secret passageway through the castle. He had some vague feeling that it was worth investigating this place; perhaps they had used it and come into some trouble there. They shouldn't know anything about it but such boys were unlikely to have such a wonderful castle secret undiscovered by them. Now, disappointed that he would have no news of any kind to impart to Gustav, Harz watched the same two women gossip to each other and then part ways. One of them made her way toward Harz with her face to the ground in a pretense of despair. "Trouble yourself to look where you go, madam," Harz said to her as she walked briskly towards him without realizing it. She looked up startled and embarrassed. It seemed surely he must have heard her friend's words, still ringing in her own ears; *No heirs, no one to succeed.* She redirected herself and walked away even faster, almost running. Harz wished they could put a stop to gossip, but they would have to wait until it died its own death and was replaced by something else. He looked down at the dirt of the courtyard the woman had found so fascinating, then sighed and headed up to the royal hall where Gustav would await the day's news with his usual fiercely guarded calm.

The first report that day was from Boris who had returned from the hunting lodge, just in case anything was happening there. Nothing was. Gustav suppressed an urge to tell him *go back and look again* but instead thanked him for his long journey and steadfast service. Boris nodded and then took a place at the buffet table but for once had no appetite. How could two able young men just disappear?

After leaving the dirt and the gossiping women of the courtyard, Harz made his way to the royal chambers where Gustav, Boris and several others were quietly passing the time, re-reading historical papers, maps and other documents merely to distract themselves. Harz entered and noted casually that *all was well* within the walls of the castle, but this standard report of his had worn thin of late for all was most definitely not well. After several minutes, Gustav asked Harz rather casually, "What of Leopold, the page to Kasch? We've hardly seen him lately. Has he too gone missing?" Trevka, present also in the room, remarked that his son had not rested since the young heirs disappeared. Leopold was as usual upset when Kasch went off on some adventure without him and had been tireless in trying to find clues as to his whereabouts. *Why won't he let me do my job as his page?* Leopold would ask his father, who could only shrug and wonder. Trevka had always delighted in having personal servants ready at his feet.

As if answering the royal question, Leopold came into the chamber a short time later and bowed on one knee to the Count who quickly waved him up and asked what news he had. "The two horses missing from the stable for three weeks have returned, both are without their saddles. They appear well enough although they seem rather hungry and tired of their time away." Gustav, along with everyone else, waited and feared to hear of some other clue the horses might have brought. Leopold added, "The horses are unharmed; no marks upon them so it appears they were just left, their riders also likely unharmed." This last was pure guessing, but if the horses had been ridden hard and far, they might have shown signs of lameness or a neglected coat, but instead they appeared to be merely hungry and weary. It could only be hoped that their riders would return the same way.

The day continued like so many before it; little talk, little eating, little accomplished. Sparrow went to Cait to discuss making new shoes, for such was a tedious process and one that required attention to detail and both of them were wanting such a distraction to make the day pass by. Although Cait was still officially her lady in waiting, Sparrow left all the small and unimaginative tasks to her other ladies, of which she now had several.

Trevka and Leopold had determined to set about finding the missing saddles. Since two were gone from the stable, they concluded that they must be between there and wherever the horses had been, and so too their riders. They set off in many directions, and day after day looked for traces of lost riding gear, a hobby that seemed to occupy Trevka no matter the reason. After a week, Leopold commented that it had been raining a lot just before they disappeared, and perhaps this was related. Maybe they had tried to cross a stream somewhere and it had been deeper or more treacherous than supposed, and they had gotten into trouble. Perhaps they had crossed a stream but then been unable to re-cross it. They would search the streams.

After returning one evening from such a search, for there were many streams they might have explored, Harz was waiting to speak with Trevka. Although he was glad that Trevka was now going along with Leopold on his many searches, he was worried that their efforts might only result in further disappearances. Harz asked him, "Have you not yet searched every stream? You must be having to go farther afield every day." Trevka nodded, weary for the long ride and wondering where his son got all his energy, and why he couldn't have more himself.

"Yes, but Leopold always has more ideas of where to go, what to look for." He busied himself brushing the road dust off his jacket as the two men walked towards the banquet hall and a much-anticipated meal. Harz asked, although they surely would have said,

"And you haven't found the missing saddles?" Trevka shook his head, so tired of looking down at the ground for up-turned tack he only saw tufts of grass when he closed his eyes. Harz shook his head also, but for a different reason. He said out loud, but not very loudly, "They may have been stolen." Trevka turned and looked at Harz; it was a rather wild theory, for lost saddles would be tiny in the vastness of the countryside and it was unlikely anyone on foot would either come across them nor wish to carry them and anyone on horseback would not need another. But Harz added, almost reluctantly, "Those two horses stolen from the stable in the village, just before Dane and Kasch disappeared, the thieves who hit you over the head just before trusty page Tag came upon them on a pig, they weren't saddled." Trevka tried to think back to the occasion. Having been hit on the head did not make the images of how it all happened come back clearly. He tried to remember, then slowly shook his head, saying

"I'm not sure. I know *I* didn't have a saddle; there was no time to put one on. But wouldn't they have taken horses with saddles?"

"Not if they were in a hurry and none were ready. Tag says he is certain that the men who stole the horses didn't have saddles." Trevka thought about it; he had become rather exasperated of late that two large saddles had not turned up in all their searching. Two prominent dark leather objects in short, dull beige grass dying in the autumn air were nowhere to be seen. And if they were out there, they should have been seen by someone. "But the thieves might have saddles now," Harz added and walked away from Trevka, back to his own quarters. Neither one wanted to wonder what else they might have. But even on foot, Kasch should have been back by now.

Two months to the day after the boys had gone missing, a snowstorm drifted into Wilker. It was gentle and quiet, as if apologetic about having to lay a cold winter blanket over the hopes of all the inhabitants of a safe return for the heirs. The snow fell in lilting flakes, with no wind to guide them down, merely floating aimlessly like lost souls cast out of heaven, looking for a place to belong. It had been snowing since before daybreak and continued all morning. With no sign of the snowstorm abating, Cait was in her room trying to sew something but having little patience with it. Harz slouched in a chair, so unlike him, looking as if perhaps he slouched low enough the snow would not be visible out the window. Finally she said to him, "You have to tell Gustav. He's sick with worry. You have to tell him and get it over with. He's going to fret to death if you don't." She looked over at Harz but he didn't say anything, merely hid his eyes behind his hand as he rubbed his forehead. Cait returned to her sewing, yanking the thread through the fabric and glad it was only an underskirt. She finished the seam and bit the thread with her teeth. She put the garment down with a thud and looked at Harz again, who sat unmoving in the hope he would become one with the chair which needed not to walk or speak or take a great part in this duty of life. But she wouldn't leave it alone. She got up and went over to him, repeating "You have to tell him. Today." She stood over him in a stance she had never used before. She was not one to insist on things when so much had come favorably her way, but she couldn't bear the waiting any more. Two months, and now it was snowing. If the heirs had had an adventure of their own making, they would have come home from it by now. Cait put her arms akimbo on her hips and glared down lovingly at Harz. He finally took his hand off his forehead and let it fall as he looked up at her.

"All right," he said. He could have added so much more to that, so many warnings about what it would mean for the two of them. In his heart he knew what it would mean, but he wasn't sure Cait knew. Still, she was the one insisting so he wearily lifted himself to stand. They gazed into each others' eyes and Cait smiled her reassurance up at him. Harz put his arms around her lovely body and hugged her gently for a long minute, then let her go and headed for the door. As he made his way down the hallway to the royal chambers, his footfalls lonely and echoing in the cold air, he began to practice in his head what he would say to Gustav. He wanted to make this speech with as few words as possible. He had no idea if Gustav would be relieved or infuriated, or simply disbelieve it. But Harz was going to tell him that he was not without an heir to leave his castle to. Gustav had the grandson of his first cousin, and Leopold would make a very fine heir.

When Harz entered the royal chambers, a man he did not recognize, obviously a commoner, was speaking to Gustav with a bundle of papers clutched in his hand. With a soft and deferential voice, he was detailing a line of descent. "So you see, it would seem that in all likelihood, my second cousin's nephew holds some relation to your good Count's third cousin's grandson." With that, he lowered the papers on which the family tree was written out, as Gustav had not reached out his hand to take hold of them. Gustav smiled at the man and said to him,

"Thank you, Mr. Turgood. Please keep your family tree a private matter. We don't want confusion or disputes to enter into any of the details." The man agreed heartily with the necessity of this, then bowed low and thanked the court for their attention and turned to leave. He came face to face with Harz, whom he had not known was there and gave him a startled bow as well, then left. They all smiled at each other after the stranger was gone, although Gustav somewhat less so. He dreaded having to hear long lines of such cases. He glanced at Harz and said to him, "I hope you have a more interesting tale than our last supplicant." When Harz didn't reply at first, everyone in the room went silent. They all were hoping for news of the missing heirs and with the continued silence wondered if indeed there were some, and all of it bad. Harz feared that his own tale was yet another plea to place a family relation into the position of heir apparent. By the time he had decided where to begin, all eyes were on him.

"When I was sixteen, I married a commoner named Robyn Swift. The morning after our wedding she disappeared and it turns out she was taken by her family to another village rather far off and I didn't see her again for many years. I thought she had deserted me." He stopped talking and wondered how to proceed. So many details he didn't even know himself. Best to be brief. "Fifteen years ago I discovered that we had a daughter whose name is Beth and who is now married to Trevka. As you know they have ten children, the oldest being Leopold who is himself now fourteen. So you see the Count has a cousin's grandson to leave his castle to, if he so desires." There was unbelieving silence for a full minute while everyone contemplated this revelation. If it had not been Harz, they would have suspected a lie. Or might have suspected his collusion in the disappearance of the heirs. But coming from Harz, none of them supposed his tale was any other than the truth. Finally Gustav asked him,

"And this Robyn Swift, where is she now?"

"In Jiltradt, with her family of a husband and sons, alive and well as far as I know. Though I have not heard from her in some time so her situation may have changed." *Again*, Harz wanted to add with a little ironic bitterness. Gustav was not deterred.

"That is most excellent news. We will invite her to visit as soon as possible." With that, Gustav motioned for everyone to be dismissed for a midday meal and when they had all left, some of them uttering impromptu words of congratulation, Harz and Gustav were left alone in the room excepting a few squires and pages. Gustav watched as the last of the people left and closed the door, then asked Harz anxiously, "When was the last time you saw this lady?"

"Fifteen years ago, at Beth's wedding. She left and went back home, I assume."

"You mean to say even Beth does not know of this?" Harz shook his head. He had never told anyone he had a wife, never told anyone he had a daughter and never told his daughter who she was. Now suddenly all these things would become public and would be gossiped and tittered about. Gustav knew Harz would hate this and was already feeling the unpleasantness of having to speak of something that was long past in his mind and now resurrected. He thought a while before blurting out the stream of questions in his mind, some of which Harz might not have answers for. Gustav realized he would not be able to extract very much detail from his cousin, and that he most likely did not know every last detail himself. Finally Gustav said to him in a happy but quiet tone, "This is really quite good, though, that you never said anything. You never sought to install your grandson as a party to the throne." Harz sighed and almost rolled his eyes.

"Until now. Some will speculate I had a hand in your sons' disappearance. *That* possibility didn't occur to me when I kept quiet about my heirs." Gustav waved off this line of thinking, concluding,

"If you had had your desire on this throne, you would have married and had a passel of children by now to plague me. Thank the gods you're too picky for that." They both smiled, Harz somewhat more thinly. But Gustav could not contain his excitement. He continued, "Do invite Robyn Swift to come for a visit. I would like to meet her, and I think it would be good for the rest of the castle to know who she is, have a chance to meet her as well. She's lived long enough away from a place she earned long ago." Harz shook his head at how easily this all came to his cousin. He said quietly, almost under his breathe,

"She was married the last time I saw her. Is this husband invited as well?" Gustav's brow crossed. A second husband would not be legitimate, but it was a misdemeanor he was willing to overlook. After thinking about how unpleasant it would be to have such a person around, Gustav amended his invitation.

"Such a husband is not legitimate. If she prefers to stay with him, of course she has that right. If she would like to come here, that is also her right, but she would do so alone as your first and lawful wife." Harz nodded and didn't say any more. Gustav thought and planned and then waved over a squire to make arrangements for honored guests. When Harz turned to leave amid all the planning and hubbub, in which he had no interest, Gustav stopped him to ask, "Do you think she'll come?" Harz turned around and replied,

"I believe she will." Gustav was quite pleased at this news and continued with planning. It was the only good news he had had since his sons had gone missing. He was at last able to concentrate on something positive. Harz walked away wondering how many awkward revelations were now his duty to make. When he had married in secret 31 years ago, he had imagined keeping it a secret. How absurdly unrealistic, yet it had worked for quite a while.

15

Getting a wife

Harz sent a message to Robyn that her presence was requested by the Count of Wilker. As a relation to his future heir, he wanted to meet her at her convenience. While he waited for a reply, he met with Beth to tell her the whole truth. Instead of her being angry or disbelieving, she was glad to find out Harz was her father. A lingering sense of unworthiness had its last dust balls swept away by the news. She had secretly fantasized it to be so ever since he had walked her down the aisle at her wedding. Beth was the mother of the future Count of Wilker and her father would serve between him and the present Count.

Robyn's return message came back right away that she would visit the castle expeditiously and as soon as a party were sent to fetch them. She was now a widow living with her last child, a fourteen-year-old daughter named Hildy. When Harz rode into Jiltradt with a contingent of officers and a carriage for the ladies, he installed them at the inn and then went on to meet Robyn with only a page beside him to assist the ladies.

Before he had reached their door, Robyn and Hildy came out to greet him. Robyn had obviously put on her best dress and was smiling grandly, hand-in-hand with Hildy, who stood next to her mother with hair combed and tied in a ribbon. The page stayed outside with the two horses while Harz went inside. Robyn had hot tea and cake on the table. Hildy, having curtseyed to the Count's cousin, sat in a corner and worked on darning some socks. When he had last visited, she had likely been the baby who slept in the corner. Ironically, it was the same corner. Harz looked at her industriously working on the socks, thinking it was the last time she might ever do so, for socks would be provided for her in abundance and any showing holes would be instantly replaced. Harz and Robyn now sat settled at the kitchen table with their tea and their conversation in front of them. Robyn was no longer the haggard mother of three truculent boys whose partner gave her little help. She was now raising a young girl in somewhat easier circumstance (having fewer mouths to feed) and living in a tidy home without rambunctious boys and a sometimes drunk husband tossing about. Harz had not told her the exact circumstances for his visit, but she looked at him across the table seeming to know what he was about to say. It was,

"I suppose you heard that the Count's sons have disappeared?" Robyn nodded sympathetically and said,

"I was so dismayed to hear it." Then Hildy looked up from her work and added,

"We kept looking for word of their reappearance," then she quickly bent back to her darning. Robyn turned back to Harz and said,

"I'm sorry it hasn't come." Harz nodded, adding,

"It makes Leopold the next heir to the throne." Robyn looked surprised and added quickly,

"After you of course!"

"After me," Harz agreed. Harz didn't know much about darning but it seemed Hildy was quite dedicated to it. He cleared his throat and stated, "Count Gustav wishes me to say that you and your daughter are hereby invited to live in Wilker castle as wife of the future Count and stepsister to Viscount Leopold. He sends assurance that you are both most welcome and will have a comfortable home there for the rest of your lives, should you choose to make it so, which he hopes." Robyn blinked and stared, a pink flush coming across her face. Hildy's hands began to shake slightly and tug at the knots in her yarn. Robyn didn't immediately say yes as Harz had expected, but instead asked him softly,

"Do *you* want me to be there as your wife?" Suddenly a scene 31 years old replayed itself. They had been sitting like this across a table from each other, two teenagers, and Harz had said he wished he could marry her even though he was a member of the royal family and should probably choose someone else. He had looked into her eyes and thought to himself, *This is the only woman I could spend my whole life with.* It was an enormous irony that most of his life had now gone by without her, with only a few memories of her visiting him now and then in dreams and daydreams. She had asked that question, *you want me to be your wife?,* and he had gazed at her and thought of how much he loved the way she saw the beauty of things against the backdrop of a harsh life. A girl who showed courage and initiative instead of simpering and dependence. A girl who smiled at him directly without coyness in her eyes but a genuine happiness to be with him. He had felt madly in love with her and had a desperate determination to marry her suddenly, for the window of opportunity seemed to be but briefly open.

Now something long lost was being returned. This time, it would stay for the rest of his life. He focused again on Robyn, the same genuine love in her eyes as there was so long ago and he gave her the same answer as long ago, "Yes, I want you to be my wife. You are still my wife. Come back with me to the castle as soon as you like, the sooner the better. We can send for whatever you wish to bring with you, although you won't need much. I'm sure new clothes will be waiting for you." Hildy suddenly dropped her darning and ran over to her mother and threw her arms around her shoulders.

"When can we go, Mother?" Robyn patted her daughter and whispered to her to go back to her darning, that they would go soon enough and she mustn't make a trouble of herself. Harz and Robyn got up from the table and discussed the plans for their departure. Robyn would have leapt onto a horse and carried her daughter under her arm then and there but instead conveyed to Harz that she would have to inform her landlord of their leaving and say a few goodbyes to her neighbors. Harz knew Gustav would be anxious to have them arrive, and so said he would be at the inn and waiting for her when she was ready, be it a day or a week or longer. She nodded quickly and watched him walk out the door and join his page to head back to the inn. She had to hold herself back from shouting after them, "Come back, I can leave this instant!" Her only slight misgiving was not being sure who wished her presence in the castle more, Gustav or Harz. Hildy came out from the house and hugged her mother, saying,

"Are we really going to live in a castle and have nice things to wear and we can eat five times a day if we want?" Robyn watched the men on horseback amble away.

"Yes, darling, it seems we are."

The next day at mid-morning, Robyn sent word to the Inn that they were ready to leave. Soon after, half a dozen men on horseback and a carriage arrived at her door where several boxes were outside the door and Hildy was sitting on one of them holding a canvas bag and pushing her hair behind her ears every few minutes. When she saw the men turn the corner, she turned to the ajar front door and said to her mother, "They're here." She stayed seated on the box as the party approached and marveled at the carriage in the middle of it all. It didn't take long for the few belongings they wished to take with them to be packed onto the back of the carriage and for them to be installed inside of it. Harz was going to tell them they really didn't need to bring anything, that they would get new clothes and new furnishings at the castle, but instead of opening up the possibility to a thousand questions, which he knew they were bursting to ask, he instead instructed his page to sit in the carriage with them and try to answer their questions and instruct them on castle protocol so that they would feel more secure about their new routine.

When they arrived, as he suspected, their questions had worn them out and they at least had their excitement contained. The page stepped down from the carriage, admirably hiding his own exhaustion as he turned to help each of the ladies step out. Another page was waiting to show them their apartment next to Harz's, which had been moved down a hallway so that they would all be together. What had previously been storage rooms, perfectly quiet and nearly devoid of traffic, were now three rooms for Robyn and Hildy. Harz was about to be dismayed at having his living quarters moved, but it was just as he should have expected from Gustav. The page opened the door for Robyn and Hildy and they walked in, Hildy no longer able to contain her astonishment as she ran to a window and bounced up and down in front of it, taking hold of the curtains there and waving them to make sure they were real. The page then led Harz to one door farther on and said all his things had been moved in his absence. Harz stepped inside with somewhat less enthusiasm than Hildy had, certain he would walk into a jumbled mess and be ready to make a noise about the disorder of his belongings, but instead looked around and felt an odd sense of displacement at seeing all of this things, neatly arranged in this larger, more light-filled room. He had already decided to take an instant dislike to all the changes, but after sitting for five minutes in his favorite chair he conceded that it was rather interesting how they managed to move everything yet keep the arrangement of furniture exactly as it had been in his old room. He even wondered if perhaps Cait had directed the whole move, making sure everything was done right. Then he was filled with an overwhelming sense that the movers had played a joke on him, showing him in great detail how little his life had changed in so long a time, then had completely changed in a very short time. So he moved the desk out of its corner and into a better spot next to a window, proving the movers were not so clever after all. He would reprimand them later, if he were still in a mood to.

After their journey, the ladies were given a day to rest and settle in. They were each given a maid, which was a grand extravagance to them but they didn't know of course that most women of importance in the castle had several. The maids directed the unpacking of trunks of dresses for the women to try on and approve of or not. Robyn found several she liked but had to remind Hildy that although she was allowed to keep anything she wanted, it would be better to accept only a half dozen, and focus on the uses she would put them to and the adjustments they could make to them. Each woman was assured they would of course be getting new clothes made just for them, but this would take time and they would need something to wear right away.

In fact, a formal banquet was planned to welcome them at the end of the week, and much of the discussion over the clothes focused on which gown would be worn to this first and most important occasion. Robyn had not seen Harz except for a moment or two since they had arrived, but he came by a few days before the banquet to see if they had everything they needed to be ready for it. They would probably have no idea how they should look. "Fear not," Robyn said to him when he inquired. "Our maids have us well prepared and we shall not embarrass you. My gown is deep blue with black trim and Hildy's is lavender with purple trim; we shall look superb." Harz didn't know how to respond to this, wasn't sure what he might have contributed to the choice of dress and realized he had nothing to say. But instead of leaving with only an acknowledging nod, he said,

"We arrive at 7pm." Robyn smiled and Hildy was twirling with her dress held up to her in front of a mirror. She turned and smiled.

One thing about Harz's new room was that it overlooked a completely different part of the castle grounds. Whereas before he had had a clear view of the dairy barn from his window, now he was on the opposite side and instead his windows looked out towards the village. He found himself entranced by the view and watched as people crossed the bridge or paused at the middle of it to gaze over the side. He did not spend more than a moment wondering what he himself should wear to this banquet. The plainest, blackest suit would do just fine but after putting it on, he realized he would appear rather shabby next to Robyn and so changed into the suit Cait had made him for Beth's wedding. He would not allow sentimentality and brushed aside memories of having first tried it on. It was now reserved for only formal occasions, funerals and such. No one had better try to congratulate him on his marriage of 31 years ago. No one had at the time and it was too late now to make up for it. What his mind dwelt on was the long years of abandonment, not the fleeting moments of happiness and excitement that came before that.

Harz had always liked to enter a room without being noticed. He was in the habit of keeping his eyes on everyone else, not vice versa. But he knew he could not sneak the guest of honor into the banquet hall. Even so, he instructed the page outside the door of the hall that their names were not to be announced in a shout over all the chatter, but he was to wait until after they were inside and the room had quieted. Harz and Robyn stepped into the banquet hall and stood by the door. Almost immediately the room went quiet and the page announced their names with a conversational volume and they then proceeded to take their seats at the table.

They had a seven course feast which lasted over two hours. After a while they heard music playing in the next room, but no one got up to dance. Gustav fixed his gaze on Harz, who suddenly realized that he was expected to take the first dance. If he had not had so much wine with dinner, he would have certainly drawn the line at this expectation and refused, somehow. Instead, knowing refusing would make more of a scene than not, he stood up and held out his arm to Robyn, who rose elegantly from her chair and glided into the music hall with him. A small crowd was there already, people who had not been invited to the more private banquet. They were instead given the privilege of watching the first couple dance. A man in black velvet who rarely danced and a woman the same height in dark blue silk glided over the floor as if made for each other. People spoke about how they must have coordinated their clothes and how perfect they looked together.

Trevka stood near his wife watching as well, but next to him Beth and her step-sister Hildy paid little attention to anything but each other. Despite Beth's early and somewhat unhappy years at home, she was very interested in becoming acquainted with Hildy. She had left before Hildy was born and never got to enjoy being sisters, but now they would. Trevka marveled that he was watching Harz dance with his wife of 31 years. Thanks to him he now had a mother-in-law and he smiled at the ironic perfection of it. While most men chaffed under a mother-in-law's watchful eye, this one had inadvertently elevated his children and his grandchildren into being the heirs to Wilker castle. He could never find fault with her for that. It had been quite enough for them to be part of the royal family, but with Gustav's heirs all but gone or childless, this revelation had brought the most unexpected of turns. He was now the father of the future Count of Wilker. Briefly he remembered Mona and wished she could see how he had indeed done better than his beginnings predicted.

Still, the reason behind it weighed on Trevka's mind. He and Leopold had scoured the woods and fields, but after Harz had put the idea of saddle thieves into his mind, he had never again expected to find the saddles lying in the grass. When snow had begun to fall, they had given up the search. This was both a relief and nagging concern. Trevka had refrained this evening from his usual habit of tucking his now two leather straps into his jacket in light of this formal banquet, but he remembered them just the same. He was certain now that they had originally been together in one three-stranded braid. One of those straps had been used in an attempt to poach an eagle and her eaglets. He had recovered that one. Another of those straps had been found in the village by Tag and he had recovered Tag. The third one was still at large, and in his heart he knew it was in the possession of the perpetrators of the poaching, the perpetrators whom he had chased but who had hit him over the head and escaped. They may have later found two saddles lying in a field, abandoned by both horse and rider. These might be the same criminals who had been around when

Sparrow lived in the forest; she had told of a time when she was almost attacked by them but had scared them off. Were they murderers? Is that why both Dane and Kasch were missing? In his way, Trevka had been trying for these sixteen years to catch these criminals and now it seemed they had escaped his grasp again, perhaps with deadly consequences.

Trevka could only imagine the worst as he stood in the hall, filled with dancing now, that he would be obligated to join. He usually loved to dance but the celebration was also a declaration: The expectation that Dane or even Kasch coming back was gone. Someone new was being put in their place. That person was his son, but neither he nor Leopold had taken much joy in it.

Leopold had used the slim excuse that at fourteen, he was not quite old enough to join in the formal banquet which was to honor his own grandmother. He could easily have found a way to be invited, Trevka had told him he could come. Trevka knew of some adults that would be at the banquet who displayed less maturity and manners than his son. But Leopold did not want to attend for two reasons: One was that it was an occasion for Robyn to become acquainted with her new life, not for him to become acquainted with his new role. There would be time enough for that later. The other reason was that he still couldn't give up hope of at least Kasch returning. The happiest day of his life was still the one six years ago when he was given the honor of being Kasch's page. Only a few years older than Leopold, Kasch had always been like a big brother to him, taking special interest in the little fellow who was born when he was just old enough to feel protective about the baby. Dane, who should have been more like a brother to him, had never cared to share the stage of attention with anyone, let alone a baby that now replaced his own position as Beth's primary charge.

On his tenth birthday, then exactly old enough, Kasch asked his father if he could make Leopold his page. But it was to keep Leopold close by his side, not to order him to fetch water and shoes and news. Pages did carry the burden of being constantly on duty for minor things, and they did it knowing it was the first step to becoming a knight. Some were more harassed than others. Kasch had wanted to ensure that Leopold didn't have to tolerate Dane's indifference. Dane had tried to make Leopold sorry for not being his page by reminding him that Kasch was not the legitimate heir to the throne. Leopold of course always knew this as Dane never failed to make it supremely clear. It made Leopold wish that inheritance of a throne was based on character and fitness, not chance of birth. Leopold heard notes of music drift faintly into his room that evening and knew that everyone was dancing and celebrating the arrival of his grandmother and the revelation that Count Gustav now had a half dozen heirs. But he could only think of Kasch, wishing somehow there was an explanation for his disappearance and bowing down in his mind to the gods for a way to find him.

16

Ladies awaiting

Beth, Hildy and Robyn were in the village. There was holiday shopping to be thinking about and Robyn was busy planning. It was so much more fun than last year when there was so little money to spend and so few people she wanted to spend it on. While she studied the wares on offer, Beth and Hildy took less interest in shopping and more in each other. It had been a month since they had been getting better acquainted and they were both half sisters and fast friends, even though Beth was fifteen years older. Hildy had brought up the subject of Harz. She envied Beth who could claim him as her real father. Her own father had never been someone she was terribly proud of or close to. She was the last child in a line of boys, and merely a footnote to her father's accomplishments. Hildy remarked to Beth, "I am guessing that Harz already had a lady love when we came barging into his life. At least that's the way it seems to me sometimes." Beth pondered what to say. Hildy was both precocious and discreet, but even so it wasn't a matter of even Beth's business. She didn't want to gossip about her own father.

"I guess so," was all she offered. Hildy had not been expecting or wanting great details. What she really hoped for was to both see her mother happy and for their situation to be secure. It was a fact that Harz had never married anyone else and was still legally Robyn's husband, despite her illegal marriage to another man who was now dead. Hildy wished she could feel as much a part of the family as Beth could. She said,

"This is really something compared to where we used to live. There's so much more to Christmas here, so many festivities. I just wish it could go on and on." Beth replied with an observation tinged with regret,

"It's nothing compared to what it usually is. With the sons missing, celebrations are all subdued." And then trailing off in her thinking she added quietly, "Although I suppose some day things must return to usual..." This gave Hildy a new way of looking at the situation and she said,

"Yes, I suppose it must be much on everyone's mind. I had thought we would see more of Harz after moving here, but we see very little of him. I know it makes my mother unhappy, she told me they were so much in love once, although I realize that was over thirty years ago." Hildy paused for a minute, watching Beth who seemed to be thinking of something far off and then asked her,

"Did our mother ever tell you about your real father or was it a secret all those years?" They were silent while their mother discussed sundries with the shopkeeper. It didn't seem as if Beth was going to say anything, which Hildy respected but she felt disappointed. Interrupting Robyn's talk with the shopkeeper, Beth went over to tell her they would wait for her at the tea shop next door, for she was in need of a warming beverage. They left Robyn and went to the tea shop, sitting at a table near the window and Hildy now hoped her mother would spend extra time in the shop instead of hurrying herself along. Beth had been composing her thoughts for a long time, then she began,

"I was thirteen when my father decided I would be sent off to Uluvost to be a servant to the royal family there. He had some vague connection, one he boasted of. I think he was just tired of me, always preferring his sons. I was terrified of leaving home, although a part of me thought it might be better away." Beth shook her head remembering. "It wasn't. But that's another story. Before I left, my mother did tell me a story about my father, although I didn't realize it at the time. She said that when she had been very young, she had fallen in love with someone. Someone serious and important whom she had admired and whom she was lucky enough to meet one day. He was impressed with her desire to read and her interest in things most girls ignored. But then it was unusual that our grandmother had wanted to read, and they learned what they could together. It was something she always thought would be important and so they deciphered signs over shops and worked their way through a favorite psalm in the Bible. So Robyn was an intellectual lady, unlike so many others her age. And this man she admired noticed that about her." Beth looked up from her tea to glance out the window; her mother was still at the shop next door. She sipped her tea and continued,

"She never told me that they eloped or spent a night together. She only said that it is possible to find someone you love, and that going out into the world might afford me that chance. I think she was just trying to settle her conscience and give me something to hope for. She had doubts about my going to be a servant. I thought for a long time that she had just made that story up about meeting someone special, about admiring him so much and never forgetting him. Now I realize, she was talking about Harz." Beth stirred from her long-ago memories and added, "And as you know, I didn't find out he was my father until just a short time ago. It's funny, he walked me down the aisle and I didn't know." She drifted off in her talking. She was never mad at Harz for not telling her sooner, only grateful that he finally did and that now she had a father she truly admired. Hildy seemed wistful and Beth reached her hand across the table and said to her, "And I'm sure he'll walk you down the aisle when you are married, and to someone wonderful I'm sure." Hildy chuckled at the suggestion. She was more interested in her painting and daydreaming and just enjoying this new life she had been given. She would be a nun at the castle, if they had such types, just for the chance to stay there all her life. Marriage struck her as a risky business and it was foolish to tempt the fates. She said to Beth,

"I think mother is still in love with Harz, perhaps as much as she was all those years ago." She sighed. "But I think Harz has lost his love for her, and now has someone else in his life. It's been too many years to come back into his life now." Beth wasn't sure about this, and hoped in any case it wasn't the case. Besides, she mused,

"That's not true; he never knew me and now we are quite close. He visits his grandchildren often and I think he was even a matchmaker for me and Trevka. He really thinks of others much more than he lets on." Beth glanced back out the window and saw the door to the shop begin to open. She added, "I think he's too distracted by Kasch and Dane being missing. You know, I took care of Dane when he was a baby. Not that he really remembers that. Once he found out he was next in line to be the Count, it was pretty much all he could think about or talk about. He made it a point to stop calling me mommy then." She didn't want to add out loud, *it crushed me when he did so, for he was always my son to me*. She also didn't say out loud what she knew: If he were alive, he'd be here. She saw their mother giving final remarks to the shopkeeper and so she quickly added, "And besides, as to anyone else in Harz's life, he is much too serious about propriety to associate with any woman besides his wife while she resides in the castle." They heard Robyn's voice bid the shopkeeper good day. Hildy knew everything Beth said was true, but she also knew that although he might not actually talk to or visit another woman, she was on his mind nonetheless and her own mother was interfering just with her presence. If she felt unwelcome for too long, Hildy feared her mother would simply go back to Jiltradt with her head held high but her defeat trailing behind her.

Genivee was sorting through some of Magnus's books when Minka came in and observed her at the task. She casually asked her mother if she could spend the day in another village if she went with some of her friends. Genivee paused in her sorting, glanced at her daughter, then tossed the heavy book in her hands aside. "I don't think so," she said casually, knowing Minka wouldn't be listening anyway. At least Minka had stopped putting up false protests to her mother's decisions, which lessened the number of pointless arguments, if not the number of unapproved outings. They were both quiet as they knew they had reached another impasse. Only the sound of books being stacked broke the silence. Then Minka asked,

"Are you going to sell these? I don't remember Daddy reading them lately. We could get a new dress for me - and you - at least." Genivee remarked,

"No, I'm not selling them." But she wondered if Minka actually questioned whether or not her father was coming back. Or was that Genivee's worry? She didn't want to discuss it with her daughter and instead asked her,

"What village is it that you intend to visit? I should know where to look in case you don't return." Minka narrowed her eyes; her mother had so little faith in her. Of course she would return, how incompetent did she think she was?

"Not far, just the next village south." Genivee knew what this meant so she asked,

"And what would be the name of this village?" But of course, Minka didn't know and therefore did not have the satisfaction of enlightening her ignorant mother, so she just said,

"I'll tell you about it later, after we've been there, you wouldn't be interested now." Genivee continued sorting, certain that if anything at all interested her about the "next village" it was only whether or not Minka returned from it. Or was she interested? Of course she cared about her daughter, although when she didn't return early on some evenings, it was more what she might have to tell Magnus that consumed her thoughts. What would he think of a wife who couldn't contain her own daughter's wild behavior? Genivee sat down to catch her breath with one particularly large book in her hands. She glanced down at *Birds of the Continent,* trying to remember the last time it had been opened. She put it aside and looked up at Minka. It was perhaps a little amazing that Minka seemed to want some sort of approval from her mother, but it was not forthcoming. Genivee said to her,

"You'd do better to stay here and read one of these than to scamper off and look for more trouble."

"Oh, I won't find any trouble, mother. I'm smarter than that." Genivee turned her back on her daughter and continued the sorting. She had observed, in the months since their fateful visit to Dr. Quilin that not only had Minka shown no signs of pregnancy, but in fact no signs of its ever being possible. Minka had always complained heavily every month and taken to her bed when that time came. Now those few days in bed didn't occur at all, every day was one in which she was free and able to cavort about. At least Genivee felt relief in not worrying about her making new demands to force some unsuspecting man to marry her. She had once had a nagging feeling that Dane was somehow going to become a part of one of her intrigues, but now with him missing, she felt a slight relief. It was curious that Minka was not more worried about him. She no longer claimed to carry his child nor even wonder about his whereabouts.

Genivee carried a stack of books to another room and when she came back, Minka had slipped out without saying anything. Genivee gazed at the empty spaces and wondered if Magnus would notice the changed arrangement. She stared out the window. If he returned, she should see him there one day. But the path was empty for now. She sat down and pulled the one and only letter she had received from him in all the months he had been gone.

Dearest Wife,
I hope this arrives to you and you are reassured that all is well here. It was difficult to find someone traveling your way to send a letter along with him. Arrived in Brylle safely. Cannot say how much longer I may be here. There is great difficulty in finding workers willing to be away from their homes for so long. They want to bring their families and I cannot promise there will be enough housing for so many newcomers. We shall continue to search for single men. Take care of yourself and Minka until I can return and do so, I know you are capable. Magnus

She wondered how capable she had been. Things hadn't gone well at all, although not much had been in Genivee's control. Would Magnus find he liked being in his homeland? Would he meet an old acquaintance and decide life up north was preferable? Genivee put the letter back in her pocket and picked up a book at the top of the stack and leafed through it. Nothing caught her interest. She sighed and put it back, then picked up *Birds of the Continent* and left.

Cait was in her room, brushing her hair and studying the courtyard outside her window. Her view was not of the whole courtyard, but of a corner of it near the entrance gate. It afforded some unexpected sights, as on this occasion when two guards were sheltering from a cold wind and warming themselves with spirits. Cait smiled to herself as she watched them rub their hands together and attempt a chuckle, waiting for the sun to rise over the tree line and warm them further. As she was smiling about her secret view of these two she went into her main sewing room to continue with a hem line that was particularly long and wide. It had embroidery at the edge and the hem followed a swaying line. It was exacting work. As she sat down with the dress on her lap she began to thread a needle and noticed across the room Harz sitting silently in a chair in the shadows. She was startled by his presence and gasped, then exhaled with a sigh.

"When did you sneak in?" She asked, not that it mattered. She hadn't seen him in the several weeks since Robyn had arrived, or was it a month already? She had expected to not see him again in private, and in fact she felt it would not be right to do so any more. Harz didn't answer her question so she asked another one. "I hear your wife is not too unpopular. She certainly wasn't what people expected. Much softer spoken for a person who lived 30 years in Jiltradt."

"What's wrong with Jiltradt?" Harz asked, defensively for a place he hated.

"Oh it's just another one of those villages far enough away for people not to know it and thus safe enough to be made the butt of jokes with no one to take offense."

"There must be thousands of such villages," Harz remarked.

"Yes, but happily for them no one knows their names." They were silent again while Cait made a knot in her thread and studied the hemline and the embroidery, deciding how to begin. Once she had, she said, "And speaking of gossip, I don't like to think what will be said when someone sees you near my room early in the morning." Harz grunted disgust and declared in a rare display of his power to do so,

"I'll tax them for it." *Tax* might mean a day in the stocks, removal of some portion of their food supply, public reprimand or humiliation. In his position, Harz could be the font of such actions occurring daily, but there had never been any in Cait's memory. As the Count's cousin, it was his duty and privilege to punish transgressions.

"Which would make them gossip more." Cait continued the imagined punishment to its conclusion. Harz waved a hand of indifference. "Which I wouldn't mind but I think it would be hurtful to Robyn." Harz stood up and walked into the light coming in through the window. No one appeared to notice him standing there as everyone about, not many, busily went about their business. He wished his own day was so ordained. He said,

"Thirty-one years ago she disappeared and I spent fifteen years thinking she had left me in sudden disgust. Then I found out she had been taken away against her will and I spent the next fifteen years wondering whether to feel sorry for her or try to rescue her, for which it was too late in any case. Now here she is, posing as my wife and I can barely remember why I married her in the first place." Cait sewed at her hem and said without looking up,

"She is not posing; she *is* your wife. And you must remember something so important as why you married her. Even at that age, I have no doubt you were old beyond your years." Harz gazed into the sky instead of the courtyard. Finally he said,

"You know Gustav is several years older than me. Back then, he was already the object of great speculation among the female members of the realm. They all wanted something in connecting themselves with him; the prestige of being the next Viscountess, the knowledge to giggle about some personal aspect of him they had gotten to know, perhaps just the trophy of having known him one night. It was difficult to watch, because I knew those women were pretenders. The few who might have been sincere were too humble to put themselves forward with the necessary vigor." He stood remembering those days. It had seemed that suddenly they turned a corner in their age and became targets for scheming people. "And I was next in line for it."

He shook his head, remembering that it was then that his ability to detect lies in others became clear, perhaps because for the first time he was exposed to so many more liars than before. "It was so unpleasant to watch them fight over him, as if they even had a right to. In the end even Gustav's father tired of it all and found someone from outside the realm to be his wife." Remembering Gertrudis, Harz wagged his head. "She was the worst of them all." Cait finished his thoughts and tried to bring them back to the material point by saying,

"And you determined to avoid all of that by marrying young and in secret."

"I suppose so," Harz said, turning away from the window so that he could speak more quietly and more directly to Cait. "Robyn actually didn't know who I was. That in itself amazed me, but I saw it in her eyes. She was much better educated than most girls, and I could hear that in what she said. She didn't chatter like a typical girl. And she was very beautiful." Cait looked up and saw Harz smiling at the memory. "Not pretty, like some girls with little wisps at the tips of their eyes and dimples at the edge of their smile, but beautiful because her eyes were filled with wonder and while she had opinions she governed them well." Harz wondered at how old that memory was and then sat down next to Cait, which he had told himself he wouldn't do, but as she was not going to relinquish the needle in her hand to coddle him, he felt safe in doing so. She said to him,

"You can forget things if you make yourself. Do you think I dwell on being attacked in Uluvost castle? Your friends Trevka and Brake saved me and whenever that memory comes back, I shift my thinking to my good fortune in their being there and their headlong rush to my aid. That is what I remember; the good at the end of it." Cait had been so relieved when no one ever arrived at the castle to question the death of a man in Uluvost. He was a monster who deserved to be killed on the spot and Cait was thankful that Trevka was there with the law on his side to carry it out. It wasn't quite how things were usually done in Uluvost. She sewed for a while and they sat in silence. At last she said, "Now go and remember her the way you first saw her and forget all the interference which came after. Push it away and replace it with the better memory and make new memories. And don't punish anyone for gossiping about her, I think she'd rather have more a more direct sort of attention from you." Cait looked over the edge of her spectacles at him; spectacles he had had made for her so that she could continue to sew and enjoy her place at the castle. "Don't worry about me, she's much lonelier than I ever was," she assured him. Harz picked up her hand and kissed it, then got up and left.

When Harz headed to Robyn's room that evening, having spent the whole day finding excuses not to do so, he dreaded it. When he passed by two women gossiping about something and figured it was Robyn or him or both of them, he was even more unhappy about the visit, but now felt obligated. The women laughed and whispered to each other, and he imagined they did so quite a bit, but there was no way to stop women from doing so. As he walked towards Robyn's door, he pictured her inside, weepy and depressed over the gossip she herself would also have heard, gossip about a pretend wife, brought from far away, whom her husband barely acknowledged and rarely visited. It was not in his capacity to know how to abate such feminine feelings, but he anticipated having to repeat several platitudes and falsities.

He knocked and a lady-in-waiting opened the door. Robyn was sitting next to a window with a large book in her lap and she looked up from it to see Harz and smiled. Robyn told the lady to bring some tea and she left to do so. Robyn turned the pages of the book slowly, admiring the drawings in them. Harz walked over to her carefully and noticed it was a book of illustrated birds. Robyn was studying the pictures with fascination. She said,

"Genivee lent me this book. She said as long as her husband was away, I might as well enjoy this. She is very kind to think of me." Harz couldn't think of how to respond to that, his usual reaction to things Genivee did and said. So instead he just sat next to Robyn and looked at the picture too. "I think I've seen this bird, but I never knew what its name was. Here's what it says: *The flicker is a golden-winged woodpecker. It flies up from the ground in a sudden flash. It has a black crescent on its breast which symbolizes a sensitive heart. Flickers are excellent parents and care for their demanding young well.*" Robyn ran her fingers over the drawing carefully, then turned the page and studied the next drawing. "What wonderful images," she murmured. Harz sighed. After she had turned several more pages he said,

"I supposed I should have been visiting you more, making sure you had things to keep you occupied." Robyn didn't look up from the page but just said,

"You've been worried about your cousin's sons, like everyone." Harz gazed across the room, not seeing it. He had mostly stopped worrying about the boys, for there was apparently nothing left to hope for. Many months had gone by and now it was winter. If they had been out on a lark, they would certainly have returned by now. Robyn added, "But then, I disappeared once too, and I was all right." She looked up from the book and gazed at Harz until he turned his eyes to her. "Except that I was wretched with missing you." Harz inwardly marveled that Robyn didn't, hadn't ever, blamed him for not rescuing her. Why did he feel guilty for not doing so? By the time he did, it seemed his part in it was very minor. It had been Gustav who insisted on bringing her back to the castle. Suddenly Harz remembered a time, after he had stopped thinking his bride had just abandoned him, when he had become convinced something terrible had happened to her. He had gone mad trying to find out where she was. But the neighbors in her village knew nothing. The whole family had disappeared one day without a word. He had had to give up looking, for there were hundreds or thousands of places they could be, and if they had left they might well be hiding, and if they were, they were likely hiding their daughter from the man she had claimed she was married to.

Now he looked back at this woman whom he had wanted desperately to find so many years ago. Now here she was, as if by magic, the girl he had been missing most of his life. After much silence between them, all he could say was, "I missed you too." Robyn heard the crack in his voice and thought he was going to shed a tear which would certainly mortify him so she put her arms around him and cried herself so that he wouldn't think she noticed. Harz wrapped his arms around her and they held each other thus while the book's pages crumpled between them. But Robyn wasn't going to concern herself with a book, even a borrowed one, when she finally had him in her arms. Still, it was perhaps too soon to expect more than sympathy. So she shifted the conversation back to the boys, for whom their immediate concern must remain, and said,

"They could still come back. They may be in a village after all, not out in the forest merely because that is the last place we knew them to be." Harz took a deep breath and stroked her hair. Her head was resting on his chest and although he had loved Cait for the last fifteen years, he now remembered that he had loved Robyn first and still did. This was his bride and he remembered holding her for the first time, the wonder of having a woman who loved him in his arms, a treat boys dream of and dare hope to attain. It was magical and unbelievable and he would never let her go again. Harz pushed her away slightly to take the book from her lap, close it shut and place it on the table in front of them. Then he pulled her back into his arms and she sighed with delight and kissed his chest through his jacket. "You love me," she murmured happily and tightened her arms around him. Harz smiled and kissed the top of her head and hugged her back. Then he said,

"Yes, I love you. But I don't want to have to explain to Magnus how his book came to be bent." They laughed together and soon after the lady in waiting came through the door with the tea. She set it on a table and looked about, wondering what to do. They hadn't noticed her, being busy with a kiss. But they looked up finally, thanked her for the tea and told her she was finished for the day.

17

Dreams along a stream

It was that same dream again; Kasch fell backwards into the water and thrashed his arms and legs against the unexpected drenching. Then he righted himself and swam, but it was only a second before he felt himself plunging over the waterfall and rolled onto his back. His held his breath as the falls carried him down, then when it was calm again he poked his head through the surface and spotted the shore, heading for it before another falls could disorient him again. But another one did before he reached the shore. After being tossed and splashed over piles of boulders, cushioned by the torrent of water over them, he pulled himself up to the surface again and looked around. He saw the river's edge and made his way over to it, climbed out of the water, caught his breath and stood up to look around. He expected Dane to be on the other side, and they would laugh about that and *about which one would have to make the crossing again. Then they would blame each other for losing their balance and who knocked over who. Sometimes in the dream Dane was on the other side and the dream made him happy; when the other side was empty the dream broke his heart.*

Kasch woke up. What he hated about the dream was that it ended there, as if there was still something needing to be done where he came ashore, as if Dane were waiting there for him. But in reality, Kasch was far away from that place and that time. He wished it had happened differently, but in reality he had climbed out of the stream and Dane was nowhere to be seen.

Come to think of it, the dreams in which he actually saw Dane were occurring less frequently. Now Kasch couldn't remember the last time he'd seen a good end to the dream. After waking from the dream, he would remember how he'd spent the day hiking downstream, certain that Dane would have to have traveled at least as far as he had and that he would see him either clinging to a tree branch or soaked through and sunning himself on a rock. He couldn't possibly be further upstream than Kasch, could he? Maybe he had bonked his head and had passed out or was just lying somewhere feeling dizzy. Whatever had become of him, Kasch was not leaving the stream until he found out and so the entire day went by with Kasch traveling so far downstream that he no longer recognized the landscape. Not that he was by any means lost; he knew exactly how to get back to Wilker, if only by traveling upstream again. But as the sun was setting, he knew it was too late by then to head back there. He found a place to sleep for the night and since it was still late summer, he would be fine. He was feeling a little hungry, but was able to eat enough berries and nuts, still on the trees, to make for a not-too-uncomfortable night's sleep.

After a dreamless night, for he had been exhausted when he finally laid down to sleep, he awoke with a start and the situation seemed dire. For nearly a whole day Dane had been without food and likely without rest. Kasch had kept expecting to see him yesterday, but with the whole day gone, he was now having serious doubts about him. Maybe Dane made it to shore and then hiked off back home without even calling out to him, but Kasch didn't believe in that possibility very much. He only hoped his brother might be so unconcerned, or possibly unhappy with him. Dane could get into a snit over nothing.

After waking that first morning, Kasch was contemplating the possibilities, sitting by the stream with his forehead resting over his crossed arms when he heard a sound behind him. Before he even turned to see what is was, he knew it was the sound of a human too clumsy to know how to disguise his footsteps. It must be Dane trying to sneak up on his brother and mock his despair. In an instant this hope vanished because it was not Dane behind him but rather two men who had the unmistakable look of desperate characters. His mother had given them a name and he knew in an instant that he was face to face with the Rogues.

That was three months ago now? It had snowed once or twice and most of autumn was gone which meant he was now in the forest spending the winter with the rogues. By now he knew their names. Bit was the smaller one who wasn't terribly bad except that his education was so delinquent it was tragic. Maw was somewhat larger, dirtier and definitely hopeless to the bone. Maw had completely managed, probably without trying because effort was anathema to him, to put Bit under his thumb and turn him to every criminal, amoral way he knew of. Kasch wasn't sure if Bit was more stupid than lazy; he might have a reachable mind if he could ever be gotten away from his cohort. When the two men faced Kasch on that shore far downstream from Wilker, they had no idea whom they were looking at and Kasch and no intention of enlightening them. To them Kasch was another countryside vagabond and he let them believe it. They were hopelessly bored with and dependent upon each other and welcomed something new in their lives.

Initially, Kasch believed that the rogues knew what had happened to Dane or had even been responsible for his disappearance. Knowing Dane, he would easily have become confrontational with these wanderers, challenged them and then been overwhelmed by them, even though they weren't terribly clever. Kasch knew it would be useless to question them about it, for it they had harmed Dane they weren't going to admit to it, so he remained with them hoping to learn something of Dane's fate or whereabouts through casual conversation. But after several weeks, it became clear they had not seen anyone else in many months and having Kasch around was something they both found new and addictive. He told them stories, lies mostly, that kept their curiosity up and by this means he was able to stay with them and therefore, be in control of them.

The rogues also allowed Kasch to become a part of their society because it was an aging one; they must be nearing their fifth decade and were becoming tired of the difficulties in living this sort of existence. They had been attempting to live in villages for the last dozen years or so, but this too had its challenges as they were forced to leave one after another when their petty thefts and other crimes were pursued. By now, an honest life was all but impossible and certainly never entered into their thinking.

After giving up on learning anything about Dane's fate from them, Kasch thought it would be useful to stay close to the rogues so that he could plan an escape and return with officials who would apprehend them and perhaps jail them for good. But the longer he stayed with them the more he decided that if he escaped, he would likely never see them again. They knew one thing; how to avoid being followed. Kasch had come to the absolute conclusion, based on Trevka's tales, based on his mother's memories, that these were the rogues she had spoken of. These were the men who had attempted to trap an eagle and then later descended upon the royal travelers headed to the Marianna Valley, intent on robbing and killing them. These were the men who, by chance, came upon his mother's home in the forest and came very close to attacking her and likely killing her baby for sport. All of these crimes were worthy of punishment by death and not for one of them did Kasch have any proof. Not that he needed any.

The law of the land was that, as a representative for the Count, Kasch had every right to execute these two outright. His suspicions would carry the weight of truth and no one would question his having carried out the law. No one except of course, the rogues themselves. They often complained at the injustice of not being allowed to hunt animals as their hunger dictated. Why should all the animals in the forest be for the Count alone? They needed to eat too, and why should he care if a hare or squirrel went to another now and then? These facts kept them from warm beds under roof at night, and as age and weariness overtook them, they lamented them all the more. They didn't know it, but Kasch was probably the only man standing between them and certain execution for their lives of crime. He was the only man, having been raised by a mother like Sparrow, who thought twice about killing people because of hunger and a law that applied to everyone except the richest man in the land.

Depressed over the uncertain loss of his brother, Kasch was comforted by only one thought: he had been glad it was himself and not Dane the rogues encountered, for Dane would have handled it terribly. He likely would have asserted his being royalty, and that they could ransom him for a handsome sum, as he was certain his father would pay it. Kasch hated the idea of Dane educating them to another crime, and helping them to rob his own family. No, if Dane had encountered the rogues, either they or he would not have survived it. Dane had no patience for what he feared or disliked. And while the rogues offended Kasch, while they disgusted and annoyed him, they did not frighten him. He was ten times as smart as the two of them put together and he had decided to deal with them in his own way. Ironically, it was what his own mother had intended for him, although he didn't know it. He had wisdom about the forest from his mother and sense about dealing with people from his father and handling the rogues was a test of his mettle and downright fun. He had spent many weeks at a time, and years all together, on his own in the forest and could do it much better than these two, but he didn't allow them to see the things he ate along the way that they passed by without realizing. They clumsily caught squirrels and rabbits, trudging far to check their traps and walking right past perfectly good things to eat. Kasch enjoyed hoodwinking them all through the day and ultimately planning their capture and removal from his beloved, and, yes, royal forest.

As weeks passed to months and still no one from Wilker found their way back to Kasch, he had come to the conclusion that either Dane hadn't made it back himself or else he was too inept to lead a party back to where Kasch might be. Even if Dane were geographically clever, Kasch had gone far downstream and was likely much farther away than anyone would suspect. Dane was back at the castle, Kasch assured himself, safe and sound and enjoying, temporarily he must certainly be thinking, a time in the spotlight with no sense of competition from his half brother. Dane was so inexplicably jealous, and Kasch decided it would be good for him to have his father to himself for a while. It was too obvious even to Kasch that Gustav favored his second-born son much more.

It only took about a week for Kasch to realize that Maw was a hopeless case. But he did want to get Bit away from him, and this was for two reasons: For one, Bit was actually decent. And he was hardworking, although he wasn't allowed to ever think it. Bit caught most of the game and he cooked all of it. An unfortunate part of his daily diet however, was being dominated by Maw. Bit thrived on, or rather starved without, regular invective from Maw about what he was doing and how he was doing it (wrong). It was a parasitic relationship. Maw was the parasite on Bit's back, and Bit had no idea that he was unnecessary, so connected were they to each other. When Kasch looked at Maw, he saw the bloated, clawing tick that Trevka would pull from a dog's skin. So fat with blood it couldn't hold itself upright and when extracted it would burst to death from its own greed. The dog would then scratch heartily at the newly tick-free wound with vigorous satisfaction. As a boy, Kasch always enjoyed watching Trevka do this; he knew it made the dog happy. But Dane hated it and ran from the room screaming in fear of a counter-attack from the defeated (and newly freed) tick army. Bugs scared him. Kasch chuckled to himself remembering this, and convinced and comforted himself by saying, *Dane has scurried back home, away from the tics and these two hobgoblins, and all is well.*

The other reason Kasch wanted to pluck Maw off Bit's back was that Maw would most certainly perish on his own without him, and that would be a convenient way for him to go. He didn't really deserve to live off Bit any more than a tick did, but unlike a tick, Kasch didn't care to dispatch Maw with his bare hands; he hadn't brought any weapons for a trip to the headwaters. Besides, killing someone wasn't so easy to do *or* forget. When Trevka told them the tale of killing an attacker on sight in Uluvost, he had been filled with rage against the attacker and killing was easy. Kasch didn't have any rage about these men, not yet anyway. He had no desire to kill them, only to rid his father's realm of their behavior. Yes, what did it matter if they caught a squirrel now and then? But it did matter if suddenly everyone believed that might be a fine idea. Then the forest would suffer for sure.

It was a cold winter morning and the three of them were sitting around a fire. It wasn't a very warming fire because the wood was damp and instead of a warm glow, there were only smokey wisps rising up, hissing now and then like a snake trying to hibernate and not being allowed to. Maw was of course complaining about the fire, having made no effort to find dry wood or even knowing how to make some. "Ye're the most worthless fire-starter in this whole damn forest. Check them traps and git us some food to put over this here fire, I'm starvin'." Bit poked at the flames. If it were colder, Kasch would be tempted to build the fire properly but he didn't want Maw to think such comforts were within their grasp and Kasch wasn't suffering the way they were. They had not been privileged to the castle diet Kasch had and he was much more ready for a harsh winter than they were. Bit kept poking the fire, not getting up to check any traps. Maw shouted at him, "I told ye to check them traps ye worthless skunk-"

"If'n I leave now it'll go out 'fore I git back so I got to git it goin' first." Kasch blew on his hands and rubbed them together to warm them. He closed his eyes to narrow slits at their conversation. It was the same one they had every morning, with Bit being lazy and Maw being snide and between the two of them so little getting done. A few flakes of snow began drifting down from the sky and the forest was quiet and calm but Maw broke the peace of it.

"That's jes great, now it's snowin' on yer fire. How's thet goin' to help it?" Bit looked over at Maw with a malevolent stare which didn't last. He went back to gently blowing on the tiny flame to get it to flare up and dry the dead leaves he'd piled on, which it did most pathetically. Kasch wondered to himself yet again how he might keep these men in one place while he made it back to Wilker. He knew they would vanish the instant he turned up missing and what's worse, would know he was not the hapless wanderer he had made himself out to be. If he left, he would lose them for good. He was the only person to come close to catching them after all their years ravaging the countryside.

The fire seemed to begin to start better, the leaves had dried out and now an orange flicker was casting a little light into the gray morning.

Bit fed it with twigs and more leaves. Maw muttered more insults and complaints of cold and hunger, all of it Bit's doing. The forest was then quiet again and Kasch closed his eyes. They were next to a rock outcrop that offered the tiniest bit of protection from the wind, which had thankfully died down the previous night. It was just a little bit better than the open fields but not by much. With his eyes closed, Kasch pondered again the worthiness of trying to bring these hopeless souls to – what? A more useful life? Was it possible for them? Not for the first time he planned an escape. It would be quite easy enough on a night with moonlight to get away from them while they slept; they tended to be very afraid of travel at night, even with moonlight, for they had been frightened by an owl that had stalked them one night long ago and they thought they were under a curse. They did not now move through the forest after sunset and so slipping away then would be easy. By morning Kasch would be long gone, but so would his chance to finally catch these men who had attempted to kill his father, his mother, possibly his mother's parents and who knew who else. He could of course knock them senseless and perhaps tie them up to separate trees, if he had rope and could keep them apart, but how then would he be any better than they? He was determined not to fall to their level.

Something imperceptibly slight made Kasch open his eyes. Behind the outcrop and peering at the three men, with just its ears and eyes visible, a wolf was watching them. Kasch blinked and looked again. Kasch had been missing his usual communication with wolf, which he usually had when he visited the forest. Immediately Kasch thought out to her, "Thank you for coming! I've longed to see you and talk to you." After a moment her thoughts came back to Kasch,

I'm surprised you're still here this late in the season. You don't have the coat for it. Kasch shivered under the small wrap he had, a tied-together collection of rabbit furs that only covered his shoulders. "You're right," Kasch agreed with her. "I could use your help." *Go back to the castle where you live and be warm,* the wolf advised. How Kasch longed to do it, but he explained, "I can't leave these men. They don't deserve to stay here and I'm trying to get them out." The wolf swayed her tail, although this was out of view and Kasch only saw it in his mind. She was contemplating. Why should Kasch care where these men were? Kasch and the wolf gazed at each other over the quiet scene, and finally Kasch thought to her, "I don't want you to be in danger. Remember the traps I showed you in my mind and look out for others. The traps are why these men should leave the forest, but you are not responsible for them so thank you for visiting me but don't come near these men again." The wolf turned and retreated without a sound. Kasch had realized then how lonely he felt here in the forest, when usually he had so many animal companions near him. But they mostly stayed away from the rogues.

Kasch always thought Maw should step into one of his own traps, if only to feel what they were like, but he never did, probably because he always sent Bit to check them. Bit had in fact gotten up to check the traps and when he returned, Maw was dozing with snowflakes landing, hissing and dying under his hot breath. Bit came back with a rabbit in his hand and proceeded to skin it and put it on the spit. He tossed the pelt to Kasch who attached it to his wrap with a series of long pine needles. Kasch continued sewing and thought of Luna, who must be despairing right now that he was ever coming back. *I'll come back to you*, he tried to send her the thought, but did not feel her receive it.

A week later they had moved off the high elevations and came down to the edge of the forest. They were closer than they had ever been to Wilker castle and they all knew it. Ironically, although they had come down from the high elevations to avoid the coldest air, it was now unusually warm and the sun shone admirably, though low in the sky even though it was midday. They hiked along the edge of the forest, hoping to stay hidden yet expecting to find game in the meadow, also escaping the winter's worst. Suddenly Bit ran ahead of them, seeing something glinting in the sunshine. Bit bent over and picked up a vessel with a piece of paper in it.

Bit held up the shiny new object and looked at it curiously. He could hear a scroll of paper tapping against the inside of the vessel but could not figure how to extract it. Maw quickly grabbed the new toy away from Bit and uncorked the bottle. He jabbed an index finger into the bottle's neck but it was too fat to pull the scroll out. He raised the bottle now stuck on his finger with a humph of disgust and was about to smash it when Kasch swung his arm and snatched the vessel off

Maw's finger. He eyed them casually as he licked his pinkie finger, put it into the bottle and pulled the scroll out. He knew neither of these men could read and he also knew, with hungry eyes, this note was from Luna. He opened the scroll and quickly read the words, devouring them. He glanced up and gazed longingly in the direction of the castle. If he left the rogues here, they would slither back into the forest and continue to poach and pillage it, and he loved it too much to let them have the run of it. He glanced from the horizon back to the scroll. It was offering him a way to possibly escape the fate he had chosen for himself a little sooner.

"What s'it say?" Maw asked suspiciously. Kasch glanced down again and re-read Luna's words, buried them into his heart, then began,

"It says: *A party of the Count's men will be passing by this point on their way to the royal hunting lodge, and anyone wishing a royal dispensation should here await their arrival.*" Maw's eyebrows crossed while Bit hunkered down as if expecting the Count's falcon to arrive soon and swoop down upon them. Maw asked,

"What's dis-suspension?"

"Dispensation," Kasch said. "It means he'll do a favor for anyone willing to wait for his party to pass by." Maw considered this and finally Kasch added, "He likes to have his subjects pay homage to him." Maw rubbed his beard.

"When's they passin' by?" Kasch glanced at the scroll again, then replied,

"Today or tomorrow." Kasch sat down declaring, "I'm waiting. This could be good." He settled down on the ground with his hands behind his head and let the sun warm his face. Bit saw what he did and decided to do the same. Maw looked at them both with suspicion. Soon he heard their steady breathing and turned quietly away to head back into the forest. He didn't entirely believe that any royals were headed their way, but if they were, he wanted to see if indeed they had anything to hand out to Kasch and Bit. He could always steal it from them later if they did.

Maw made his way into the forest, looking for a tree with lower limbs to climb so he could watch from a distance. He was looking up at the branches and assessing the sight line to where the other two were waiting, now almost out of view, and took a turn around a tree, thinking that if he could jump a little he could catch the lowest branch. Just then a trap snapped onto his leg. He was so shocked by the pain. speechlessly gasping for breath. He looked down at the metal teeth latched onto his lower leg like the fangs of a wolf. Blood ran out his leg and washed his dusty shoe. He managed to undo the trap with trembling hands. He leaned against the tree and clutched the bloody trap, still gasping in big gulps. He swore every blasphemous word he knew and then began a determined hobble back to his companions, asleep in the grass. *I'll kill them both for setting a trap on me.*

18

Travelers Return

The afternoon was calm as Kasch dozed in the grass. He had become accustomed to how much time they wasted and now used it to contemplate. The sun was still warm on his face and he was re-reading Luna's words in his mind over and over. It was a not unpleasant way to while away the time. He was just between awake and asleep, a state he savored drifting through but was rarely able to keep when in his comfortable, warm bed in the castle. On this day, however, being the middle of the afternoon, he was not so sleepy nor so comfortable. His mind imagined his adventure ending: The three of them walk back to the castle and Bit and Maw confess to their crimes and pay the consequences. Probably a sentence of hard labor, but saved from death by the fact that they had surrendered instead of being caught and putting the Count's men to more trouble. Kasch liked this outcome and watched it again in his mind. The three of them walk through the castle gates, Luna runs to see him and they are happily united. Maw cannot interfere in his life any more and is slowed in his pace, as his days of running away are over. In fact, he is limping. Kasch looks back at the pair and Bit is helping him to walk. Kasch peers more closely and sees that Maw's foot is hurt. He tries to look more closely and see why but then an angry, growling Maw crashes into his reverie and his eyes fly open to see Maw grab Bit off the ground and shake him violently with promises of death on his lips.

"I'll kill ye for settin' a trap on me–" Maw raised the heavy metal leg trap in his hand and aimed it full force at Bit's head. Bit himself was only half awake, dazed with confusion and offering no resistance. Kasch flew into the pair and grabbed Maw's arm to snatch the trap away from him. Maw collapsed backward, his arm twisted and two of his fingers broken. He was screaming loudly and lying more helplessly than a few broken fingers warranted. The two stood over him as he writhed, noticing with alarm that his bleeding ankle was turning the dried grass red with blood. Kasch looked down at the sprung trap in his hands, shreds of fabric in its teeth. Bit noticed it too and pointed accusingly,

"I never set no traps down here, swear to it!" Maw groaned out,

"Like ye'd ever remember." His words trailed off as he clutched his twisted arm, then his leg. His foot trembled from the effort of hobbling back from the forest. Kasch knew he should try to wrap the bleeding ankle but there were only the shirts on their backs and neither of them was willing to give them up. Kasch declared plainly,

"You're going to bleed to death." Bit and Maw gaped at him; they knew he was wise about things and both of them feared he was telling the truth. Maw shrunk from his own mortality and Bit had a horror of seeing a man die, especially if he himself had set the trap and forgotten it. It was possible after all. Kasch added to Bit, "We'd better leave him here so we won't have to watch this. It's going to take a while, anyway." With that, Kasch turned and headed for the forest, this time holding a stick to test the tall grass in front of him. Bit looked at Maw lying helpless in the grass, then at Kasch's back heading away. Maw could only bemoan his sorry fate and knew they would soon walk away and leave him there, slowly freezing to death as his blood poured out, its scent attracting wolves that would slather over his still-living flesh while ravens pecked out his eyes. Suddenly Bit remembered.

"The royal party – they'll be by and help." Kasch just shook his head, turning back so they would hear him when he said,

"If they haven't come yet this afternoon, they won't be by till tomorrow. By then it will be too late to save him, although he'll probably still be alive. Well, barely. In any case, they want homage, not problems." Kasch turned and continued walking away. Bit glanced down again at Maw and then started to follow Kasch. He wasn't used to thinking for himself. Maw raised up his hand to Bit and then let it fall. Bit caught up to Kasch, walked a few paces, then asked,

"Tain't there a hamlet 'tween hare and the Count's castle? We could mebbe take Maw there and git some doctorin'." Kasch turned and looked at him, then back at the groaning heap in the grass. He studied in silence for what seemed like a very long time to the suffering Maw and agonized Bit.

"You want to ask someone for help?" Kasch said.

Bit looked down, doubtful anyone would give them help and there was a hopeless wail from the man on the ground. He dreaded dying in the grass as the sun set, the cold air congealing his blood. Bit knew he would never be able to help Maw on his own. Bit looked up at Kasch and nodded his head to him. Kasch sighed and walked back over to Maw, leaning over him so that he would hear. He annunciated plainly, "Bit wants to drag you to a town. Do you want to die here or there?" Maw groaned and rolled. Kasch looked over at Bit and shrugged his shoulders; he couldn't understand a word. Kasch glanced toward the forest again, then up at the sky. There might be a few hours of daylight left. Bit saw Kasch losing interest and said,

"Town, he said town!" Kasch looked over at him dubiously, shrugged again and between the two of them, Kasch and Bit hefted Maw up, ignored his shrieks of pain and together they hobbled to the hamlet on the other side of the meadow, which took over an hour.

By the time they reached it, Maw had bled out most of his life through his ankle and Kasch and Bit were exhausted from hauling him down the foothills. At one point Kasch almost dropped him and left him for dead, but he had energy from being jubilant over finally heading home. They begged a night's stay in a barn and some rags to wrap Maw's ankle. Kasch gazed down at the passed-out man and merely said, "If he wakes up tomorrow I guess he'll live." They were both nearly passed out themselves with fatigue and fell asleep on the damp and dirty straw.

In the morning, a much-subdued Maw opened his bleary eyes and gazed up at his saviors. Kasch declared that he was not about to drag him another foot and said he would travel to the castle to get help, unless they preferred to continue living off the forest through the winter as they were. They both shook their heads at the grim prospect and said they would wait for Kasch to return. Kasch reminded them, "You'll have to face whatever the Count says you deserve, and I've seen you poach his game."

"You ate it too -" Bit added, confused.

"I'll take whatever punishment he has for me. Will you both?" Again the two looked at each other and nodded their heads simultaneously.

Kasch added darkly, "If you aren't here when I get back, I'll hunt you down and kill you both for running away. And I'll have the Count's men to help me." They nodded their heads again and Bit said meekly,

"I'll stay with Maw, tho he wouldn't do the same fer me."

Kasch left the barn and informed the owner who he was and who his prisoners were. He added, "You'll be paid for jailing these offenders until the Count's men take possession of them later today. You might want to lock them in." The barn-owner nodded and hurriedly gave Kasch the use of his best horse. Kasch mounted up and rode away at top speed, smiling all the way. He would be back at the castle for the noontime meal.

Before noon, however, another rider approached the gates of Wilker castle, and this one had an entire party traveling with him. It was Magnus, returned from his surveying trip and bringing with him workmen and engineers to construct the bridge that would connect his homeland with Wilker along a path that would take one week to travel instead of three. Trumpets blared as he crossed the gates and people came out to see who had arrived, Genivee among them. As a lunch banquet was prepared, Magnus and Gustav talked about all the news each had missed in the intervening months. When Boris broke the news that both the royal sons were missing, Magnus turned quiet. The silence was broken by the announcement that the celebratory banquet was ready and they all wandered toward the dining room. Magnus was hungry, but his appetite, like everyone else's, was slight.

Chatter had begun to return to normal as the banquet hall filled with people who rejoiced at Magnus's return and the engineers he had brought with him spoke of their plans for the bridge, the work it would entail and the vastly increased traffic and commerce it would bring. Then the trumpets blared again. A herald outside the castle was yelling to open the gates with all haste; a rider was headed for them at full speed and was to be allowed inside without breaking his pace. The diners went to the windows to see what was about, for it sounded as if there were an invasion upon them and the heralds and gatekeepers were making them welcome. People along the path of the rider on horseback cheered and shouted, jumped and ran after him, even though he was dressed raggedly and was not bearing any regalia. Inside the gates, the commotion had caught like fire and people came pouring out of the doorways either to join in the cheering or at least see what it was about. By the time Gustav had got to a window the man on horseback was in the center of the courtyard with people happily greeting him, excited and clapping his horse and their hands all at once. Gustav wondered why they were all so enamored of the vagabond when he looked up at the window, waved his arm and declared, "Hello, Father, I'm home."

The following spring, plans were underway for the investiture of Leopold. It would not take place until the end of summer, when, if an entire year had passed and Dane had not yet returned, Leopold would become the heir after his grandfather Harz. The somberness of Dane's never returning slowly lifted as winter gave way to spring and Kasch having returned salvaged some happiness out of a sad situation. Kasch reversed his position with Leopold such that *he* was Leopold's page instead of the other way around. This took much convincing of Leopold on Kasch's part and they continued to confuse outsiders as to whom was showing deference to who.

Bit and Maw were retrieved from the hamlet where, to Kasch's amazement, Maw still clung to life and Bit still remained by his side. Eventually, with Quilin's ministrations, Maw was able to gimp about very slowly, although too much walking became painful fast and any ideas of his escaping anywhere were laughable. Gustav wanted to banish them to the dungeons for the rest of their lives, but Kasch convinced him this would undo all his diligent work throughout the fall. He wanted them to realize useful occupation and after much debate, it was decided that Bit could work at carving a wisent out of a huge tree trunk that was dragged from the forest. Maw was allowed to sit nearby and make editorial comments, which was not much different from how he used to treat Bit, but now both of them knew which one was beholden to the other and which could now ignore the other. Bit worked away at his carving - Kasch had seen him whittle little animals when he wasn't roasting a squirrel - and a wisent in fact began to take shape outside the castle grounds. When it was finished, if Gustav liked the resemblance, he would have it moved to the courtyard and start Bit on another one.

Magnus's entourage of workers, a few of whom had brought their families, began construction on the bridge over the river. It had taken a while to find the exact right location, somewhat away from the castle but still close to the village, before work began. Magnus spent every day visiting the progress and making it known that soon there would be increased opportunities for commerce and new sources for garnering revenue. His return to home coincided with a lessening of Minka's trips abroad, and although she continued to try, she failed to attract a man of sufficient status to lure her into marriage.

Sparrow was so overjoyed to have her only son return to her that she spent every day in wonderment of it. She ceased to lament the fact that she might never have any more children and instead looked forward to the day when she would have many grandchildren around her just as Harz did. It seemed like a very likely prospect as Kasch and Luna prepared for a summer wedding. That of course was after Kasch "rescued" her from the nunnery where she was when he returned from the woods. It was just a small nunnery next to the church in the village and she was only there to help out; cook, clean and tie the shoe laces for the oldest nuns. Of course Minka made derisive remarks about such work, but Luna knew that if someday Minka needed such help she would regret having spurned a friend who did not shy away from the task.

Kasch continued to wonder if his fantasy about Maw stepping into a leg trap had had any influence at all over its actually happening. Perhaps he had simply foreseen a future event. Perhaps he had set the event into motion, he could never be sure. It had brought his adventure to an end and for that he was thankful, and Maw had survived the ordeal and was now a subdued man, probably because he was in almost constant pain. Even complaining took an effort he could not spare, and he mostly spent his days (when he was able to rise from his bed) giving Bit advice that Bit happily ignored.

Cait continued to sew in her room and make dresses for the ladies connected with the royal family, all of whom were her good friends. She had several apprentices and didn't have to do the very tedious work, but instead enjoyed buying the materials and even going on trips, once the bridge was finished, to suppliers farther away. She had never imagined going so far afield or making the decisions in purchasing new and unique fabrics. It was a great adventure for her to take these trips, always with friends and escorts and pages that made sure the party from Wilker received the best accommodations and attentions.

Trevka, father of the future Count of Wilker and still a knight, was no longer out and about proving his prowess on horseback or with a sword but rather was often found under the beech tree in the castle courtyard with a group of children gathered around him, many his own. He would slowly pull one and then another leather strap from his inside jacket pocket. Beside him, his faithful page Tag would have the third lanyard in his own jacket pocket. (Kasch had given it to him as a gift, saying he had liberated it from the Rogues one day while they dozed on the forest floor.) When all three lanyards were braided back together, the wide-eyed listeners would marvel at how the scratch across all three parts connected perfectly. With the braid complete, Trevka would then relate various aspects of the tale; how he had freed an eagle and saved five eaglets, how he had stalked dangerous criminals over the mountains towards Elster, how he had found these same men years later, or how he now surveilled over these apprehended vagabonds as they slaved out their sentences. The fact that only a few select men had even ever seen a real live wisent was in fact also thanks to him, for he himself had lured one to the meadow through the use of magic cards. As his wife Beth watched from a window above, she would smile as she heard the little listeners' voices cascade with oohs and aahs, and all the while Trevka would assure them he was never exaggerating. Tag always confirmed the truth of this.

Made in the USA
Charleston, SC
12 June 2014